"Mayb

school. "I've ...

self and my wits."

he snorted lightly.

"Glad you haven't had any trouble," he said. "Part of my job is to make sure people in town stay safe."

"I thought your job was to uphold the law."

"Figure it's the same thing."

His words only served to make her feel guilty. How would he feel if he knew Clear Springs harbored a fugitive from justice?

Author Note

Gemma, my heroine in this story, strives to do her best—even though things happen to derail her plans. Isn't that how it is for many of us? Unexpected obstacles thwart our best-laid plans. Some are good. Some are difficult. How we choose to face them is up to us, but always the choice takes us on a new path.

I hope you enjoy Gemma and Craig's story, which is set in Southern California's gold country. If you have read my other stories you may recognise some familiar names and faces in Clear Springs.

I love to hear from my readers. You can write to me at kathryn@kathrynalbright.com.

CHRISTMAS KISS FROM THE SHERIFF

Kathryn Albright

Published in Great Britain 2016
by Mills & Boon, an imprint of HarperCollins*Publishers*
1 London Bridge Street, London, SE1 9GF

© 2016 Kathryn Leigh Albright

ISBN: 978-0-263-91743-7

Kathryn Albright writes American-set historical romance for Mills & Boon. From her first breath she has had a passion for stories that celebrate the goodness in people. She combines her love of history and her love of stories to write novels of inspiration, endurance, and hope. Visit her at kathrynalbright.com and on Facebook.

Books by Kathryn Albright

Mills & Boon Historical Romance

Heroes of San Diego

The Angel and the Outlaw
The Gunslinger and the Heiress
Familiar Stranger in Clear Springs
Christmas Kiss from the Sheriff

Stand-Alone Novels

Texas Wedding for Their Baby's Sake
The Rebel and the Lady
Wild West Christmas
'Dance with a Cowboy'

Visit the Author Profile page at millsandboon.co.uk.

I'd like to dedicate this story to my sister-in-law, Marlana—a constant supporter of my writing ever since I married into the family. From the bottom of my heart, thank you for always being there for me through life's ups and downs. You light up my life. Love you!

I'd also like to acknowledge my editor, Julia Williams, for her encouragement and help in honing this story to a much better version of the original draft. Thank you for all your hard work, Julia!

Chapter One

Southern California—1876

Gemma's warm breath turned to ethereal vapor in the frosty air as she marched determinedly toward the one-room schoolhouse. *Unruly!* That was the word. The children had been so full of energy yesterday that they had scarcely settled the entire day. Whether they had learned anything at all in the space of the seven hours was a mystery. The closer the days drew to Christmas, the more challenging it was to keep their attentions. Did all teachers suffer this problem or was she somehow lacking in the correct process of discipline?

Of one thing she was well aware—her education by tutors had not prepared her in the least for the life she now led.

Thank goodness for the one year she attended

the university in Boston. Teaching was not so very different from being a lawyer or judge— particularly in the area of divvying out discipline. Her father had prepared her well in that regard.

She adjusted her small lunch pail and the books she carried to a more comfortable position in her arms and turned from the main road to the dirt path that led to the new school building. Fresh tracks marked the tall damp grass—an oddity this early in the morning. Unease rippled through her, making her shiver as she stared at them. The sun glistened on a thin layer of frost, but where the imprints occurred, the weeds and grass were crushed down and wet. The footprints circled from the front steps of the building around to the small attached woodshed at its side. They were large enough to be those of a grown man.

Now who would be lurking around the school at this hour?

She climbed the two front steps and pushed the skeleton key into the lock when the door moved freely. Odd… She had locked it last thing yesterday. Quietly she opened the door and glanced about the one large room, taking in the vague lingering scent of varnish that still clung to the new benches and the loose clump of pine garland that she had deposited on her desk before leaving yesterday.

To her left, in the back corner of the room, one of her older pupils sat at his desk slouched over a book. Fingers from one hand threaded through his stringy blond hair as he rested his head on his hand, completely absorbed in whatever he was reading. He hadn't even noticed that she had entered the room. "Billy!"

He jumped in his seat.

"How long have you been here?"

"Got my chores done early and skedaddled afore Ma could find something more for me and Tara to do."

She walked over to stand beside him. He was halfway through the book *Robinson Crusoe*.

Even though she was pleased to see him reading she couldn't pretend to be happy about him breaking into the school. "How did you get inside? The door was locked."

The excitement of the story dropped from his expression and he swallowed. "I didn't hurt anything, Miss Starling. Honest."

"That's not the point. You shouldn't have come inside at all. That is what a locked door indicates."

"It weren't locked all the way," he said, his chin raising.

She cringed a little. "The proper use of the verb is *wasn't* locked. And this isn't open for debate."

His confidence wavered slightly. "Maybe

it was just half locked and when I jiggled it, it opened."

She studied his earnest expression. No matter how he'd entered, rules were rules and he needed to follow them. "You are not to do it again. Understand?"

"Yes'm," he said, contrite now, his face red.

She stared at him a moment longer, just to make her words stick. "For now, please see to lighting the stove and then go outside until you are called in with the others."

Sullen now, he rose to do her bidding.

A twinge of guilt pricked her. Had she handled that correctly? It was important that she appear strong and capable. It was a fine line, she was learning, between keeping control of her classroom and yet not squelching her students' zeal to learn. Billy was fifteen years old after all. When she was that age, she'd been full of the confidence of youth. She had considered herself practically grown no matter that her father called her his little girl still. At that age a dressing down by her teacher would have been humiliating. Perhaps she should have been more aware of that before chastising him. But then, perhaps given his age, he should not have trespassed in the first place.

The conflicting thoughts hounded her as she walked to the coat closet, setting her lunch pail on the shelf above the long row of pegs. Shrugging from her night-blue woolen coat, she hung it on the last wooden peg and then rubbed her hands together to warm them. The mornings had been chilly for weeks, but of late, they were downright cold. Snow was expected any day and with the snow—Christmas.

Billy walked by on his way to the door. She glanced down at his feet. The footprints she noticed must have been his. His shoes were as large as any mans, although the rest of him hadn't caught up yet. He was as tall as her, lanky and still growing.

"Mr. Odom? Are you enjoying *Robinson Crusoe*?"

He shrugged noncommittally, before stepping outside and closing the door behind him. Boys were funny creatures. As an only child and female, she had little experience with what happened in their brains.

Staring at the closed portal, she breathed a sigh of relief. For her first teaching job she had thought she would feel a bit more secure. Things came easier with the younger children, but the oldest ones… Billy and Duncan…she had more difficulty with. It hadn't been that long ago that she was a schoolgirl herself—five years at most if she didn't count the year at the university. She'd thought it wouldn't be anything at all to slip into the role of teacher after her own exemplary education. Finding herself questioning her decisions and second-guessing herself had never entered her mind until she'd taken this position.

The sounds of chatter as more children arrived outside made her push those thoughts to the back of her mind. She surveyed the room with a critical eye, making sure everything was ready for the lessons ahead. The schoolhouse seemed more comfortable than when she first arrived. Then, construction had been nearing completion and with the help of a few determined souls and the supplies her friend Elizabeth had brought from La Playa, the schoolroom had quickly come together.

Picking up a sliver of chalk, she turned to the wall behind her desk and wrote the day's morning lessons on the slate board. Fifteen minutes later, she withdrew her father's watch from her skirt pocket and checked the time. Nine o'clock. Time to ring the—

"Miss Starling!" Moira Bishop rushed through the door. "C-c-come quick!" she cried in her high-pitched voice.

Outside came the sound of one boy taunting another. "I ain't doin' it, ya crazy goat!"

Gemma hurried out. In the schoolyard, all the children stood to one side and watched Duncan

Philmont and Billy Odom circle each other like two feral dogs. Billy already sported a cut above his left eyebrow and a growing bruise there. This was a first. The two had never gotten along well, but they'd never come to fighting before.

"Both of you…stop this immediately!" She rushed into the yard. "This is no way for civilized people to act."

Billy, his flannel shirt torn, never moved his gaze from Duncan. Blood dripped into his eye from the cut. He blinked, and then swiped his sleeve across his face to clear his vision. Duncan, a year older and standing a good foot taller than Billy, crouched down and moved closer, his angular face set in a menacing scowl. His tousled black hair contained bits of dried grass and small twigs and a large grass stain smeared his right shoulder sleeve.

She may as well have not spoken at all for all the reaction it gained. "You must stop! What is this all about?" she demanded.

"Back up, Teach," Duncan said. "This ain't no concern of yours."

Her spine stiffened. Teach, indeed! He knew better than to address her like that.

"It *is* my concern if it happens here at my school."

Behind her one of the Daley boys bet on Duncan to win and two other children piped in that they'd put in a bet too. Shocked, she roared, "There will be no bets!"

A few younger children backed up, their eyes wide at the first true display of anger she'd revealed since starting her position.

However, her tone didn't faze either of the two who continued to circle each other. Duncan inched closer, intent upon his next move and completely ignoring her. Blood dripped from his swollen and purple upper lip.

Billy trembled with suppressed anger. Sweat streaked with mud ran down his face and neck.

Suddenly Duncan leaped at him and grabbed behind his neck, pushing him, facedown toward the ground. Hunched over like that, Billy punched him hard in the gut—once and then with his other fist. With an *oof*, Duncan went down, pushing Billy with him. In the dirt and grass they grappled, their tempers gone, their only thoughts to pound the other to dust. Really, this was entirely out of hand!

She must do something. Now. She raced back into the school and picked up the bucket of water she used to clean the slate board—filthy rag and all. Running back outside, she stepped up to the two and sloshed the cold contents of the bucket over both boys.

"Yeow!" They rolled off each other and spit the filth from their mouths. Then they scrambled to their feet and stood there glaring at her, the water dripping off their messy hair.

"I'm disappointed in the both of you. Christmas is nearly upon us! It's a time that embraces a generous and giving spirit, and I find you both *fighting*!"

Neither one said a word but their expressions said they absolutely *hated* her interference.

"Nothing is worth fisticuffs. You must both learn to discuss things and compromise. That is the way of a civilized people."

Billy snorted. "Tell that to my pa."

She glared at him. "It takes a big man to keep control of his emotions. That is the mark of a gentleman."

"Who says I want to be a gentleman?" Duncan mumbled under his breath, a mutinous frown on his face.

She chose to ignore his attitude. "All right then. Billy, go down to the creek and clean up, and then take your seat inside."

That she had singled him out first only made his anger more palpable. He picked up his flat tan cap that was now streaked with dirt and grass stains and slapped it against his thigh.

"To the water, Mr. Odom."

When he'd finally shuffled off, she turned to the other boy. Duncan needed to wash up also, but she wasn't about to put him in the same proximity with Billy so soon after the fight. "I'll get you a cloth for that lip. You may take your seat now."

Duncan smirked, a half smile on one side of his face that made only one eye crinkle up, and took his time picking up his own flat cap from the grass. "Yes'm, Teach," he said, before turning away and swaggering toward the schoolhouse.

She didn't like it…his belligerent attitude or the rude way he spoke to her. In the ten weeks that she had been teaching, she'd learned he had little respect for anyone, likely owing to his father's position in the community. "Mr. Philmont. I will thank you to address me as Miss Starling."

He didn't slow down, didn't acknowledge that he heard her, and she found herself addressing his backside as he disappeared inside the building.

She let out a frustrated sigh before catching herself. The other schoolchildren stood in a half circle, wide-eyed and watching to see what she would do next. It had been the first fight at the new school. What tales would they take home to their parents? Not once in all her years had she witnessed a schoolyard fight.

She took a deep breath and then picked up the

empty bucket. "Inside with the rest of you. It's time to start school."

As the younger children scrambled into the building, Gemma watched Billy leave the edge of the clearing and trudge through the mix of pines that sloped down to the water. Why did people so easily turn to violence to solve things? Out here in the West, it seemed even more so than in Boston. One minute Billy had been reading and the next he was fighting. So quick to anger.

It made her all the more determined to impart a decent education to her students. They depended on her. "'The law is reason free from passion,'" she quoted under her breath. Aristotle. Which meant in this instance…hmm…she must not let her emotions interfere with her judgment when she handed out a punishment to Billy and Duncan. She could take it further, she supposed, and make sure her emotions were not transmitted to the students. Calm, cool, collected—that was the attitude. She blew out another breath. Thank goodness for Aristotle.

Billy Odom never came back to class.

Craig Parker pounded the nail into the last plank of wood that now boarded up the entrance to the Farnsworth Mining Company's one and only mine. He took a moment to check the sturdiness of his handiwork and figured it would do the job of warning off any curiosity seekers. He'd been around long enough to know that the lure of possible riches, even from an abandoned mine, still called to opportunistic men. There was always someone who thought they knew better than anyone else and could find a sliver of gold if they just looked hard enough—the danger be hanged.

For a mining town it had come as a surprise that so many of the men were family inclined and wanting to settle here in Clear Springs. The boom on gold had played out except for a few of the mines and those were dwindling. It's why the town had gone from nearly two thousand folks, mostly living in a tent city, to just over one hundred. Those that had stayed were putting down roots, strong roots. They built a church. And just finished a permanent school. It was a lot like the place he'd grown up in farther north.

He stowed his hammer in his saddlebag and mounted his horse, Jasper, then reined the gelding toward town. When he'd taken the job of sheriff, he hadn't considered closing up a mine would be part of his job, but Chet, the owner of the mine, had become something of a friend. After facing down thieves, Chet had been laid up healing from an injury. He was now back to work at a viable mine, but Craig figured boarding up this millstone was the least he could do for the kid.

Since that first bit of excitement things had been fairly quiet in town. The next haul of gold from the Palomino Mine made it down to the bank in San Diego without so much as a whisper of trouble. He wasn't complaining, but other than jailing obnoxious drunks overnight so that they could sober up, he'd like to feel that he was doing more for the community that had hired him.

Pressing his legs against his horse, he urged him into a gentle lope. The morning haze was gone, the sun high overhead and filtering through the boughs of the tall pines. The crisp, dry air crackled with a static charge every so often and held a clearness he never got tired of seeing.

He followed a self-made route every day. Now that school was in session, he had taken to riding by the new schoolhouse. He told himself that it was because the school was part of the township, but deep down, he knew he wouldn't mind a quick gander at the pretty new schoolteacher. He'd seen her once in the yard, and watched amused as she played ball with the children. He was fairly sure that she'd seen him too. For a moment her gaze had caught his. She had quickly extricated herself from the game, brushing back the tendrils of dark brown hair that had fallen into her line of vision, and then refocused on him. With a flounce of her skirt, she had disappeared inside the schoolhouse.

He took the deer trail across the meadow and through the pines until he came to the shallow creek a short distance from the school. He found his usual spot where the span of the creek was twenty feet wide and the water rippled gently over the submerged rocks, creating small whorls in the shallows. Dismounting, he released the reins and let his horse drink.

Fifty feet upstream something yellow flashed.

Along the bank a young girl had laid across a large boulder, stretched herself as long as possible and was trying to retrieve something from the ripples. She wore an overly large green knitted sweater over a yellow pinafore smudged with dirt. Blond braids hung down and skimmed the surface of the water as she reached for whatever eluded her in the water. He hoped it was worth a dousing, because it looked like that was going to happen in about two seconds.

"Here, now!" he called, striding toward her. "What are you up to there?"

Startled, she drew back her hand. When she caught sight of him she swallowed hard and then scrambled to her feet, wiping her hands on her wrinkled pinafore. Now that she was upright rather than horizontal he judged her to be about six...or perhaps seven years of age.

He stopped fifteen feet from her so as not to scare her or make her trip. With his big frame, he had that effect on some children. "I'm Sheriff Parker, miss. What are you up to this fine day and shouldn't you be in school?"

Telltale red blotches immediately blossomed on her cheeks, answering that question. He'd done his share of playing hooky when he was younger. He figured it did a boy good to have some freedom. But girls? He had never considered much what a young girl would want to do in her spare time.

"What is it you were after there in the water?"

"Nothin'," she said in a high, airy voice.

"So you can talk." Now that they had established a small amount of comfort with each other, he stepped over to the bank and peered into the shallows. A new copper penny shone through the mild ripples. He retrieved it easily and held it out to her.

She snatched it from his fingers as though he might take it away in the next instance.

"Time for you to get to class now. It just so happens that I was heading that way. We can go together."

At that she looked a bit nervous. Suddenly she

concentrated on her feet as she shuffled through the crisp brown leaves that littered the deer path leading back to the school. He grabbed his horse by the reins and followed at a short distance, amused that her steps slowed the closer they came to the school. Was she anticipating a scolding from the new teacher? The woman hadn't looked that ferocious, but maybe to such a small girl everything looked big and scary.

They came to the side yard and he stepped ahead of her. "Wait here." He tied his horse to the tie line.

He rapped on the thick wood door before entering. A young girl in the first row was standing and reading aloud. At the front of the room, Miss Starling paced slowly, back and forth with a book resting open in her hand as she followed along with the reader. The white blouse she wore tucked in at her waist to a dark blue skirt, giving her a crisp, professional air. She looked like a no-nonsense schoolmarm, pinched mouth and everything, in complete control, but he had to smile to himself at the amount of chalk dust streaking her skirt at her hips.

He started down the center aisle that separated the girls from the boys.

She stopped pacing and looked up from her book, frowning at his interruption.

"Sheriff? What can I do for you?"

"Miss Starling. I need you to step outside for a minute."

"What? Now? But I'm in the middle of class."

Not the response he was looking for. "It won't take long."

She looked like she had just sucked on a lemon. Yep. The expression marring her pretty face at the moment was decidedly miffed.

She closed her book with a whump, the sudden noise startling half the class, and set the book on her desk. "Moira…" She addressed the young girl who had been reading. "Continue to the end of the page and then hand the book across to Uriah who will read on."

As she strode directly in front of him and out the door he caught a whiff of the soap she had used that morning. It hinted of jasmine. A scent like that you didn't forget. For a woman who was all business such an exotic soap was more than a little intriguing. He was pretty sure it wasn't perfume—only ladies of the night used such devices—not sensible teachers. His mouth twisted in amusement as he followed her out the door.

"Now what is this all about?" she asked, turning abruptly to confront him at the base of the steps. Her deep brown eyes held his gaze, challenging him to make this worth her while.

"Found someone I believe is supposed to be here instead of down by the creek." He nodded toward the girl that, despite his instructions, had moved and now hid halfway behind the shed.

Miss Starling's shoulders lowered from their rigid set. Disappointment filled her voice. "Not again."

Not again? "I ran into her downstream about half a mile from here."

"I see. Thank you for seeing her safely here."

She seemed to have thawed a bit for which he was grateful. That first look she had given the little girl was heavy enough to bow her small back with the weight.

"Tara Odom. What have you to say for yourself? Was it a rabbit this time? Or a squirrel? What was so fascinating that you would forgo class again?"

Tara didn't answer at first, but stepped into full view. A second later her chin quivered and she hung her head. "I was looking for Billy."

Miss Starling pressed her lips together as she seemed to consider her reply. No hint of a smile. No softening of her voice. "You have a responsibility to yourself. Your job is to learn. Concern about your brother is an admirable quality, but he made his own choice not to return after what happened this morning."

Tears appeared in the little girl's eyes. "I just want to know if he is okay," she said in a small voice—a voice that now had a catch to it.

It seemed that the shiny copper penny had been forgotten. He wondered what had occurred that morning.

Miss Starling squared her shoulders. "I'm afraid that I will need to speak with your parents about this."

The girl's lower lip trembled. "My...my ma?"

The teacher didn't appear in the least affected by the girl's tears. Craig couldn't say the same about himself. He'd always been a sucker for a female's tears—his mom's, and Charlotte's.

"Yes. And your father."

"He...he ain't home."

Miss Starling's mouth tightened further. "I'm very disappointed in you. For the rest of the week you will stay inside at noon and work on your studies to make up for your lovely half day of recess today."

"Yes'm."

"You may take your seat now."

With her shoulders hunched, Tara shuffled into the school.

He told himself to keep quiet. It wasn't his

place to say anything. Yet he wasn't happy with the woman's attitude. Didn't she notice the girl's distress? It wasn't like he'd caught the child stealing or setting fire to something. She had just been enjoying a little freedom and apparently looking for her brother. Guess it would be best if he left before he said something he'd regret. He walked over to the tie line to get Jasper.

"You don't approve."

Her voice carried a hint of the Eastern Seaboard. Maybe that's why it had sounded harsh to him. With a tilt of his head he indicated the school door where the girl had entered. "Seemed to take things a mite rough."

"It is her third infraction in four weeks. She has to learn she can't come and go on a whim. She'll never get anywhere being lackadaisical. Life takes discipline."

"I know all about discipline and I don't need a lecture on it," he said quietly. From what he'd heard, this was her first year of teaching. He hoped she loosened up before too long or her students might make things real rough for her. He happened to know a bit about that—having been one of those students himself at one time. "Her brother is usually with her. He looks out for her."

Her lips parted and for a moment she looked unsettled, as though she hadn't actually thought about the two as family. Not really. "As sheriff, I'd think you would be on my side."

"Not on any side. Just an observation. Kids play hooky all the time. It's part of growing up."

"The last time I checked, I was the teacher here. Tara needs to tend to her own troubles rather than worry about her brother's issues. He has enough to worry about as it is." She picked up her skirt and ascended the steps.

Where had she grown up? Under a rock? "Family loyalty means something to most folks." The words tasted bitter in his mouth. *Most folks*, he reminded himself didn't include his own.

With his words, she faltered on the last step, but caught herself. "I appreciate you seeing her safely here. I'll take care of it. Good day, Sheriff."

"One more thing," he said, stopping her before she disappeared inside the school.

Her nostrils flared. She had a small nose. Cute. Distracting. And she wasn't happy about his interruption in her life.

This was more important. If he remembered correctly, the Odoms' property was about as far afield as a person could live and still be considered a resident of Clear Springs. The family's low-slung cabin was little more than a shack hidden among the giant boulders on the eastern face of the mountain. The trail was nearly impassable.

It was a wonder the girl made it to school at all. She was fortunate to have her brother's company and care and likely wasn't looking forward to traveling home on her own at the end of the day. "Have you ever been to the Odoms' property?"

"No. But I have a good sense of direction. I'm sure I could find it."

"It's a fair distance, especially on her short legs. You told her she had to look out for herself. Well, I think she was doing that. It looks like her brother took their one and only ride."

She shot a glance at the tether line. A long-eared mule usually stood there throughout the school day, stomping the ground and occasionally braying for attention. He'd heard it a time or two. Finding the animal gone took the starch out of her bonnet and for a moment she seemed at a loss for words. "So you *do* spy on me."

"Just making my rounds. Keeping things peaceful. Quiet. Don't want anyone lost…or hurt."

She stared at him long enough that he wondered at it. "I'll… I'll see that she gets home."

"You?" He didn't need a lost teacher as well as a lost little girl on his conscience.

"Yes. Me." That cute nose rose a little higher. "I can walk with her. I should speak to her mother anyway."

He rubbed his chin, considering her—her clothes, the thin leather shoes she wore peeking from beneath her skirt. They didn't look sturdy enough to hold up on a hike through the woods. "You won't make it back to town before nightfall," he said, none too happy about the prospect of heading that far out of town that evening. The Odoms stayed to themselves. The one and only time he had been to their cabin he had been greeted with a shotgun in his face. "The way I see it is…I'm taking her. It is my job to see to the safety of the people here."

She arched a brow. "That's commendable—and rather far-reaching for a description of your duties."

He hadn't expected her irritable attitude and wasn't sure what to make of it, but this verbal battle wasn't getting either of them anywhere. He wasn't budging and neither was she. "I'll come back at the end of school. We may both get a break and find that her brother has returned with the mule."

She exhaled. "Fair enough. Thank you for bringing Tara back. If something keeps you from arriving at the end of the day, I will see that she gets home safely." With a swish of her long blue skirt she disappeared into the schoolhouse.

Fine by him.

Chapter Two

It took the rest of the day for Gemma to calm down from Sheriff Parker's visit. He rattled her. That's what he did. *Keeping things peaceful* indeed! Where was he when the fight broke out between Billy and Duncan?

It was an unfair thought, but she thought it just the same. He couldn't have known it would happen. The fight had taken her by surprise herself.

She'd thought over their conversation at least twenty times and come to the conclusion they had both been concerned about Tara's well-being and that was a good thing. They simply went about it at odds with each other.

It hadn't helped that his appearance happened right in the middle of Moira's reading. It was the first time the Bishop girl had actually read more than one sentence without stuttering! She had

gone on for nearly four sentences! Gemma had
been so excited that she was holding her breath,
afraid to break the spell, afraid that the least little
wind would blow Moira back to her old pattern
of refusing to read aloud at all. Even the other
students realized something different was happening and were quietly amazed.

And then enter Sheriff Parker. Tall, blond, im-
posing Sheriff Parker.

Most of the men she had been introduced to
in Clear Springs were married and fathers of the
children she taught. Oh, she had met a few single men in church—a few miners, ranchers and
cowboys. She had been careful not to be overly
friendly. Actually she had quickly discouraged
them, admitting truthfully that she had too much
to do with this being her first year of teaching to
entertain thoughts of a social nature.

It was only a half-truth.

But Sheriff Parker hadn't approached her after
the first and only time she'd been introduced to
him—when he had arrived on Molly's doorstep
with her good friend Elizabeth. Since then in the
course of walking to and from school, she had
seen him about town. His office stood on the
northernmost point of Main Street—the same
road that led out of town and passed the school.

He had kept his distance. Only a tip of his hat

brim or a brief nod indicated he'd even noticed her. It should have been a relief to her in a town where the men so unevenly outnumbered women. Unfortunately, all it had done was make her more aware of him. She told herself that it was because he held the office of sheriff and considering her past, that was a worry in itself.

It couldn't be that he stood head-and-shoulders taller than other men, even though he did. He must be at least three inches over six feet. And it wasn't that his square, strong jawline, and perfectly straight Roman nose made him more handsome than the others—which they did. He was just so…male. Even in his dealings with others, she had noticed that his deep voice and spare words held more import than if he'd spewed out the entire dictionary. He was manly, composed, dignified. And it was so very unsettling to know that her thoughts dwelled on him more than they should.

Today, he had said he was just making his rounds. Making sure everything was quiet. But all his lurking had done for her was kick up some very *unquiet* sensations. She had come West to leave certain things of her past *in* her past and start anew. She couldn't afford to have a sheriff snooping around. If he found out the truth about her, he might send her back to Boston… and to jail.

While she washed off the large slate board at the front of the room of the lessons and examples she had posted, she kept an eye on Tara. After the girl had donned her heavy sweater and hat along with the other children gathering their coats, she watched them head out the door to their homes while she returned to sit dejectedly on the first-grade bench. Her small shoulders were slumped as she swung her legs back and forth and stared out the window. Gemma was halfway through sweeping the floor when a sharp whistle sounded.

Tara jumped from her seat and ran to the door. She looked back up at Gemma. "That's my brother. Can I go?"

"May I go," Gemma corrected.

"May I go?" Tara repeated.

Gemma leaned the broom against the wall and then walked to the door, wanting to make sure it really was Billy. Billy—who had never returned to class. At the edge of the woods, Tara's brother sat astride the old mule. He didn't dismount or attempt to come any closer, but stared at her, an obstinate expression contorting his face along with the bruise that had blossomed into a swollen purple discoloration closing his right eye.

He wouldn't be persuaded to come talk to her. Not now. His anger was too fresh. If only she'd stopped the fight sooner. There might have been hope then to talk things through. She felt terrible that she hadn't been paying attention more to what was happening outside while she wrote out the daily lessons on the board. She wouldn't make that mistake again. What had caused the fight? Should she even make the attempt to discuss things with him? By the stubborn scowl on his face he wasn't in any mood to talk.

Well, truth be known, she wasn't either. It had been a trying day. Perhaps it would be better to put some distance between everything. Emotions were still raw, but in another day things would blow over. Things always looked better after a good night's sleep. Always the next morning she was more clearheaded. "Go ahead, Tara. I'll see you and Billy tomorrow."

Tara's little forehead wrinkled up. "Ain't you comin' to my house?"

"Not today. Let your mother know that I'll be there Saturday." She could only hope time would put everything in better perspective for them all.

Tara rushed down the steps and ran across the clearing to her brother. Once they'd disappeared down the lane, Gemma went back inside to finish her daily chores.

After stacking her papers and anchoring them with an iron paperweight, she grabbed her heavy blue coat and slipped into it. All that remained was to bring some kindling from the shed so that the stove would be ready come morning.

She walked around the side of the building to the shed. As she cracked open the door, a loud angry hiss sounded from the deep dark inside. Suddenly the door slammed outward and crashed against her shoulder. She lost her balance and tottered backward. One step. Two… And then she fell, going down hard on her derriere. Before she could think to move, a large furry ball raced out through the open door and scrambled frantically over her legs, its long claws scratching through her heavy woolen skirt as though it were thin paper.

"Aagh!"

The varmint raced toward the creek and disappeared.

She sat there stunned, her heart pounding, her breath coming in gasps. By its size and coloring it was a raccoon. She hoped it was a raccoon. She shivered, hoping it wasn't a groundhog or badger or some other dirty animal. Did those even exist in this part of the country?

Nothing like this ever happened in Boston! She dragged in a deep breath, trying to calm her racing pulse when suddenly her eyes started to burn. She was frustrated and discouraged at

the same time. She didn't like feeling helpless...
frightened. And that's just how the scare had
made her feel.

Shakily, she gathered her wits about her and
rose to her feet. She dusted herself off, straight-
ening her coat.

How had the raccoon trapped itself in the
shed?

Stepping up to the shed, she worked the latch
on the door. She had heard that raccoons were
smart, but were they smart enough to work this
latch and open the door in order to enter on their
own? Even then, the latch was fairly high off the
ground. And with no food, nothing to bait it, why
enter? It didn't seem likely.

Unless, someone had put it there.

The image of Billy Odom's angry glance before heading to the stream filled her mind. Was
this his way of getting back at her for interfering
with the fight? Maybe he had thought she slighted
him when she sent him to the creek and didn't
require Duncan to go too. She had just wanted
them to stay separated until their tempers cooled.

Perhaps it was simply a prank to garner excitement. After ten weeks, the newness of coming to
school had waned for most of the children. With
Christmas coming, it was much more difficult to

keep their attentions. Likely, teasing the teacher was considered fair play about now.

But not fair at all by her book. She didn't like this type of teasing. She didn't care to be startled out of her wits.

Inside the shed a few remaining logs were strewn over the floor from the short, stacked pile. Either the raccoon had done that in its unsuccessful attempt to escape, or whoever put the animal inside had. Either way, she would soon need more wood. She made a mental note of the fact and picked up two small logs to take into the school. Still a bit wobbly and shaken, she shut the door and latched it securely.

Inside the school, she prepared the stove for lighting in the morning. Then, because of her scattered thoughts of raccoons and badgers, she pulled out her chair and climbed up onto her desk, searching the crux of the crossbeam with her hand. After a moment of patting along the beam, she touched on the box that held her father's gun. She breathed a sigh of relief. Still there. It was good to know she and the children had protection but she hoped none of them ever learned of its hiding place.

And she hoped she never had reason to use it.

Sheriff Parker always had a gun strapped down at his hip. Had he had reason to use his in his position here in Clear Springs? The man's holster and weapon fit to his hips like it was a part of him. He would look odd without it. She shuddered. Was it the thought of him firing it from a low, crouched stance? His jaw tight and his eyes squinting the way she'd seen it on the cover of dime novels? Or was it the image of that weapon riding low and casual on such a trim, broad-shouldered form that made her extra aware of him as a man and stole her breath?

He could be waiting outside right now. He had said he would return to escort Tara home. Gemma climbed down from her perch. She picked up her empty lunch pail and stepped outside. There was no sign of him in the schoolyard. Perhaps something had come up. Perhaps he'd seen Billy arrive with the mule. Whatever his reason for not showing himself to her, she was glad of it.

After making sure to lock the door behind her with her skeleton key, she headed to town.

Molly Birdwell's lips twitched at the end of Gemma's tale of the fight at school and then the raccoon. She slipped the supper dishes into the tub of warm water and soap and began to wash them. "Boys can be mischievous. I wouldn't put it past my two young'uns to do something like that once upon a time."

The woman hummed as she washed. Molly was broad in her hips and had a round face topped with fluffy white hair that reminded Gemma of a sweet Mrs. Claus. The woman's husband had passed on four years back and she'd opened up her house to boarders to make ends meet. Gemma also suspected, with as much as the woman liked to talk and bake, that she enjoyed having company.

"Are you saying I should have handled it differently? That it's a case of boys will be boys?"

"Oh, I ain't saying that at all. Their pa would have walloped my boys good if he'd heard tell of them causing a ruckus at school. No—you did the right thing there. You couldn't let them keep a-fightin'."

Gemma rose from the table and grabbed a cloth to dry the dishes. She valued Molly's advice. The woman had been through good times and rough times and had a commonsense approach to life that reassured Gemma.

Molly eyed her skeptically. "You ain't never run into a situation like that?"

Gemma shook her head. "I didn't fight with my tutors." Just the thought of stern Mr. Allen rolling in the dirt in a bout of fisticuffs produced an unexpected giggle. She slapped her hand over her mouth.

Molly chuckled. "No…guess you wouldn't, at that."

"And what about the raccoon?"

"Now, *that* you can't let them git away with. They'll only try something worse next time."

Next time? Gemma swallowed. "What do you mean…worse?"

"Oh, likely you got nothing to worry about. They was just trying to get a rise from you. 'Course, if it was mean-spirited, that's another thing entirely."

It could have been mean-spirited. She hadn't gotten on well with Duncan or Billy for the past few weeks. Maybe she was pushing them too hard. They both had so much potential and she had encouraged their competition, hoping it would spur them even further in their studies. She hadn't counted on it being quite so adversarial as an out-and-out fight.

"Then you don't think the raccoon could have found its own way into the shed and the door just happened to slam shut?" she asked hopefully. She really didn't want it to be because of a student.

Molly shrugged and kept right on washing. "Guess you'll have to talk to your class and figure that out."

"Molly, they are not going to confess to something like this. No one would."

"No, but you might be able to tell something from the way one of the kids acts. And though I don't hold with squealin' on your neighbor, one of those children might feel a need to tell on his classmate."

Gemma contemplated the woman's attitude and wondered if she would ever feel that self-assured. An education in Boston sure didn't translate to real life in the back country. People here set more stock on common sense and survival than they did on head knowledge.

"I learned one thing from today. I'd better make sure the shed has a way to open it from the inside. I wouldn't want one of my students to get trapped in there like the raccoon."

Molly nodded. "That'd be hard on a young'un for sure."

"Let alone trying to explain to the school board how I let it happen."

"Could be something that would leave a soul scar."

"A soul scar?" Gemma asked. She'd never heard of such a thing.

"Something that hurts a body. Something you can't see with your eyes. It ain't on the surface like a limp or a burn that puckers the skin. It's deeper than that. It's something real hard to heal from. Something that's always there inside you for the rest of your life."

Like her reason for leaving her home. She understood Molly perfectly now. "I wouldn't want to inflict that on any child."

She stacked the last dish on the shelf before speaking again. "I had a visitor today."

"Other than the raccoon?" With her grin, Molly's round spectacles rose up on her apple cheeks.

"Tara Odom decided to go looking for her brother after the fight. The sheriff found her by the creek and brought her back to school."

"He's earning his pay then."

"He didn't care for the way I disciplined Tara. It's just…she's so far behind the other children and I know she has it in her to do so much better. I was…strict with her. And I'm afraid I wasn't very nice to the sheriff."

"Now, don't let that bother you. You have to handle things as they come and as you see fit at the time." Molly wrung out the dishrag and turned to wipe down the kitchen table. "He's new in town himself. Just been here six months or so. That's barely enough time to get settled into the place and know what's what."

"It's just…"

"Just what, dear?"

Gemma sighed. "I don't know. He's so…big and…and…"

Molly raised her brows, this time tilting her snowy white head. "I'd think that would be a good thing for a sheriff."

The thought of Sheriff Parker had her insides twisting into a knot. What was it about the man that set her senses so off-kilter? She probably shouldn't have mentioned anything to Molly. From all she'd heard of the man, people thought he was doing a solid job as sheriff. They only had good things to say about him—Molly included. But still…

"Is he married?"

The woman eyed her with curiosity. "Heard tell he was engaged. Some young woman from his hometown up north of here, but I ain't never heard of her coming to visit."

Gemma should be breathing easier by the minute. The Sheriff had a sweetheart. "Well, that has to be the best news I've heard all day. Perhaps once he marries he'll stop coming by the school and criticizing me."

Molly chuckled. "Oh, he was likely only trying to help. My Mort was the same. Men always think we gals need answers like we can't figure things out for ourselves. We just go about it different is all."

"I didn't like it," she said stubbornly, unwilling to give the good sheriff an inch of grace.

"Well, seems you had quite a day, all told."

Gemma snapped out the wet dishtowel and then took her time spreading it out to dry over the back of the kitchen chair. "Yes," she murmured. "Quite a day."

Chapter Three

Craig Parker stood with his weight shifted to one leg while he leaned against a support four-by-four in the back of the town hall. He crossed his arms over his chest and listened to the proceedings of the Clear Springs School Board meeting. The board was made up of four men, each with children benefitting from the education Miss Starling was handing out. Patrick Tanner was the head of the board and had done the hiring of the new teacher. With four children in the school—two girls and two boys—he had a keen interest in seeing they were educated. Tanner had come with his wife. She, along with Mrs. Winters contributed enough of their opinions that it was obvious they felt their own particular viewpoints should be written into school law.

None of it mattered much to him. He didn't have kids in school. He hadn't even planned to be here tonight, especially after Miss Starling's sound refusal of any kind of help yesterday, but ever since then her abrupt attitude had sat crooked in his judgment. He couldn't reconcile that woman with the one he'd seen playing in the schoolyard and the one the children liked. It was enough that he wondered about her. He had to trust his gut feelings. They were there for a reason. He'd learned that well enough from Sheriff Talbot in the time he'd worked as his deputy. So here he was...

Tonight Miss Starling wore a dark, forest green skirt and pale green blouse. A fitted vest made of the same stiff dark green material as her skirt gave her the no-nonsense appearance that she seemed determined to portray—at least around adults. She appeared at once appealing and distant. As though a body would have to wrangle through a stiff layer of starch and burrs to find the real woman underneath.

She sat looking reserved and collected among the others in the small circle of chairs, her appearance calm with the exception that she kept fingering the high lace collar at her neck as though it was too tight. Something had her on edge. No one else in the room seemed aware of it however, but he couldn't help but notice everything about her, from the thick dark brown

braided bun at the back of her head that seemed
to prop up her felt bonnet, to the tips of her newly
blackened shoes.

She was pretty, all right. He'd noticed that
when he'd gone to the party dedicating the new
schoolhouse in September. He hadn't danced with
her. She had been busy enough with meeting all
the parents and their children, so other than a
very brief introduction, he'd stood back and observed. Since then he had seen her a few times
a week from the doorway of his office as she
walked past on her way to the school, her pert
little nose in the air and a resolute expression on
her face.

That's all he would do—look. He'd had all he
could take of a woman messing with his mind.
After Charlotte scorched his pride when she
chose his brother over him, he intended to steer
clear of the female half of the world and tend to
his job.

The door behind him opened, letting a brace of
cold air swirl into the room. He straightened away
from the post and turned to see Ryan Philmont
enter. The tall, lanky man dismissed him with an
uninterested glance and then strolled toward the
small circle of people with a swagger and confidence that said he belonged there despite the fact
he wasn't a member of the school board.

"Philmont," Tanner said by way of acknowledgement. His wife puckered her face with disapproval of the man.

Ryan Philmont smiled—an oily smile if there ever was one—and tipped his hat to Mrs. Tanner and then to Miss Starling before removing it, slicking back his black hair with his hand. "It can't hurt to know what my son is being taught now can it? Especially after his fight yesterday."

"Fight?" Mrs. Winters gasped. "I hadn't heard about any fight!"

Neither had Craig.

"Guess you haven't got to that part of the meeting." Philmont slipped into a vacant chair, slightly apart from the circle of board members.

The look he turned on Miss Starling was a mite too condescending in Craig's estimation. For a moment she maintained a tight smile, but then her dark lashes shuttered down. After her self-assurance at the school, Craig wondered that Philmont could bully her so easily. He also wondered if she had hoped to get through the meeting without calling attention to the fight.

"My son been behaving in school?" Philmont asked.

She notched up her chin. "I don't think this is the right time to discuss indi—"

"You stopped the fight…but only after they'd

been going at it for a time. Only after that Odom boy knocked out a tooth from my boy's mouth."

Her mouth dropped open and she leaned forward. "Is Duncan all right now?"

"Seems you should have asked that right after it happened yesterday."

She frowned. "I believe speaking with Mr. Odom would be the correct course here as it was his son involved with yours."

Ryan smirked. "Right. He's long gone. Left his family high and dry."

"That's enough, Ryan," Mr. Tanner interjected. "Miss Starling shouldn't have to referee any fights. That's not why we hired her."

Philmont snorted. "I said to hire a man, but you wouldn't listen. Good thing Duncan only has till the end of the year." He settled back into his chair, drawing up his leg and resting his foot on his other knee.

Craig had never gotten on with Philmont. The man thought he was somebody big in this small town. Since he ran the land office, anyone with a claim had to go through him to own it legally. Craig didn't have an issue with the way he did his job—only his attitude about it and nearly everything else.

He hadn't planned on staying the entire meeting, but now, seeing how Philmont had planted himself for the duration, Craig reconsidered. He'd stay awhile and see how things shook out. He took a seat near the door—close enough to listen but far enough away to make the point that they needn't include him.

The meeting continued for another thirty minutes. Talk of the coming Christmas presentation by the children had the women getting all a-flutter and putting in their two bits. Women sure thought things down to the smallest of details. Holly sprigs? Mistletoe? Nice but wholly unnecessary by his way of thinking. Somewhere between the pies and the eggnog he stifled a huge yawn.

Tanner followed suit thirty seconds later. "I think we've covered most of the items we needed to discuss," he said, breaking into the conversation.

"Not quite," Miss Starling said in her clear northeastern accent, raising a finger for attention while she glanced down at her notes. "I wonder if I might have permission for one of the older boys to do custodial help about the school. Things like cleaning out the ashes in the woodstove and sweeping the floors after class. And for the winter, starting a fire in the stove to warm the room before school starts every day."

Mr. Philmont immediately lifted his chin. "Not Duncan. He helps me at the land office."

"'Fraid we can't afford that," Tanner said. "And when you signed your contract…"

She pressed her lips together. "I am aware of what I signed. I was thinking that the chore would help foster responsibility in one of the boys. Not necessarily *your* son, Mr. Philmont."

Craig about choked on her dig. His gaze sliced to Philmont. The man didn't even comprehend the double meaning of her words. Or if he did, he wasn't about to acknowledge that he had been one-upped by a woman. From the determined expression on Miss Starling's face, she wasn't about to give up her quest for help. Like just about any woman he knew, she was a woman who bristled at the word *no*.

The meeting ended and Craig stood with the others. Miss Starling neared, deep in conversation with Mrs. Winters. She stopped when she came abreast of him.

"Sheriff Parker. I am surprised to see you here."

He cleared his throat. "Thought I'd walk you home."

Was that fear in her eyes? It disappeared so fast he wasn't sure.

"I'm capable of seeing myself to the boarding house."

Considering the way things had gone between them at the school, he was ready for her rebuff.

"It's not an offer. There is something I need to discuss with you."

She pressed her lips together. The effort brought out her dimples.

"Official business," he said, gruffly.

"Oh," she said, her voice tight with resignation. "I'll get my coat."

He slipped his Stetson on and headed outside to wait.

On Main Street, the others had all started toward their homes with the exception of Patrick Tanner and his wife.

"First time I've seen you at one of these meetings," Tanner said, tugging his coat closer to ward off the wind.

Craig shrugged. "Thought it was about time."

Tanner's gaze flitted back into the meeting room for a second, and then he turned back to Craig and lowered his voice. "Do you ride by the school much?"

"On my rounds. Two, three times a week. What's on your mind?" It was obvious Tanner was mulling something over.

"Sounds like these older boys could be more than Miss Starling can handle."

"Maybe you should have taken Philmont up on his idea and hired a man."

"Tried to. Right after we lost Miss Talloway to marrying last March. I was sick and tired of hiring a new teacher every year—sometimes two in a year. Single gals just don't last long around here. Even the older ones get snapped up."

Craig commiserated with him, but didn't see what could be done to change things now. Miss Starling had already signed a contract.

"I brought up hiring a man at the town hall meeting in the spring," Tanner continued. "Just about had a riot on my hands from the single men hereabouts. Must have been right before you started as sheriff."

Craig had started in July. As far as he knew, he and Miss Starling were the newest additions to the town. He didn't know much more than that about her. "Guess it makes sense moneywise. The town can pay a lot less for a woman teacher than a man."

He snorted softly. "That had nothing to do with it. People here wanted the diversion."

"By people you mean men." He could understand the miners' attitudes. While working all day in the mines it would be enjoyable for most men to hope for the chance of crossing paths with a pretty woman in town. And it would be near heaven to have a chance at courting a soft and willing woman. He frowned. Miss Starling didn't quite fit that image.

Tanner sighed. "At least she agreed to finish out a complete year. I've heard she has discouraged the few cowpokes that have tried to pound a path to her door. She's keeping her end of the bargain."

So she'd had a few callers? Already? "Well, don't include me in your stampede. The one time I interrupted her class she got real prickly. Left me to understand that she didn't appreciate my interference."

"You don't say?" Tanner seemed to take hope at that. "Maybe she'll stick around two years—at least until my oldest finishes with her schooling."

"So how did you find her?"

"Well, I'll tell you. I didn't want anybody real young. I was hoping for a widow or an old maid. Someone with experience. By August, when nobody like that had answered the advertisement I placed in the San Diego newspaper, I was starting to sweat. Here the new school was almost finished and there was no one to teach in it—at least no one with the right qualifications. I happened to mention it to the traveling preacher one Sunday. He passed along the word down in La Playa. It wasn't but a short time after that, Miss Starling wrote and agreed to an interview."

"So…in the nick of time."

"Yep. Last-minute. And when she came she had all her things with her, just like she expected to get the position and stay on. But you know? That gal has more education behind her than any woman I've ever met. My children are learning things—things I never knew which isn't saying a whole lot. We are lucky to have her."

There. Another inconsistency with Miss Starling. Craig blew out a breath. If what Tanner said was true, why would Miss Starling come here? Why not some private, rich school in the city where she could draw a better salary?

He'd leave Patrick to his fantasy. Miss Starling was too pretty to stay single long, but it wouldn't be because of him that she left teaching. She was too full of starch for him. Besides, he wasn't planning to go down that road again anytime soon.

Even as he said it, the memory of her playing ball with the children in the schoolyard came to him. A woman who was stiff and starchy wouldn't do that. Was it just around him…or maybe men in general…that she put up a barrier?

Just then the woman of their conversation emerged from the building and headed their way. As Miss Starling neared, Craig breathed in the scent of jasmine that circled around her. That clean-smelling soap she used was headier than any perfume worn by the saloon women he'd met in passing. Miss Starling should have more sense. He stopped midbreath when he noticed Tanner watching him.

Tanner shook his head once, then bent down and locked the door to the town hall. "Good night, Sheriff. Miss Starling."

"Good night," Gemma said with a pert nod, at the same time tying her hat ribbons under her chin, while crunched over to hold on to the loose papers tucked under her arm. Not surprisingly they didn't fly off into the night the way they would with most people. *Starch and burrs.* When she was all together and her notes folded and contained within her satchel, she turned her face up expectantly. "Now. You wanted to speak with me?"

He indicated with is hand that they could start walking and then started down the boardwalk toward the boardinghouse. The town was buttoned up for the evening. As the other members of the school board disappeared into their respective homes or rode out of town, their figures absorbing into the dark shadows, the road became deserted. Even the two saloons were quiet, although lamplight from each of them could be seen trickling through the windows at each end of the road. The miners, by this time of evening, had finished their beers and were probably too tired to stand up. If they were smart, they had headed home themselves.

With one gloved hand, Miss Starling gathered the edges of her coat closer about her neck. "It smells of snow in the air."

He glanced upward. A blanket of clouds moved slowly in from the west, snuffing out the stars all the way to the horizon. The moon in the eastern sky still shone bright—to the point that its light cast shadows on the dirt road. Her comment at once distracted him from his agenda and what he wanted to discuss. Strolling and observing the night sky was…well, it was romantic…and at the moment not a word he would use with Miss Starling. He glanced back at her upturned face which was cast in a silvery blue as she caught the moonlight. Just what was she up to?

He was curious about the fight, but he figured it was none of his business unless one of the kids really got hurt. Kids scuffled. That's all there was to it. And it sounded like she had handled it. 'Course, he wondered how she had handled it. Billy was her height and Duncan five inches taller. How had she stopped them?

"I'm new to the community by most counts, miss, but I gather that you've been here even less time than I have. At school you were talking about going out to the Odoms' place."

"Yes. On Saturday."

"Have you got someone going with you? Someone who knows the way?"

She looked perplexed at his question. "Well… No. But I'm sure there is a road…or a trail. Tara and Billy—"

"Are country born and bred."

She stepped down from the boardwalk and started across the first crossroad. "Why would that matter?"

He studied her pert nose which she had notched up stubbornly in the air. "You don't strike me as someone who grew up in the country. For example, can you tell me which way we are headed? North or west?"

She was quiet.

"This isn't like a city where there are names for roads and easy-to-remember storefronts. It's easy to get lost in these hills. One boulder starts to look like another. One tree the same thing. I can't have you walking…or riding…all over the mountain. You'll be lost within half an hour."

"*You* can't have me walking…" she echoed, a trace of sarcasm in her voice.

Guess she didn't care much for his interference. It couldn't be helped. He wasn't about to let her wander the mountains on her own. He walked another half a block with her in silence, hoping she was absorbing the truth of the matter.

Her steps finally slowed and then came to a stop. "What do you propose?" she asked, facing him.

"To go with you."

"I don't think…" She shook her head doubtfully. "That's really not necessary."

"Not. Necessary. Hmm. Then tell me which way you are facing now."

She sucked in a breath and let it out slowly. "I can't."

"Well, until you can, you need an escort. I'm offering."

She frowned. "Sheriff…I doubt the etiquette of the situation allows for you to accompany me."

So that's what was bothering her. "It doesn't allow for a woman to go alone either. Sometimes out here you have to be practical."

"Well…perhaps Mrs. Birdwell or Eileen Gilliam at the dry goods store could accompany me. I'll ask one of them. You needn't trouble yourself further."

"Fair enough." He had plenty of other things to do.

She started walking toward Mrs. Birdwell's again "Do all the other women here know their directions?"

"If they were raised in the country they do."

"Day or night?"

"While the sun is up for the most part. There are a few who know the stars too." He couldn't imagine growing up without that knowledge. His father had impressed it on him by the time he was ten. "Just where are you from anyway?"

"Obviously not here," she grumbled.

"So…?" he prompted.

She eyed him with a speculative look. The light through the saloon window danced in her eyes. "Guess."

He hadn't expected that. He raised his brows. A challenge. "Big city. North, I think."

She smiled slightly.

"Your clothes are fancier than most. Your shoes wouldn't last more'n a day on a hike."

"My shoes?" She stopped and looked down at her feet. "When did you check my…? Humph."

"San Francisco? No…" he answered himself. Not with the way she said certain words. "Back East somewhere."

"I have a feeling not knowing the answer will trouble you immensely," she said smugly.

"It may take me a while, but I don't back down from a challenge."

She stared at him a moment and then dropped her gaze. "There are a lot of people here from the South. I noticed that some harbor ill will toward northerners."

He had witnessed a few slights, and then realized she might have been a target. He sliced his gaze toward her. "Toward you?"

She shook her head. "No. But I am surprised. Especially so far away from where the fighting occurred."

Was she really so young not to understand? "They lost everything. The War Between the States might as well have been yesterday for those that had to leave their homes and start completely over. You might want to give that some thought before you teach about it."

They turned down the side road that led out of town. Widow Birdwell's boardinghouse was the last house on the road. The light from her parlor blinked dimly through the rustling pines.

"It's a good thing Molly doesn't feel like that or I might be out of a place to stay. Thank you for the reminder to be sensitive in its instruction." Her tone became more thoughtful. "Surely Mr. Tanner wouldn't have hired me if he thought there would be a problem."

"He was just relieved to have a teacher of your caliber for his kids."

She stopped walking. "He said that?"

Craig nodded.

"Well, I suppose that is reassuring," she murmured, looking at him with a puzzled expression. "I arrived on the tail of another teacher leaving. I thought…perhaps…" She blew out a breath. "The Tanner children have had a total of four teachers in seven years with three of them marrying. I assured Mr. Tanner that that wouldn't happen in my case."

"I thought all young ladies wanted to marry."

"Not. Me." She started toward the boarding-house again.

He caught up to her in three strides.

"May I ask you something, Sheriff? You're a man… I mean that you understand boys a tad better than I would. Why would two boys old enough to know better get into a fight? They should be setting an example for the younger children— not fighting."

"I take it you don't have brothers."

"No. And I'll admit that I was so intent on stopping the fisticuffs before more bloodshed occurred that I didn't think to get the real reason for the fight out of them."

He slanted a glance at her. "The best time to wrangle an answer out of them is while they are still fighting mad. Things tend to spill out from the gut."

She sighed. "Then I've lost my chance."

"So you haven't come across much fighting in your other teaching jobs." Tanner had said this was her first teaching job, but he wanted to hear it from her.

"This was a first." She looked up at him. "This is my first teaching position."

He tucked that bit of information away. "Sounds like you did okay. You stopped the fight. No one died."

She stepped up on Mrs. Birdwell's stoop. "An interesting way to put it."

He reached for the door handle. "Just out of curiosity... How *did* you make those boys stop fighting? Hard to believe they'd stop just because you told them to."

Her lips twitched and then those dimples appeared again as her smile grew. "I threw a bucket of cold, dirty water over them." She stepped inside. The parlor lantern lent a yellow glow to the right side of her face. "Good night, Sheriff."

He tipped his hat even though she was already closing the door in his face. "Night, Miss Starling."

The woman might have no idea about staying safe on the mountain but that smile of hers could sure pack a wallop.

* * *

On Friday at noon, the sudden realization that the schoolroom was quiet made Gemma turn away from the window. She'd been staring at the road, wondering when Sheriff Parker would come riding down the lane. Twice now in the past three days, he had appeared at the beginning of the noontime break. He had stopped his mount just this side of the stand of pines and leaned on his saddle horn to watch what was happening at the school, remaining there a good three or four minutes, as he observed the children—some who lived nearby heading home for their meal and others sitting on the front steps with their lunch tins and baskets.

The first day he'd come upon her, she'd been outside after finishing her own lunch and well into a game of kick the can with the children. When she spied him, she had reluctantly stopped. She wasn't sure if playing games was a "teacher-like" thing to do. Having grown up with tutors, she really had no idea if it was acceptable. When he showed up again, she made sure to stay inside even though the children had asked her to join them.

He had come a time or two before over the months that she had been teaching, but this was more often…and more obvious. Had Mr. Tanner said something to him? Were they worried that she could not handle the students on her own?

The quiet in the schoolroom once more permeated her thoughts.

"I'm sorry, Mr. Shalbot. Please continue."

Charley Shalbot began reading again in a halting voice. He was having difficulty with the long paragraph, but he bravely plowed through it. Gemma had to admire his tenacity. In the back row, Duncan sprawled across his seat looking bored and restless. Actually, a number of the children had had enough book learning for the morning. It was time to break for the noon refreshment whether it was timed to the sheriff's arrival or not.

When the end of the day came, she dismissed the class and followed the children outside. She watched over them as they started on their way home—something she did every afternoon. Her gaze wandered to the tie line. The old mule hadn't been back—just as Billy and Tara hadn't been back to school since the altercation between Duncan and Billy. Hopefully, she would be able to speak with the children when she saw Mrs. Odom tomorrow.

A movement near the bend in the road caught her attention. A short, bent-over man with a shock of stringy gray hair showing under his brown hat stood watching the children head off in different directions. He leaned on a walking stick that came up to his chest. His overalls and cotton shirt were stained with grass and mud. A wave of unease filled her. It was the second time she'd noticed him on the edge of the clearing since the beginning of school.

"You there!" she called.

Either he didn't hear her or he was ignoring her. She started toward him.

At her movement, he raised his head and stared at her for a moment. Then he turned and shuffled into the trees.

"That's Larabee."

She spun around, startled at the deep voice so near to her.

Duncan Philmont stood only a few inches away, his arm above his head as he leaned against the doorframe.

Her heart pounded as she splayed her hand over her chest. "Duncan! I thought you'd already left."

A cocky grin inched up his face and amusement filled his green eyes.

She didn't enjoy being startled—even less so after the raccoon incident. She pressed her lips together. He stood a bit too close for her comfort, close enough that she could see he was growing dark facial hair now. "Larabee, you say?"

"Yeah. He's an old-timer around these parts."

"Is he…friendly?" Her heartbeat slowed back to normal.

Duncan shrugged. "He don't talk to folks much."

"Why?"

The familiar cynical glint returned to his eyes. "Most think he's off in the head."

Duncan always seemed to challenge her, and she wondered if he still resented her earlier treatment when he and Billy had their fight. Then she recalled the footprints in the grass. Could they belong to Larabee instead of one of the older boys? "Would he be a danger to the younger children?"

Duncan straightened.

For a moment, he looked surprised that she would ask him his opinion. She supposed that was to be expected. Usually she didn't ask her students questions unless they were rhetorical. That's what her experience had been growing up with her tutors. "I'm sure you know better than I would. You are from here. You know more of the local people."

He cocked his head and peered down at her as if debating with himself whether to answer or not.

The look reminded her of his father the other night at the meeting. She had had enough of his attitude and to show it, she fisted her hands on her hips and faced him. "Is this about the other day? The fight?"

He didn't answer.

"What was the fight about, Duncan?"

His lower jaw jutted out stubbornly. "Ain't nonc of your business."

"None of my business! I should say it is! It happened on school property."

"It's between me and Billy. Gave our words and spit on it."

That didn't make any sense to her. They made some sort of spit bond and then had a fight? She would never understand boys. Never. "Do you realize that some of the younger boys were betting? And I'm sure their parents have learned of it by now. There could be ramifications. I need to know why you were fighting. If there is a problem between you two and it isn't resolved, how do I know it won't happen again?"

"It won't," he said sullenly.

"I cannot force you to tell me," she said, disappointed. "I hope someday you will. You and Billy are both intelligent boys and you have a good future ahead of you. I hate to see you bent on hurting each other." He was a bit too much like his father, but hopefully those sharp edges would round out as he matured. "I…I wish you'd told me about your tooth."

"You heard about that?" He asked, his tone guarded, but much less antagonistic.

"I should have asked if you were all right. I'm sorry I didn't."

He lifted his chin. "Weren't nothin'."

"It must have hurt. And you didn't say a word."

He swallowed. "You shouldn'ta got so near Billy and me. Stupid thing to do, Teach."

"Should not…" On the cusp of correcting his grammar she stopped herself. It was more important that he was talking to her—that they were actually having a conversation. It was a first between them without his belligerent attitude getting in the way. Instead, she asked gently, "Please don't call me Teach. Is there something you wished to discuss?" She wasn't entirely sure why he was hanging around.

When he didn't answer, she persisted. "Something about your homework?"

He snorted. "Naw."

"Well, won't your father be waiting for you at the land office?"

He blew out a breath, his scowl deepening. "Yeah. Guess so." He grabbed his coat from the bench, hooked his finger into the collar and slung it over his shoulder. "See you, Miss Starling," he mumbled as he strode by and down the steps of the school.

At least he hadn't called her Teach.

Chapter Four

Saturday morning, Gemma slipped on her felt hat, tugging on the wine-colored ribbons beneath her chin and then shrugged into her dark blue wool coat. Stepping out into the sunshine, she closed the boardinghouse door behind her and headed for the livery at a brisk walk. The snow she had been sure would fall during the week had not fallen. Instead a heavy frost had clung to the shady areas of the town every morning and as soon as the sun rays found it, it quickly melted away.

She had arranged for a buggy. Eileen had agreed to accompany her, although she was not sure of the way herself. Molly was busy finishing Christmas gifts for a group of Clear Springs' unfortunates at the church. Remembering her talk with Sheriff Parker she had thought to mention something to him yesterday, but Eileen had said he was busy at one of the mines.

She stepped inside the stable and the odor of horse and leather and fresh straw permeated her senses, overpowering the crisp freshness of the day outside. The livery had two sections, divided by a railing. The stalls on her left and the large open area that housed two buggies and one carriage to her right. In the latter, Gil Jolson bent beside a horse, cleaning mud from its hooves with a metal pick. When he saw her, he dropped the horse's leg and straightened.

"Got you all set up right over here, Miss Starling." He walked to the smallest buggy that he'd already hitched to a horse.

She looked about the stable. "Has Miss Gilliam come by?"

"Haven't seen her."

"She must be detained. Well, no matter. If you will assist me I'll drive by her father's store and fetch her."

Just as Mr. Jolson started toward her, Bradley, Eileen's younger brother rushed into the livery. He stopped short just inside the large door.

"My sister ain't comin', Miss Starling. She ain't feelin' good. Had me come to tell you."

"Oh." Gemma lowered her shoulders as his words actually sunk in. "Oh… Thank you for letting me know. She's ill, you say? Should I come check on her?"

"Naw. She's just got one of her headaches. Can't stand the sun." He turned quickly and raced back out of the stable.

What was she to do now? She really had to get out to the Odoms'. She couldn't let things go until after Christmas break. It might be too late by then to entice Billy and Tara back to school.

Mr. Jolson stood by the buggy, waiting to see what she would do.

"I won't be needing the buggy after all," she said, disappointed.

"Sorry, miss. I'll leave it hitched for a while, just in case you change your mind."

"Thank you." She stood there, undecided on what to do next.

Mr. Jolson watched her a moment more. "I got to take ol' Tartar here down to the blacksmith," he finally said, taking up the reins of a dun-colored pony.

"Oh…of course. Please go ahead. I'll see myself out…"

When he'd left with the pony, she surveyed the stable once more.

"You wouldn't have gone far with the buggy," a deep, familiar voice said from the darker corner of the stable.

"Sheriff Parker. You've been eavesdropping!" She glared at him as he came to stand before her.

He wore a deep brown leather jacket, tan canvas pants and brown boots. A dark stubble shadowed his strong jaw.

"That I have. It's a good quality to have as a sheriff." He tipped the brim of his tan Stetson. "I heard you were looking for me yesterday."

"Yes. Only to ease your mind that Miss Gilliam would be accompanying me today."

"Seems those plans have changed."

"Unfortunately."

"You wouldn't have gone far past the school in that buggy. The trail requires that you ride horseback."

She scowled. "Now, there is a bit of pertinent information that you could have shared with me."

His blue eyes twinkled. "I can tell by that determined look on your face that you are still considering heading out of town."

"You cannot stop me." It was a stubborn, childish thing to say.

He raised one brow. "Sure I can. You are not going alone. I won't have that on my conscience."

"You would use brute force?"

"Might. Or handcuff you to that post." He indicated a nearby iron ring for tethering horses.

She was appalled...and frustrated. "That would be most indecent."

They glared at each other. After a good long while, he indicated with his chin two horses standing near the farthest stall—a black and a chestnut. "I took the liberty of saddling the mare."

He wasn't giving her the choice. It was either go with him, or not at all. Very well. She tugged her gloves on tighter and started toward the horses. Halfway there, she stopped and stared at the saddle on the smaller animal.

"What's wrong?"

"I'm used to sidesaddle."

His eyes narrowed. "I'm getting a new appreciation of your upbringing, Miss Starling. This must be quite a change for you from... Boston."

"You have no idea." Then she realized what he'd said. She had hoped he would forget trying to figure out her past. The game had been unwise. She realized it the moment he had started asking her questions. "You found out."

He nodded. Once.

How much had he come to know about her? She swallowed and with a forced casualness, stepped up to the mare and stroked its warm neck. "How?"

"You dropped a few clues." He tilted his head, indicating he'd help her mount. "You'll figure out the saddle."

She was relieved that he wasn't going to pursue more of her past. She would be more careful with her information from now on. The horse ignored her ministrations, but for a flick of its ears. "I'm sure I can adjust. There can't be much of a difference. It's not like I'm riding an ostrich. It is still a horse."

An amused grin inched up his face. "Now, there's a picture to think on. I'll give you a leg up."

She felt a bit nervous and it wasn't about the horse or the saddle, but about him standing close as he laced his fingers and waited for her to place her boot in his hands. She steadied herself—her right hand on the saddle horn and her left one on his strong thick shoulder. She was so close she could smell the clean scent of the soap he'd used that morning. It mixed with the scent of leather and horse and was altogether…pleasant.

He shifted under her hand, and then straightened, a question in his eyes. She realized she'd hesitated.

"Ready now?" he asked, his brows raising, and the brilliant blue of his eyes capturing her for a moment.

She nodded and took hold of the pommel and the cantle. She placed her boot in his hands and he boosted her up. In the space of a heartbeat she was on the saddle and then sliding…

"Whoa, there!" he said, and clasped on to her waist to steady her.

She blew out a breath. "I've got it."

He let go and backed off, yet all the while her skin tingled and her waist felt like it was on fire beneath her layers of clothing. She tugged at her coat and then straightened her felt hat in an effort to make herself feel "all together" again. Then she realized that he was waiting for her to settle, and she stopped fidgeting.

He handed her the reins and then walked around her horse, adjusting her stirrups to the length of her legs. "All set for this?" he asked, a doubtful look twisting his expression.

She nodded gamely. "Lead on, Sheriff."

He led her horse out the smaller back door of the livery and handed the reins up to her. "I'll meet you at the school in ten minutes. Take it slow to give me time."

He had surprised her. She hadn't expected him to be sensitive to the situation. His unstudied competence suddenly made her feel secure and protected... She blew out a slow breath. And all the more aware of him.

It was a bit...unsettling.

"Thank you, Sheriff." She urged her horse to the small side street. When she looked back over her shoulder, he had already reentered the livery.

Her seat felt foreign at first—and hard—and she wished she had thought to wear thicker undergarments. At this rate, her derriere would have a pink glow—if not a blister or two—by the time she returned to Molly's. She passed Mr. Winters with his young son in tow as the two entered the barber shop.

"Out riding, Miss Starling?"

"Yes. I couldn't resist. Just for a bit."

"Well, it's fine weather for it. Good day." He turned into the shop.

He hadn't seemed off in the least! Not about her riding astride, or about her riding alone. She sat a little taller in the saddle.

She passed Molly's boardinghouse and then turned north, following a trail away from town that led diagonally through the woods to the schoolhouse.

Once she arrived at the school, she waited for the Sheriff. Five minutes later he appeared riding up from the stream.

"Ready?"

She urged her horse up beside his. "I would appreciate you taking it slow. It's been a while since I rode—more than a year."

"You will understand why a buggy won't work once we turn off the main road."

They continued for a mile in silence, persisting farther north. A light wind gently rocked the branches of the tall pines and rustled the naked branches of the few oaks that lined the route. On each side of the road, curled, dead leaves and acorns littered the ground.

"Here we go. It gets steep in a few places." He reined his horse through a stand of manzanita and headed east, following a deer trail. Beyond a massive boulder, it skirted the southern side of a mountain that was speckled with large granite boulders and sumac. The scent of mountain sage filled the crisp air. Suddenly she was quite thankful for his presence. She doubted that she would have been able to find the way on her own.

A blast of cool air rounded the hillside, whipping up the ends of her scarf. She gasped and tightened her scarf around her neck, tucking the ends under the collar of her coat. "No wonder Tara and Billy don't make it to school when the weather is bad," she murmured. She was gaining an appreciation for what a struggle it must be to take this trail daily.

"Probably why she was worried about her brother...and about getting home the day of the fight."

It was the gentlest admonition she had ever received. "I see why you insisted she not go on her own. A little girl has no business out here on her own."

"Neither does a lady from back East."

She reined back and stared at his broad back, only slightly miffed that he'd been right. "Point taken, Sheriff."

A small lizard scrambled off a boulder that stood next to the trail and skittered away into the brush.

"Do you know how to shoot, Miss Starling?"

Her gaze flew to his face. Why would he bring up guns all of a sudden? He couldn't know, could he? She glanced at his holster and gun. "Why do you ask?"

"I realize the school is only a stone's throw from town, but it is close enough to the creek that you are sure to see animals stopping by. This isn't Boston, where I suspect the largest wild animal might be a rat."

"A rat! Of all the outlandish things to say. Just what part of Boston do you think I am from?"

His look was curious…assessing. "I wouldn't know."

Every time they spoke she seemed to give more of herself—her past—away. She had to be careful. The sheriff wasn't a fool. Quite the contrary. Each time she was with him, she became more and more convinced of his innate intelligence.

"I've seen a few snakes," she admitted in a clipped tone, but then became more thoughtful. "Just what type of wild animals are you talking about?"

He blew out a long breath. "Bears, cougars…"

"Wolves?"

"Not around here, but there are definitely coyotes."

"Nothing has bothered me so far."

"Maybe you have a guardian angel."

"No," she said. If she had an angel watching over her she would be safe and comfortable at home. Perhaps by now she would even have finished law school. "I've found I must depend on myself and my wits."

He snorted lightly. "You could be the smartest person around and your wits still won't help you outrun a bear."

She wasn't about to let Sheriff Parker know about the gun she had hidden in the rafters at the school. He would commence with all kinds of questions and then what would she say?

"Glad you haven't had any trouble," he said, looking more relaxed. "Part of my job is to make sure people in town stay safe."

"I thought your job was to uphold the law."

"Figure it's the same thing."

His words only served to make her feel guilty.

How would he feel if he knew Clear Springs harbored a fugitive from justice? Here he was helping her, yet she wasn't being honest with him.

She eased her horse up over the crest of a hill and started down into a small valley. The trail split, and she reined back slightly to see which fork the sheriff would choose. When he moved ahead and to the left, she found herself staring at his broad capable back as his horse made the way down a particularly bumpy patch of ground. He held himself square and confident, the ends of his leather jacket brushing his thighs and saddle. He did not appear concerned about the trail…or rattlers…or bears. All of which put her that much more at ease. Had she been alone, she would have been just the opposite—nervous and timid.

She could see now why Molly and Eileen thought highly of him. They both had mentioned more than once, his commanding nature and his handsome face. Eileen in particular had bemoaned the fact that he was engaged.

"I could not have found this trail," she admitted softly.

He glanced back over his shoulder, his deep blue gaze sliding to hers as he quietly acknowledged her words. Something shifted between them. Something that felt…comfortable.

"Sheriff?"

"Call me Craig."

She hesitated. That might be a bit too comfortable, especially considering his engaged status. In fact, it surprised her that he would mention it. "I don't think that's a good idea."

He was silent for a moment, and then murmured, "Suit yourself."

"It's just…in Boston it would be considered much too familiar."

"This ain't Boston."

"Isn't Boston," she said, the words rolling off her tongue out of habit.

"This isn't school," he said, his voice clipped. "And I'm not in your classroom."

She was mortified. How could she have corrected him when he had been helping her this morning! It was inexcusable. "I…I beg your pardon, Sheriff. I meant no offense. It was simply… habit."

His jaw tightened. Then, after a minute he continued. "The town *isn't* that big. We will run into each other more often than we would if we were in a city. It's easier…"

"I agree. But I'm sure your fiancée would prefer—"

"Where did you hear I was engaged?" he asked sharply.

Now she'd put her foot in it. "Mrs. Birdwell mentioned it a few days ago. Is it…true?"

For a moment, he did not answer her. She began to think he wasn't going to when she heard him continue.

"It *was* true."

Was? Past tense? "I'm sorry to hear that. May I ask what happened?"

"No," he said curtly. He let out a sharp whistle and urged his horse to pick up the pace.

Warmth flushed up her cheeks. Apparently a first-name basis with him didn't translate to questions about his fiancée. She had overstepped in presuming it did. They weren't exactly friends…but they weren't enemies either. She tapped her mount's flanks lightly with her heels, encouraging the mare to quicken its steps and follow before he moved too far ahead and out of sight.

Twenty minutes later they came to a small, dilapidated spread nestled in the dip of two boulder-strewn hillsides.

"That must be it," she murmured as they passed a small outhouse snugged up against the mountainside and surrounded by a few straggly pines. It was the end of the trail. The path they were on dwindled out ahead of them before a slanted wooden structure—a homestead that appeared barely large enough for one room, let alone a place to house four people. The mule that the children rode to school stood forlorn in a small, dusty corral next to the house. On the other side of the building, a frame sat in the sun with what she thought might be four rabbit skins stretched from top to bottom.

The sheriff dismounted and tied his horse to the corral post. He walked over, helped her down and had almost released her when her legs wobbled.

He grasped her again and she gripped his forearms, steadying herself further. His arms were hard as stone, so muscular that her fingers couldn't span but half the width. Holding on to him was like holding on to a tree trunk—sturdy and immoveable.

The look he gave her carried a hint of uneasiness. "Steady?"

She nodded…but couldn't bring herself to smile and smooth over the awkwardness of their situation—not after the words they had each spoken. "It would be prudent for me to ride more often." She stepped back to a more suitable distance.

"You're not in Bos—"

"Not in Boston anymore. As you reminded me

earlier." She glanced at the dismal scene before her and couldn't help recalling the cozy restaurants and cobbled, clean streets of the city where she had grown up. There was no comparison. And she would—she must—adapt. She couldn't go back. "I'm trying to accept that very fact."

"Then you might want to brace yourself."

At a noise from the direction of the house, they turned. A small, birdlike woman stepped out on the porch holding a rifle before her at hip level with both hands. "State your business," she said, her voice sharp and suspicious.

Gemma opened her mouth to answer, but then stopped at the woman's appearance. Her faded dress hung loose on her body with a dirty apron hanging from around her waist and she was barefoot. Barefoot! And with cold weather already here! She looked to be about forty-five but Gemma wondered if that was accurate. She hadn't bothered to put her hair up, but simply tied the stringy blond strands back with a faded piece of frayed ribbon at the nape of her neck.

"I recognize you," she said, training the barrel of her rifle at the sheriff's chest. "You brought my young'uns home from town over the summer when the weather turned."

"Glad to see you remember. They were sell-

pline...daily. Got...
doin' all rig...
drifted down her...
the sheriff again. "Wh... we doin..."

"This is Miss Starling, the...
in Clear Springs."

Gemma took one step closer. She couldn't very well say that she was upset with Tara's and Billy's attendance right off. And in the light of their upbringing, suddenly it seemed insensitive to broach a criticism right at the start of the meeting. "I am visiting all of my students' families to introduce myself."

"Oh?" Mrs. Odom lowered the destructive end of the rifle only slightly.

"Sheriff Parker offered to accompany me since I didn't know the way."

Finally, the woman lowered her rifle completely and walked over to the corner of the porch to wedge it against the wall. "I'd offer you a seat but there ain't none. What can I do for you?"

"Are the children home?"

Mrs. Odom. So, if
asking out of curiosity, what
chores?"

"Tara's got her rabbits and the chickens and
Billy's got his trapline."

Gemma caught Tara peeking from behind the
half closed front door, her light gray eyes clouded
with worry. She looked afraid to join them. With
sudden insight, Gemma remembered how the girl
had acted at school at the mention of her visit to
her home. There had been tears in her eyes then.
She certainly didn't want to make things more
difficult for either of the children. "Tara and Billy
are very bright, Mrs. Odom. You must be proud
of them."

"'Course they are." Her shoulders relaxed.
"Got their father's ways about them."

"Is Mr. Odom home? Perhaps he would like
to join us too."

The woman stared at Gemma. "I'll tell you
straight, since you ain't from around here. Elias
is good and gone for better'n two months now.
Took off north to do some prospectin'."

"I'm sorry to hear that. The children must miss
him, as well as you."

. Mrs. Odom raised her chin. "We get along.
Elias always says there's things a body needs to

know that ain't all book learnin'. Got to depend on yourself."

"Independence is an admirable quality."

Mrs. Odom stood up straighter.

"How do you yourself feel about school?"

The woman looked startled at the question. She blinked and then tilted her head as though she'd never been asked for her own opinion before. "Well...don't rightly know. I ain't never been to school."

"That's another reason I came today. The class is preparing a small presentation to begin the Community Christmas Dance next Saturday. Tara and Billy both have a part. I'd like to invite you to come and see what they have been doing in school."

"Well...I see this hullaballoo means something to you. You wouldn't have come all this way if it didn't." Mrs. Odom seemed to mull it over. "Don't usually bother with town stuff."

"Not even at Christmas?"

Mrs. Odom shook her head. "Nope. Got chores. Things to tend to here. So do my chillun."

"Is that why they haven't been to school this past week? You needed them at home?" Gemma felt a nudge at her arm from the sheriff but ignored it. "Your Billy is smart. And I suspect Tara is too, although she is very quiet."

"She's got a hard path ahead of her. Might as well learn right off it ain't easy."

Gemma could see that hard path in the woman before her. "But don't you want better for them? Tara is quick with her numbers and figuring. And Billy has the makings of a fine businessman."

Mrs. Odom chortled. "Don't 'spect that will help much at the mine."

"At the mine!"

"Miss Starling…"

She heard the low warning in Sheriff Parker's tone. She ignored it. It was important that the woman understand that an education would give her children choices. "You have to see that he can be a lawyer, a judge for that matter. Anything he chooses!"

Mrs. Odom's expression was incredulous. "You are crazy. All that book learnin' done addled your head! Miss—" The woman leaned forward and lowered her voice, as if trying to keep her words from the sheriff's hearing. "You ain't got no more sense than a rabbit if'n you're tryin' to teach him more than he needs."

Gemma gasped, completely at a loss. She had never heard such an attitude before.

"Now… I don't want you fillin' his head about bein' smarter than the others. It would make him prideful. He'd get all high 'n' mighty and I would have to take a strap to him."

"For being smart?" She was appalled. "You wouldn't!"

Mrs. Odom stiffened and crossed her arms over her chest. "I've made things clear. Now I'll ask you to get off my land."

"I just want what is best for your children."

The woman's gaze hardened. "Think I can figure that out without your help."

"Miss Starling?" The sheriff took her elbow, his grip firm. "Time to go."

She didn't budge. There had to be a way to reason with this woman.

"Gemma…"

Hearing her Christian name, she looked up at him. "But…"

His eyes pinned hers. He shook his head, one tight move.

And she let out a sigh, defeated. "I'm sorry. It's just…"

"I know."

She doubted that Tara or Billy would show up for school or the program now. Clearly she had offended Mrs. Odom. She sighed. Only one thing left to do. She loosened the cinch on her satchel and pulled out the book she'd brought along. Stepping forward, she held it out to Mrs. Odom. "I thought Billy might like to have this. He didn't get a chance to finish it at school and was enjoying the story. There's no hurry. He can bring it back when he is done."

Mrs. Odom took the book and stared at the dark red woven cover with a disapproving crimp to her mouth.

Craig tipped his hat brim and tugged Gemma as he stepped back. "Good to know that you're faring all right way out here. Send Billy into town if you need anything. Good day, ma'am."

Mrs. Odom looked up from the book. Then she gave both the sheriff and Gemma a tight nod before disappearing into her house.

Craig walked to where they had tied the horses and snapped both lead lines from the corral post. She surveyed the house once more and the small dismal plot of land that Billy and Tara called home and then ran to catch up to him.

He rode a good horse's length in front of Gemma, mulling over the meeting. Something about Edna Odom today troubled him. He couldn't quite figure it out. She'd been friendlier when he'd brought Tara and Billy home to her that time—after she'd lowered her gun, that is. At the time, her husband had been working in one of the mines. Soon after he'd been caught stealing gold and had been fired. After a brawl in the saloon, he had left the area. Maybe Mrs. Odom was having a tough time now and didn't want to admit it.

Behind him, Miss Starling clucked to her mare and he heard the light tapping of the earth as the smaller horse trotted up beside him. Miss Starling was doing all right on that horse of hers. Too bad he couldn't say the same for what had just happened with Mrs. Odom.

"How can she think like that, Sheriff?"

He shrugged. "It's her way. Nothing that a little honey couldn't fix."

Miss Starling frowned, her face perplexed. "Honey? You want…honey?"

"Not for me, although that could be interesting," he said, amused when she colored slightly. "You might have thought to hand her that book at the start of the range war."

"War?"

"Over her kids."

"Well…she's the one who greeted us holding a rifle!"

"Only to protect what's hers." He glanced over at her. "Didn't think of that, did you?"

She shook her head, lowering her shoulders.

"You can't force someone to see a different point of view."

The woman immediately bristled.

"I wasn't trying to force her!" she said, frowning. "I only want what's best for Billy and Tara."

"I know that. And you know that. But that's not what Mrs. Odom heard. She heard a woman at least fifteen years younger than her criticizing her as a mother. A woman who doesn't even have a child of her own."

Gemma pulled back on the reins and slowed her mount.

He slowed as well. "Folks like her—without any classroom schooling—are still smart. She wants her children to know how to survive and she's doing a good job of teaching them that. You saw the skins?"

"Yes. On the frame. You're saying I might have complimented her on Billy's skill with trapping?"

"That's what I meant about the honey. You catch more flies with honey than you do with vinegar."

Her gaze went to the trail ahead. "Benjamin Franklin."

"Smart man."

Something raced through the underbrush. He eased back on the reins to stop his horse and listen. Four hooves pounded the ground.

"What is it?" she whispered, reining in her mare beside him.

He put his finger to his mouth, indicating she should keep quiet, and then reached carefully for his rifle and slipped it from its scabbard.

Gemma's mare sidestepped and snorted, its ears flicking forward nervously. She reached down and stroked her mount's neck in an attempt to calm it.

A grunt. A snort. And again hooves thumping the hard earth. A small pig? Had something scared it or was it chasing another smaller animal? Two animals to search for.

Gemma's horse tossed its head. Something was making her anxious. He grabbed hold of the horse's bridle to steady the mare. At least, whatever the animal was, it was downwind from them. He strained to listen.

The cry of a cougar whipped through the air and then the frightened squeal of a boar. A moment of silence, in which no bird chirped or crow cawed, and then a commotion started up just ahead of him. He heard the hiss and growl of a large cat and more squealing from the pig which was obviously in pain.

Beside him, Gemma gripped her reins tighter in a white-knuckled clench. Her face paled and her brown eyes widened as she listened. Crows cawed angrily in the trees overhead, spectators to the dance of life and death happening on the ground. A Steller's jay swooped through the clear blue sky, screeching.

And then it was quiet.

He waited a moment and then slowly released her mare's bridle. "You all right?"

She let out her breath and nodded in answer, her eyes wide and fearful. She looked stunned—and not in a good way. "Are we safe? Will it bother us?"

"We should be able to continue on without a problem." He didn't want to alarm her, but the cat was close. Too close for comfort, in his mind. He pressed his knees into his horse and urged him on.

Another thousand feet and they came across a splattering of bright red blood on the path and against a boulder. The earth was disturbed where the cougar had dragged the boar across the trail and into the brush. The strong odor of blood filled his nostrils and Craig knew Gemma's mare smelled it too. The horse flicked her ears back and forth nervously.

Suddenly, the cougar cried out. It crouched, ready to spring, on a large boulder overhead. At the sound, Gemma's horse whipped up its head and bolted, taking off toward the road at a terrifying pace.

Gemma screamed and grabbed the saddle horn.

By the time Craig could react, she was already more than fifty feet ahead. He spurred his horse into a gallop, chasing after her. "Hang on!"

Thank God she kept her head down whether by intent or by accident. In doing so, she ducked below the pine branches that would have knocked her off her horse. Once she slipped slightly to the side, but then determinedly scrambled back atop the horse.

He couldn't get abreast of her. To force his way close would pin her leg against the hillside or scrape her against the boulders or tree trunks that lined the narrow trail. All he could do was stay close behind. When the hillside leveled out, there was finally an opening to come up beside her and grab the mare's bridle. He pulled back firmly. "Whoa…" He pulled on his reins. Both horses finally slowed and then stopped.

He breathed hard trying to catch his breath while looking back and listening to make sure they weren't being followed. With any luck on their side, the cat had been protecting its kill. When they left it would have settled down to eat. He turned back to attend to Miss Starling. "I think we're oka—"

She gripped his vest hard, and tucked her face into his chest, breathing hard. Her small shoulders shook.

Surprised by the sudden change in her, he didn't know what to do at first. "It's okay, Gemma." He looked down on the straight part in her brown hair. Her hat had fallen off during her wild ride and now hung by its ribbons on her back. "We're safe. You're fine."

Her breaths came in disjointed gasps.

He didn't know what the heck to do with his arms, flummoxed as he was by her sudden move to cling to him.

"Is it gone?"

"I think so." Her hair knot was half out of its coil and falling down her back. He breathed in her jasmine scent. What had happened to Miss "I can do it myself"? He was beginning to realize there was a lot more to Miss Starling than she cared to admit.

"Wh-what happened?" She spoke into his chest, her breaths still coming in gasps.

"Not sure. Probably the cat was being protective of its kill."

"Are we safe?"

"Yeah." He said it but he wasn't all that sure. He listened for the big cat, which was foolish since cats hunted quieter than any other large animal. It would be on them before they knew it wanted them.

Finally, he slipped his arms around her shoulders and simply held her. It was awkward at first. He felt stiff. She hadn't wanted to close the gap to call him Craig, but here she was in his arms. He didn't know what to make of it. Then she shifted on her saddle, moving closer. He tightened his hold. "Take a big breath and let it out slow."

She did as he said, her breathing still unsteady, her body still shaking. She was a tiny thing. The only other woman he'd held in his arms was Charlotte who was a good five inches taller than Miss Starling. Bigger frame too. Feeling Miss Starling's shoulders heave with every small gasp made him want to hold her tighter and ease her fear. He brushed the tendrils of hair off her cheek. Her skin felt even smoother than it looked. His fingertips tingled and the urge to repeat his stroke tugged at him.

After a while her breathing evened out. She pushed away from him, breaking the moment of comfort. "I'm all right now."

He studied her, liking the way she looked all disheveled with her cheeks flushed and her brown eyes soft and self-conscious.

She pushed a hairpin back into place.

He snorted softly. "Don't think that'll do it."

Her cheeks pinked up.

She was embarrassed. He found it rather fetching.

"If I may just take a moment…" She then proceeded to comb out her hair with her fingers.

The sight of all that rich brown hair flowing loose, the sunlight glinting on it, did odd things to his gut. This was a most intimate part of her day and he was suddenly privy to it. He would have liked to reach out and stop her. He would have liked to do the combing with his own fingers and touch those silky waves. Instead, he gripped his reins tight and simply stared, fascinated.

She rewound the thick strand with a practiced hand and coiled it again upon her head. She repinned it and then set her hat just so to cover the slightly mussed-up appearance of her hair knot. Her gaze skittered to him as she tied the ribbons under her chin. "I hope my horse was running the right way."

It took him a moment to pull out of the spell she'd cast over him. He pointed with his chin to the small cross section of road ahead of them. "Smart horse. Knows the way home."

She dragged in another deep breath. "I feel immeasurably safer knowing that. I am more than ready to leave this wood." She reached down and gathered the reins. "I think I'm set now. We can go."

He stowed his rifle back in its scabbard and then turned his mount toward the road. When they arrived there and started toward town, he made sure to keep his horse alongside the mare. Both animals were still a bit skittish and he didn't want any more galloping runaways.

"I understand…what you were saying about Mrs. Odom. You know I do that with the children in school—try to meet them where they are knowledgewise and then expand their learning from that point. And what you said…about the honey…" She looked down at her gloves for a moment. When she met his eyes again she was serious. "I do that with the children as well when I am trying to interest them in a subject. It is reasonable to assume that adults do well with that same approach. I will remember it. Honey. She probably thought I was a foolish, prideful city girl."

It would be best to keep his mouth shut. He knew that. Still he let the words slip out. "From Boston."

She smiled. "How *did* you find out?"

"Church register. Your first visit you wrote where you came from."

"It could have been a lie."

"In church?"

She started to nod, but then shook her head. "No. At least not something I could do." She looked askance at him. "Where are you from, Craig?"

So…it was to be Craig after all. Good. "North of here. I was a deputy at Bartlett under Sheriff Talbot. Learned a lot from him."

"Do you have family there? A mother? Father?"

"And an older brother." He glanced sideways at her. Seemed something had changed in the course of the morning. Up to now, he'd been asking all the questions. Suddenly she was the one wondering about him. He'd cut her off when she'd asked earlier, but now, considering things…

"When things didn't work out with Charlotte, I decided a fresh start was something I could use. I took the job here six months ago when I heard through the grapevine that they were looking for a sheriff."

They arrived at the school. He found he was reluctant to leave her. Trouble was, he had no reason to spend the rest of the day with her and he did have work to do back at his office.

"I believe here is where we part ways. If you will help me down?"

He dismounted and then assisted her. "Steady?" he asked, before he let go.

"Yes. Thank you. For everything."

By the look in her eyes, he knew she meant the holding bit.

An impish smile moved her lips. "I would not have made it to the Odoms' and back on my own. And if I had, the woman would probably have shot me. Then on the way back, being startled by that cougar I'd probably be halfway to the Mexican border by now."

He was glad he'd gone too—because of the big cat, because of Mrs. Odom's rifle. He could almost convince himself those were the only reasons. Almost. That hug lingered in his mind a bit too long for him to wholly believe it. "Just doing my job," he murmured.

Her gaze clouded over. "You have been stopping to check on things at the school more often. Is that just doing your job?"

So she had noticed.

"You heard Mr. Philmont," she said before he could answer. "After that fight last week parents are worried that I can't take care of things myself."

There she was again, trying to take on the world armed with only a pencil and stubbornness and that pretty pout. "You do all right."

She stared at him with a look of disbelief. Suddenly her brown eyes sparkled. "Was that a compliment, Sheriff?"

He guessed it was. He handed the mare's reins to her and his fingers brushed hers. A tingling sensation skittered up his arm. "Miss Starling." He tipped his hat brim. "Been a pleasure." Then he mounted Jasper and headed toward the creek to take the long way to the stable.

Chapter Five

On Monday the Odom children returned to school and settled back into their regular routine. That is if one could call the swell of anticipation about the coming Christmas holiday a regular or routine happenstance. The children's excitement bubbled over in all aspects of their lessons. The boys were louder and the girls seemed to giggle about any small thing. The coming Saturday—the day of the program and dance and the subsequent break from school—was on everyone's mind.

Now as Gemma sat on the outside steps after finishing her noon meal with the children, even she was starting to get excited about the holiday. She had bundled up against the crisp air in her coat and scarf. On her lap she held a large bowl filled with popcorn—compliments of Molly. Tara sat at her side, sifting through the popcorn for the next "perfectly popped" kernel to be strung on the thread Gemma held. Every once in a while, Tara popped one into her mouth and then glanced up slyly to see if her teacher had caught her. Gemma pretended not to notice and let her have her fill. She couldn't imagine that Mrs. Odom had popcorn— or even a Christmas tree to decorate.

As she busied herself stringing popcorn the children ran about the yard playing tag. Gemma hummed as she strung and started thinking about the evening to come. Molly Birdwell had invited her to the weekly quilting bee. The group needed help to finish the last quilt on time for Christmas. The plan was to then hang it in the town hall where the community dance was being held. It would help decorate the room. They were meeting tonight right after supper.

She looked forward to getting to know other women in Clear Springs—those that didn't necessarily have children in school. Maybe there would be someone her age. That was the reason she hadn't admitted to Molly that she knew next to nothing about quilting. By the end of the evening, all the women would know she couldn't quilt and would either snub her or take her under their collective wing. She hoped it was the latter.

As busy as she was, she found herself missing her good friend Elizabeth and wondering how she was faring as a married woman in La Playa.

Last Christmas when she had surprised Elizabeth by arriving on her doorstep fresh from Boston, Elizabeth had welcomed her with open arms and enlisted her aid to dress up her mercantile for the holiday season.

"That man is here," Tara said, staring across the open field.

Gemma looked toward the road. Craig sat astride his big black gelding on the edge of the clearing. He didn't come closer and for the first time she almost wished that he would. Something had changed with their adventure on Saturday. She wouldn't mind now if he rode up and said hello. Wouldn't mind if he stopped to chat a moment. She handed the bowl to Tara and stood, waving to let him know that she saw him. After a moment, he tipped his hat. Despite the distance she could tell that he didn't smile. He was just doing his duty…

By two o'clock in the afternoon the temperature began dropping and soon after, snow started falling. Gemma dismissed the children at the regular time and watched as they headed for their homes. She tidied up the room and then stepped outside to bring in wood from the shed. As she rounded the corner of the building, she spied the man called Larabee shuffling away from the school and down the slope to the stream. He was dressed in the same clothes he'd had on the other times she'd seen him, his shirt and pants grungy with old dirt.

"Mr. Larabee!"

He ignored her and kept walking. She didn't like him lurking around. Not one bit. She had a notion to hurry and speak to him, but even as she thought it, he disappeared from her view down toward the water. Next time she saw him she would confront him, but not today. Today, Molly was waiting for her.

Remembering the incident with the raccoon, Gemma stepped up to the shed and gingerly opened the door, ready to scoot back if something else dashed out of the small building. Nothing did so she swung the door wide. And paused. How odd. More wood—a lot more wood—had been stacked against the far back wall. Had one of the school board members stopped by over the weekend to do this? If so, why hadn't they said something to her in church yesterday?

Stepping inside, she selected a large piece of wood and stuffed it in the curve between her hip and arm. One more piece of the same size should do for the morning. She spied the perfect-sized log at the back of the pile and reached for it. Suddenly the light dimmed and went out as the door swung shut with a loud bang. She jumped at the sound. A split second later she heard the ominous sound of the outer latch dropping into place.

No!

She tossed the wood aside and pushed against the door.

No! No! No!

Gathering her energy, she rammed her shoulder against the door. It wouldn't budge! Her heart pounded. She rammed her shoulder against the door again—and again. Nothing happened.

Well, this was a predicament! The possibility of being stuck inside the shed through the night flashed through her mind. That simply would not do! No one would come by until tomorrow morning. By then she might be frozen stiff!

Muted late-afternoon light shafted through slits in the uneven wall boards. She jiggled the door, hoping to displace the latch, to no avail. Then she searched the floors and walls of the small shed for any sign of an ax or bar to pry open the door. Nothing. At a loss as to what to do next, she cried out and beat against the door. "Is anybody out there? Somebody help me!"

The winter wind rustling through the tall pines was the only answer. There had to be a solution… a way for her to get out. *Think!*

It was her own stupidity that had brought her to this end. She could only be glad it had not happened to one of her students. That would have been so much worse. How would she explain that to a distraught parent? Yet the niggling worry that something hadn't been right for the past week or two permeated her thoughts. Strange things— the footprints, the unlocked door, the raccoon.

You're letting your fears run away with you, she mentally scolded herself.

She picked up a piece of wood, took a deep breath and rammed the end of it against the door right where the latch held.

Nothing happened.

She sighed. This would take time. A long time. But giving up wasn't an option. She might freeze if she did. Readjusting her grip on the wood, she gathered her strength again and rammed the block against the door. Over and over, she repeated the motion. Her arms began to ache and her fingers—rubbed raw from the rough wood— began to bleed. The light, muted at best, dimmed further until only darkness surrounded her.

The sound of snow being crunched underfoot made her pause and listen. Was someone out there? She dropped the wood block and pressed her mouth against a small crack between the wood slats. "Hello! Help! I'm in here!" she yelled, her throat scratchy and weak from the last time she'd called out.

Heavy breathing. No answer.

Disconcerted at first, the feeling quickly turned to fear. She shrank away from the door. Who was out there? Was it the man called Larabee? Or someone else?

She picked up the wood block, keeping quiet now, and crouched down.

The whirring of the sawmill had been quiet for over an hour by the time Craig doused the lamp in his office and shut the door. Across the snow-covered road, the bank and the dry goods store were dark, but a light still shone through the windows of the restaurant. He headed that way, his stomach grumbling for want of a good meal. He passed the Rawhide Emporium and as he did he checked through the front window. The few men inside looked subdued and quiet as they played a game on the only billiard table in town.

He passed the side road that led to Widow Birdwell's and once again Gemma's image came to him. Ever since their ride out to the Odom place she had lingered on his mind—enough that when she had waved to him today he had responded with only the politest of nods. He didn't want her to get the wrong idea.

He had liked being ready with his rifle and

the protective feeling he'd gotten when he held her, but he wasn't looking for anything more than that. It had been a year since he'd seen Charlotte. A year since he'd seen that working long hours and late nights could shrivel up a relationship like a raisin and send the woman you loved into the arms of another. At least with Charlotte, he'd found out before they married. He was breathing free, and free he meant to stay. It was the only way he could do his job well.

He wished Tanner luck with his bargain with Gemma. Women as pretty as her were married in a heartbeat. With the ratio of young buck to doe being ten to two in the area he figured some young cowboy or miner would come along who would try to talk Gemma into a wedding by the end of this year. He hoped that she held out for someone who could match her spirit—and was on a level with her intelligence.

It was obvious she had been educated beyond most of the women here in Clear Springs. It was also obvious she came from wealth. Why would she leave all that to come teach here? What had caused her to come all the way out West in the first place and so far from home?

And why the heck did he care? He didn't have to ask…he knew why. Puzzles naturally fascinated him. When he sensed a puzzle he had to ponder it until he solved it. And Gemma Starling was a puzzle.

She sure could be stubborn—to the point of being exasperating! An enchanting kind of exasperating, he amended. One minute he wanted to shake sense into her and the next he'd remember how soft and warm her body felt tucked against his and wonder if he might get a chance to know that feeling again.

Even thinking about it now his chest expanded a little. He was a man and wouldn't apologize for the urges that came with that title. Yet he knew he couldn't let it happen. He wasn't about to get any closer to that pretty filly. He would just content himself with the memory.

The questions lingered as he entered The Miningtown Restaurant and Daisy Finley threw him a familiar look of exasperation. "Always a-workin', ain't you, Sheriff? It's a wonder indigestion don't follow you like a rain cloud. But I figured you'd be coming. Saved back a bit of the beef stew for you."

"Thank you, Daisy." He removed his hat, taking his regular seat at a table against the far wall where he could see everyone who came and went in the room. He was late enough that most of the supper crowd had already left. Only two couples remained, along with Daisy who did the cooking and the owner who dozed in the corner, his head lolling at an uncomfortable angle against the wall.

A minute later, Daisy set a steaming plate of stew, a hefty chunk of sourdough bread and a mug of strong coffee in front of him. The steam rose up, filling his nostrils with the inviting aroma of meat, gravy, potatoes and carrots.

"I'll be done soon…" she said, her words soft and tentative. "Walk me home?"

He sighed inwardly. She'd had her eye on him from the start—a pretty redheaded local girl— but he'd never encouraged her. She was sweet and innocent and just too young for him. She was also the best cook in town—a thing he would hate to part with because his own cooking stank. "Miss Finley…" he raised his brows. "What about Chet?"

Her lips twisted in a cute, perturbed frown. "He's just a boy."

"He was handy on that gold heist a few months ago. Who knows what would have happened if he hadn't been along."

"Oh, I know he's smart. Good-lookin' too. He comes around here now and then."

"It'd be more if you gave him the least bit of encouragement."

"I guess." She let out a disappointed sigh and began washing off a nearby table. "I heard you went a-riding with the new schoolteacher this week. She ain't much older than me and I know for a fact she can't cook."

Word traveled fast in a small town. "Saturday was official business and I haven't been privy to her cooking. It would be hard for anyone to beat you in that area."

"And don't you forget it."

Her easy agreement made him smile. "You are the best cook that I know of in these parts." For added emphasis he forked a slice of carrot.

"Maybe in the whole state," she said, notching up her pointed chin.

"Could be." He played along. "Chet would be lucky to have you cook for him every night."

She finished the table, scowling slightly as she did so, and faced him, her head cocked. "Not you though."

"I'm not the settling type. You know that," he said, keeping the conversation light. Daisy was the type of gal who needed a safe, comfortable life. One that could be planned out with few surprises and wouldn't move her far from her own folks. In that respect, she reminded him of Charlotte. She would be perfect for one of the men from one of the ranches nearby, but a life like that would surely choke him. He wasn't sure how long he would stay on here…but he liked to keep his options open.

Should he ever come close to settling down again—which was unlikely at this point—he would have to be sure beyond a doubt that the woman could handle the life he led. She would have to have enough sense of self to endure his late nights and nights alone when he didn't come home at all. Above all, she'd have to be honest with him. He could abide just about anything but a woman who lied. Charlotte's image started to rise up and choke him. He pushed aside the unwelcome memories and concentrated on eating the rest of his meal before it got cold.

"Well, would you look who just walked in," Daisy said.

He glanced up. Chet stood inside the restaurant door and surveyed the room. Once he spied Craig, he made a beeline to his table. When he got there he removed his hat. His face was a little ruddier as he self-consciously nodded to Daisy. "Miss Finley. Good to see you." Then he focused on Craig.

"Widow Birdwell is looking for you. She's worried about her boarder. That new schoolteacher didn't come back to the boardinghouse after school let out today."

Craig wadded his napkin on the table and stood. "Where is Molly now?"

"On her way to the Tanner place. She figured he should know since he's head of the school board."

He reached into his pants' front pocket, removed two quarters and tossed them lightly on the tabletop.

"Wait, Sheriff. You ain't done eatin'!" Daisy said with a petulant twist to her mouth.

"Can't be helped. Official business." He slipped on his leather coat. "By the way, Chet, Miss Finley needs someone to escort her home soon. Would you mind?"

Chet stood a little taller. "Be happy to."

Craig strode out of the restaurant. By the time he turned the corner, he was pulling his collar up against the cold wind. He hoped, wherever Gemma was, that she was tucked inside on a night like this. He caught up to Molly as she started up the front path to the Tanner house.

"Mrs. Birdwell!" he called.

"Oh, Sheriff!" She turned and hustled quickly to him, holding her scarf over her nose so that only her eyes peeked out at him. "Miss Starling is—"

"I heard," he said, interrupting to save time. "You are sure she didn't have other plans?"

"She always lets me know when she expects to be late. Tonight she was supposed to accompany me to meet the ladies for quilting. I thought she might have gone straight there, but I checked at Ruth Winters's and she hasn't shown up. I'm fearful something might have happened."

"I can see that. I'll ride out to the school and see what I can find out."

"Should I tell Mr. Tanner?"

If this turned out to be nothing and Gemma was all right, Craig knew she wouldn't be happy about half the town being put on alert. But on the other hand...if she were in trouble... It came down to his decision and he'd rather err on the side of caution. "He should be aware. But just him for now. He can make the call whether or not to round up more people to search once I report back."

He strode across the street to the livery and saddled his horse. Jasper must have sensed his agitation, because the moment Craig mounted, the horse took off like a shot. With the moon obscured by the blanket of clouds dropping snow, there was enough light to see varying shades of black and gray but not much more. Craig pulled back on the reins, slowing the gelding. He didn't want to chance running up against a low-hanging branch or into a deep rut in the road that would injure his horse. Two inches of snow had fallen in the past three hours. Two inches that would cover any tracks that could help him. He sure hoped Gemma wasn't out in it.

Even though it was so dark the outlines of the trees blended into the boulders and the ground behind them, since Craig had made a point of riding more often past the schoolhouse, the road leading there was familiar. When he arrived, the building was dark. He jumped from his horse and hurried up the three steps. Surprisingly, the door wasn't locked. He rushed inside the building, scanning the dark interior for any sign of her. "Gemma? Miss Starling? It's Craig Parker."

"I'm here."

A woman's voice—Gemma's voice—thin as if it were all used up, came from the direction of the dark cloak closet.

He walked to the doorway and could just make out movement inside. "Are you all right? Molly was concerned when you didn't return to her place." Heck—*he* was concerned.

A soft thud sounded as something hit the floor. Alarmed that it could be her, he moved toward the sound. "Where's the lamp?"

"Don't light it. I'm just—"

Her voice sounded closer and very tired. Something soft stumbled against him.

"Oh!"

He grasped on to her, steadying her by the

shoulders. She held something against her chest that had cushioned her when she bumped against him—her coat?

She didn't sound fine. She sounded spent, exhausted, her sweet voice thin and airy. And she was shivering.

"You're freezing. I'll start a fire in the stove."

"No," she squeaked faintly. "Please. I... I just want to go to Molly's. I'm cold and hungry. Would you mind taking m—"

At this point he'd do whatever she wanted—he just knew he had to get her warm. He took her coat from her arms and spread it over her shoulders.

She shivered. "The silk lining is as cold as I am."

He hesitated only a moment, and then stepped close and rubbed her upper arms to create friction and warm her further.

"Thank you, Sheriff," she said weakly. "Thank you... Oh, Craig. That feels so lovely."

Her unguarded, heartfelt words sent a surge of pleasure through him. His given name sounded special—intimate—in her husky, tired voice. He swallowed, torn between listening to his own smart counsel and keeping clear of her or pulling her against him and warming her further with a hug.

A delicate sob emerged. It tugged dangerously at his heartstrings.

She was all done in from her ordeal. He shut out the voice in his head that told him to keep his distance and pulled her against him. He rubbed her back, keeping the friction going. Slowly, she circled her hands around his waist. He blew out a sigh. "What happened?"

"It's my own silly, stupid fault."

He hated to hear her berate herself. "You are not stupid—not by a long shot. Tell me what happened."

"I…got myself locked in the woodshed."

"You what?"

"I stepped inside to get some wood and the door swung shut. Whoever built it certainly made it to last. I beat against the door for what seemed like hours before it gave way." Her teeth chattered and then she sniffled into his coat. "How did you know to come look for me?"

"Chet found me. Said Molly was worried about you."

"Chet?"

"A buddy of mine."

"Molly and I had plans this evening. I should let her know that I'm all right. I'm not up to going now, but perhaps she can still make it."

"'Fraid that's a lost cause. Evening is over."

She sighed. "It is? Then a cup of tea sounds heavenly."

"I've got my horse. If you are ready, we can go."

She fumbled with something. A feather tickled his nose and he realized she was tying on her hat.

Once outside, he left her to wait on the steps. Then he mounted and walked Jasper over to her, holding out his hand for her to grasp.

She hesitated a second.

"Don't go all Boston Proper on me now, Gemma. I promise that I won't bite," he said, amused. "It is more important to get you back and get you warm all the way through."

She stepped close and he drew her up to sit in front of him.

She shivered again, but held herself rigid as if she were afraid to touch him while he reined his horse toward the road and headed back to town. He leaned forward and whispered in her ear. "You'll be warmer if you lean against me. I will too, if that makes any difference."

She didn't change her position. "I did fine on my own. I got myself out. I'm not some helpless female."

So that's what this was about. "Never said you were."

"You thought it. The day we rode out to the Odoms'."

"There's a big difference between being helpless and being uninformed. You were simply uninformed—about the country, about cougars."

"Among other things. I didn't know there were people who thought like the Odoms. People who don't want a better future for their children. My father always wanted the best for me. He tried... so hard..."

Whether it was the darkness that loosened her tongue or her fatigue, he was pleased she was confiding in him. "That's why teachers are so important. Some folks can't see beyond their own circumstances. Teachers help them see the possibilities. That's why Clear Springs needs you."

"Mmm..." she murmured, her voice soft and dreamy as she sank back against him. "Thank you."

"For what?" he asked and wondered if she even realized that she'd pressed back into him.

"For coming to find me."

He smiled to himself. Independent, stubborn, beautiful woman. And she was in his arms. Again. He tightened his arms around her. He had an excuse. He couldn't very well let her fall off Jasper.

Every once in a while her head lolled back to rest against his chest and he was able to see the vague curve of her nose and cheek beyond the small brim of her hat. He could like this softer side of the woman who had finally emerged.

He tucked her against him further. Surprisingly, she didn't resist. Instead, she snuggled closer…and warmth rushed to parts of his body that hadn't experienced heat in a long time. His heart, for one. Here it was below freezing and he felt his chest expanding like a bellows.

A few moments later and he could see the lights winking through the trees from the Rawhide Emporium on the north edge of town. For the first time in a long time he wished the road into town were longer…and while he was busy doing his wishing, that the night was warmer.

The gentle rocking stopped.

"Gemma?" Craig murmured, his breath warm like the whisper of summer on her ear.

She hated to move. She was finally comfortable. The shivering had stopped. And the sense of protection she felt in his strong arms was like nothing she'd ever experienced in her life since losing her father.

Couldn't she stay right where she was for a few more minutes and pretend all was really so perfect. Safe, strong, secure…she knew she could come to believe it, however false that belief would appear in the light of day. She was beginning to think there was more to Craig Parker than she had thought at first. With the exception of her father and perhaps Mr. Ross, his butler, most men she had encountered only looked out for themselves. Even in the end, Roland had shown his true colors.

Roland. That name more than anything else jarred her back. Back to Clear Springs—as far away from Boston as she could have traveled. Back to the present. She opened her eyes slowly. The straggly black mane of Craig's horse, barely visible in the dark night, appeared. Then the heavy leather-clad arm of the man who held her.

This was a dangerous game that she played. The sheriff? She was a "duty" to him. Oh, he cared about doing his job well but that didn't translate to actually caring about her. She must remember that above all else. Otherwise, she might reveal more to him than she should. She mustn't rely on anybody. Ever. All she had was her wits.

"Gemma?" Craig said again, more firmly this time. "Ready to get on your feet?"

She blinked and then straightened. Molly and Mr. Tanner, both wearing worried expressions, hustled down the front path toward her.

Craig handed her down to Mr. Tanner.

"I'm all right," she said, protesting and pushing away. "I can walk." It had only been a moment of weakness…a moment best put in the past now.

Craig dismounted and despite what she'd said, took her by the arm and led her inside the house. He was gentle about it…but also firm. And she recognized that he meant to take charge of the situation. She was too tired to argue the matter.

"Bring her into the parlor," Molly said as she set aside her sewing basket from the settee and fluffed a pillow. "Stir up the fire, Patrick. I'll see to the kettle."

Gemma's thoughts couldn't catch up with the quick movements of the woman. "I didn't say a thing about tea. Did you?"

"No," Craig said.

He steadied her as she plopped—rather ungracefully—on the settee.

"That's Molly for you. A step ahead of most folks and tea is the universal answer to all things. Oh…please don't make a fuss." As she settled into her cushioned seat, she caught the amused look in his blue eyes.

The distance between them diminished to a more intimate level as he lowered his voice conspiratorially. "Don't tell her that. You'll ruin her chance to feel useful."

She studied him as he took a chair on the opposite side of the hearth. It wasn't just Molly that made her feel special. It was him. The way he acted she could almost believe that he really cared for her—more than just as a responsibility. The thought alarmed her. It could never be. She shrank away from him, pressing back into the settee and trying to dispel the intertwined wisp of hope and fear that would not leave. He didn't know anything about her. Not really. And she'd made such a muddle of things in the past by believing what others said too easily.

His dark brows knit together. "Are you feeling up to a few questions?"

She nodded.

He moved back to sit across the room from her. On the other end of the settee sat Mr. Tanner. Molly returned with a tray of cheese sandwiches and teacups filled with steaming tea.

"Everyone, help yourselves," Molly instructed, but then handed Gemma a saucer and cup herself. "So, tell us what happened, dear?"

She was starting to feel foolish with all this attention. "At the end of school, I tidied up the room and then went to the shed to gather a few logs for the woodstove. The door slammed shut behind me...probably swept closed by the wind. The latch dropped and locked me in. It took me all evening to pummel my way out."

"Humph," Molly said, settling into her rocking chair and shaking a small sandwich at her. "Like the raccoon. I thought you were going to see about that."

"What raccoon?" Both Tanner and Craig asked at the same time.

Molly would bring that incident up right off. "I planned to say something at the next board meeting. Obviously it was folly to wait."

"What happened?" Craig asked.

She proceeded to explain to them about the surprise visit from the raccoon.

When she was finished, Craig asked, "What exactly do you keep in the shed?"

"Just wood, at the moment."

Mr. Tanner frowned. "Wood wouldn't attract a raccoon. I get the feeling one of your students played a prank on you."

She sighed. "Those are Mrs. Birdwell's thoughts as well. I'm not sure how I should handle it in class. I hate to accuse anyone. Whoever it was, I don't want him to gain any notoriety on my account. That would only encourage him."

Craig raised his brows. "So you think it was a boy?"

"Don't you?"

"An older one probably. He would have had to trap that raccoon first and then open the trap just enough that it would run into the shed instead of racing away. Knowing a raccoon's nature, that would have been a feat in itself."

"Billy is the only boy I know that has a trapline. After seeing his home situation, I really didn't want to add to his mother's worries."

"It could have been anyone," Craig said. "A few of the younger boys have traplines too. Anything else happen that day?"

"The fight...and you bringing Tara from the creek." She was growing frustrated. It seemed they were talking in circles when she'd been hoping for answers. "The only other thing, now that I think of it, were the footprints in the grass early that morning."

"Probably belonging to whoever placed that raccoon in the shed. Billy, Jordan and Duncan are the oldest. Whether or not the two incidents are related—the raccoon and tonight's lock-in—is still questionable."

The more Craig tried to puzzle out the answers, the more she relaxed. She felt a little guilty—letting him take over—but not enough to grab back the duty. It was late and more than anything she just wanted to stop thinking about it and finish her tea. It had been a long day. In the morning she would be able to put it all in better perspective. And this...whatever it was that had her analyzing everything Craig did and said, would evaporate in the light of day.

"Anything else?" Craig asked.

"Well…while I was locked in the shed, I thought I heard footsteps and called out. I thought it must have been that Mr. Larabee. I've seen him a time or two when the children head for home. But he didn't help."

Molly clucked. "He's near deaf, dear. An explosion… Happened a long time ago."

"That explains why he didn't help." She felt a bit more charitable toward the man knowing that.

Mr. Tanner stood. "It's getting late. I better get home to Clarice before she locks me out."

"Now, Patrick, you know that woman wouldn't do such an ornery thing as all that!" Molly exclaimed, rising to her feet.

"I'm sorry about the latch," Gemma said. "It will need fixing."

"I'll take care of it—and make sure when I do that it can be opened from the inside."

"Thank you. Oh…and thank you for bringing out another cord of wood and stacking it. I knew my supply was getting low, but hadn't thought to tell anyone."

He frowned. "I didn't. Must have been Mr. Winters that brought more."

He walked to the door with Molly following

to see him out. "Good night, ladies." He slipped out, closing the door behind him.

Craig attempted to stifle a yawn.

She glanced at the clock on the mantel. *My goodness! Nearly midnight!* Now that her hunger had been appeased it was no wonder that she was growing tired again. The events of the evening were taking on a strange dreamlike quality.

Molly picked up the tray of empty tea cups and disappeared into the kitchen.

"I'm going too," Craig said, standing. He motioned for her to stay put. "I can see myself out."

She got up anyway. She had had her moment of weakness. It was over. She should have never allowed Craig to see her like that. Once more and he would think she made a habit of clinging to men. "I'm not weak."

"I don't think that." His eyes twinkled with admiration. "You got yourself out tonight. Besides, any woman who can keep up with her students playing kick the can has more energy than me."

"You did see." Her cheeks warmed.

"I won't reveal it unless I need to blackmail you."

"And here I had such a high opinion of you."

He studied her in such a way that any further banter simply slipped from her mind.

"Why does it bother you that I saw you playing?"

"I don't want the school board and the parents to think I'm being lax in my duties."

"They don't think that." A furrow formed between his brows. "You do know that other teachers take time to play with their students."

She met his gaze and then slowly shook her head. "I had tutors. Two. They were older. Any games we played were to challenge my mind. Games that required math, or wordplay or reasoning."

"Tutors," he repeated, looking at her strangely. "And you left all that to come here?"

He had caught her off guard. Her silence confirmed it.

"I'd like to hear about it."

"Another time perhaps. It's late," she said, hedging. "Thank you for coming for me. I know you were just doing your duty, but it meant a lot to me. It was scary in there. Dark. And with the footsteps. I thought my mind was playing tricks on me. To see a familiar face, hear a familiar voice…" The emotions that she had experienced in the shed rushed back full force and clogged her throat. She couldn't speak. She blinked back the burn in her eyes and turned away from him, walking over to collect his hat from the iron stand at the door. By the time she faced him with it, she had her emotions under control again.

"I'm glad you are all right, Gemma." He took his hat from her outstretched hand, all the while studying her intently. "It was my job, but I would have come after you either way, job or no job."

Surprised, she took a step back.

He didn't blink at her retreat. "People look out for each other here. It's like that in small towns. Just the way it is." He put on his Stetson and strode out into the darkness.

Chapter Six

Craig didn't sleep well. Things Gemma had mentioned disturbed him. Namely, the footsteps that she had heard...and Larabee. Were they related? Just how hard of hearing was this Larabee? Gemma preferred to believe that the old miner had not heard her but Craig had learned long ago that assumptions could be costly—and wrong. Larabee could have left her in the shed on purpose, although Craig couldn't begin to figure out a motivation for that. He needed to speak to Winters about that wood too.

Craig didn't want to alarm Gemma, but after her remarks he was determined to have a look for himself. That's why he dragged himself from his cot, half-frozen, and headed to the livery as soon as it was light outside. He needed to take a look before the children obliterated any tracks or marks.

Gemma was determined that everything go

well with her new teaching position. She didn't want to dwell on the fact something might be amiss and she didn't want to appear incompetent in front of the school board. He couldn't fault her for that. Just about everyone he knew felt that way to some degree. That's why it frustrated him no small amount. It made him want to protect her even if that meant protecting her from herself.

He had figured out a few things during the night. Things he hadn't been too keen on facing. When he rushed to find Gemma after learning she was missing, the impulse racing through him was not just the desire of a sheriff doing his job, but the anxious acts of a man worried about someone he cared for. And on the ride back to Mrs. Birdwell's when she had surrendered to her exhaustion and the soft curve of her body was flush up against him, things inside of him had stirred. Ever since then, thoughts had galloped through his mind that had only been a nudge before.

He'd best keep his distance. He wasn't about to open his heart up to another flaying. He'd learned his lesson with Charlotte. Besides…the inkling he'd had that Gemma was hiding something from him wasn't going away… It was growing.

A thin carpet of snow covered the pines on

each side of the road and scattered in patches beneath them. Fog clung to the low areas in the small valley and grew thicker down by the creek, floating over the ground around the school giving it an eerie aura as he rode up to the clearing. Four mule deer bolted across the meadow and dashed into the woods. He stopped in front of the schoolhouse and dismounted, and then tied Jasper to the tie line.

Striding over to the shed, he moved aside the broken door that hung on one hinge now, and peered inside. As Gemma had mentioned, the wood was stacked neatly against the far wall— plenty of it. It nearly touched the ceiling, and was far enough back that a person had to step all the way inside to reach it. The items a man would expect to see in a shed—an axe and a shovel— were missing.

He pulled back and checked the ground outside, walking the perimeter of the building. *There.* He stopped suddenly. The night's light snowfall filled in the tracks, but he could still see a slight indentation in the smooth white carpet compared to the surrounding snow. He looked around and found another. Then another. He followed them to their source where they emerged from the copse of oak and pine trees at the far side of the clearing.

He took a deep breath. So it wasn't just Gemma's imagination. Someone *had* been here and whether or not they'd had anything to do with her getting locked in the shed...they certainly had no problem with leaving her there.

Whether she wanted his help or not, he wasn't going to let her handle this one alone.

A flash of movement on the road drew his attention.

He straightened and waited for Gemma. She carried a large rectangular satchel at her side that the light wind tossed and tangled against the swing of her long dark blue coat. As she neared he could hear when she took a step—her shoes crunching through the top layer of snow on the ground—and see the flush of color staining her cheeks. Likely from the cold. Then he remembered his words of the night before. *I would have come after you either way, job or no job.* It was the truth, but he probably should have worded it differently.

"You're up early," she said, stopping before him.

"Mornin'." The pale skin surrounding her eyes bore smudges of last night's ordeal. She was still tired. He hated to worry her more, but it was important she stay alert to...to what? He wasn't sure what was going on—if anything. "I found something."

Her gaze clouded immediately. "Show me." She followed him to the shed.

He took her elbow, steadying her as she stepped over the pieces of broken door and then leading her out behind the school where he had seen the footprints. The sun was melting the snow more, already obliterating some of the tracks as the grass sprang back to life. He pointed to the ground.

She swallowed, her gaze arrested on the indentations. "Then it wasn't my imagination." She faced him. "They might not mean anything. I noticed footprints before—just last week. They easily match those of my oldest pupils. They could be Duncan's or Billy's or even Jordan's."

"Maybe…" he said slowly, but he wasn't getting that feeling. His gut told him otherwise.

"You don't really believe it. I can tell by your expression."

He shook his head. "No."

"Who would want to frighten me? I don't believe it was a student."

"An upset student might turn over a bench or two, or write something strong on the blackboard. Letting you stay locked in the shed goes beyond that."

She glanced back down at the prints. "I know you are thinking Billy did this. It can't be. He would have let me out if he knew I was locked in. He wouldn't have left me to freeze."

Craig didn't share her conviction. Boys didn't always think things through to the consequences of their actions. "Just the same, when he arrives today, I'll have a word with him."

Her brows drew together. "I hope you are wrong." She looked past him toward the road.

He followed her line of vision. Billy was dismounting from the large brown mule.

Billy looked up from tying his mule. His dirty blond hair obscured half of his face until he tossed his head in an effort to clear it away from his eyes. He shot Craig a quick look filled with tension as he walked back to his sister and helped her down.

Hmm. "Need to talk to you, Mr. Odom." He tilted his head, indicating Billy was to stay back from entering the school.

"Come on, Tara," Gemma said, holding out her hand to the girl. She glanced back at Billy, a disappointed expression on her face, but then walked up the steps and entered the school.

A group of children arrived, chattering and laughing as they walked down the path from the road. When they spotted Craig, they quieted, their gazes curious as they looked from Billy to him.

Craig walked Billy far enough away from the building so that his voice wouldn't carry to the curious onlookers standing at the school window.

"Got a few questions for you."

Billy tensed, his chin raising slightly. "What about?"

"About that raccoon found in the shed. About the fight you had with Duncan. And about where you were last night. Take your time answering. Don't leave out one single part."

He covered every detail he could think to check. By the time he was satisfied, school had been going on a while. He sent Billy inside to ask Duncan to step out.

A few minutes later, Duncan emerged from the school. He wore his usual arrogant expression that Craig had noticed around town. It made Craig wonder how Gemma got through to the boy at all.

Duncan and Billy together would be a formidable wall of obstinacy. He wasn't surprised that she was reluctant to confront them. Her confidence and self-assurance would certainly take a battering between these two. Towering over her, they would put her in a defensive position from the outset. How plain water had stopped the fight was a mystery unless the boys had been ready to quit.

Craig started his questioning the same way he

had approached Billy. Duncan wasn't as eager to explain, but slowly, as his side of the story took shape the details lined up.

A dead end.

"We're done here unless you have anything more you want to add."

Duncan's lower lip jutted out, but he shook his head.

"Then return to your seat and send out Miss Starling."

Craig paced the path that led to the road while he waited, his gaze on the gravel and small melting patches of snow. When Gemma appeared on the steps he walked up to her. "The door?"

"Shut tight."

She gripped her coat collar tighter together, whether to protect herself against the chill in the air or as protection from hearing an uncomfortable truth, he wasn't sure.

"I found out a few things. Neither boy admits to being anywhere near here after school yesterday. Both boys had a hand in the raccoon incident. Jordan wasn't involved. Seems disagreement over the raccoon was the basis for the fight. One wanted to go through with it and one got cold feet. It was just a prank. It started as a joke…and then a dare. No harm to you was intended. I think they are telling the truth."

"So those footprints that day were Billy's?"

"Yes. But when it came down to it, he didn't want to go through with it. That's why they argued before class. It escalated into a drag-down fight."

She glanced away, toward the shed. "A foolish joke." Her shoulders slumped.

"It wasn't a personal attack on you. Just boys being stupid."

"It feels personal." She brushed a few strands of flyaway hair off her forehead. "I'll have to consider how to handle this. I can't just let it slide by."

He shifted his weight. "About those footprints from yesterday…"

"It had to be Mr. Larabee. If he's as deaf as Molly thinks he is then he didn't hear my call for help."

"I'm not so sure." He hated to alarm her, but it had to be said. "The length of the stride doesn't look like that of a shuffling old miner. More likely, it's the longer stride of a man in his prime."

Her shoulders sank. "That's disturbing."

"I'm going to talk to Winters today and see what I can find out."

"All right. Thank you." She turned toward the school with a troubled air. "I had better get back to my students."

"Gemma? I'll be back at the end of the day."

"It's really not ne—"

"Don't say it," he said, interrupting. "Don't say it's not necessary…"

She stared at him, her eyes wide, startled by his tone.

"I don't want you walking alone." He had a gut feeling about all this…and it wasn't a good one. "Wait for me."

Chapter Seven

Gemma wobbled on the tips of her toes. She stood on her desktop, her body stretched to its tallest height as she searched the top of the wood bcam overhead. The box had to be here. She had waited until the end of the day after the children left for home, so that she could retrieve it without them learning of its hiding placc.

"What are you doing?" Craig asked sharply.

She gasped and snatched back her empty hand. Her heart pounded in her chest. She hadn't expected him so soon. She lowered her heels to the surface of the desk. "You startled me!"

He strode briskly down the aisle between the children's benches. "All I did was walk in."

He was right. Perhaps, after her recent experiences she was a bit jumpy.

He stopped at her desk and peered up at the

rafters. "Just what have you got up there that's so all-fired important?"

"My gun," she admitted.

His brows raised. "What?"

"My gun. Or…more correctly, my father's gun." She reached again, up on the toes of her boots, and felt along the top of the wooden beam with her fingers. In the crux of the truss she came upon the wooden box. The weight of it always surprised her. She brought it down to waist level. Slowly she opened the mahogany box, almost fearful of seeing the weapon again. As the silver barrel and hardwood handle appeared, the memories rushed back—mental images of pulling the trigger, feeling the kick and then seeing Roland crumple to the floor. How had that been her?

His family might come after her. They might even be the source of the footprints, but she just couldn't bring herself to believe that. Surely they would not come so far for revenge. Surely she was safe here even though she would always have to live with the shadow of discovery hanging over her.

She met Craig's gaze. "I…wanted to make sure it is still in working order." It was only a half lie. She had wanted to become more familiar with it. To load it. To be ready.

The weighted look he gave her spoke volumes.

She wasn't fooling him at all. He knew she was frightened.

He assisted her down to the floor. His large hand holding hers was still cool from the outdoors.

She set the box on the desk. The red velvet of the box's interior was worn in places and tattered slightly. Situated in one corner was a second, smaller green cardboard box full of cartridges. Gingerly, she picked up the gun. It felt foreign in her hand and holding it she felt strange—like she was a different woman altogether. She handed it to him.

He turned it over in his palm. Everything about the way he handled it spoke of his easy confidence with the weapon. "Smith & Wesson. Older model."

"My grandfather's."

"It won't do you much good. It isn't loaded."

"I know. I believe it is time to remedy that." She opened the smaller box and picked up a cartridge, then took the gun back from Craig. She fumbled with the chamber.

Craig frowned. "How long has it been since you handled a gun?"

"There was never much of a need..." Up until a year ago, she'd had her father and the butler Mr. Ross to protect her. "But now...with the footsteps... I know this may be a drastic response and I could be overreacting..."

"But your gut tells you different."

She straightened her shoulders. "It never hurts to be prepared."

"I agree."

She took a deep breath and then exhaled. "I was hoping that you'd teach me."

He measured her solemnly with his blue gaze. "You aren't thinking that you would have used it to stop the fight, are you?"

"Good heavens no! Never with the children. Not even to shoot in the air!"

He took the gun back from her, peered down its barrel as if checking its alignment.

She stepped closer. She would either have his help or she would figure it out on her own. "It would only be for self-defense...against animals. Or to protect the children."

He clicked slowly through each chamber. "An animal reacts differently than a man. The noise of firing the gun will often scare off a wild animal, but not always. Some will attack. But if you threaten a man with a weapon, he will try to get the upper hand. He might rush you and try to disarm you. Or, if he has his own gun he'll shoot you. It is best he doesn't even know you have a gun unless you are willing to use it. You can't hesitate."

She shuddered at the thought of Roland's face looming toward her. She had hesitated then. She had been scared to death and beseeched him to leave her alone. He hadn't listened. He was so sure he could make her do what he wanted.

He studied her a moment longer. "All right. I'll teach you."

He shoved the papers and stone paperweight on her desk to the side. Removing his neckerchief, he spread it out on her desk. "If you are going to be responsible for a gun, you should know how to care for it—clean it, load it and shoot it. Anything done poorly could result in a misfire, which could end up hurting you or someone else."

The next fifteen minutes she listened as he explained the proper care of a gun. He was patient, answering her questions, making sure she repeated certain steps as he watched so he could be sure that she understood. He was methodical in his instruction…sure. When he was finished and they were heading outside to practice a few shots, she asked, "When did you learn all this?"

"When I was twelve. My father taught me."

She hustled, trying to keep up with his long strides over the uneven ground. "That's young for such responsibility."

"We had a small ranch. A pack of wolves decided stealing our young calves was easier and probably tastier than hunting wild game. My brother and I had to protect the herd."

She was impressed. "You learned from such a young age about taking care of things." It was probably rooted so deep that he didn't even realize that's why he chose being a sheriff. He probably couldn't help looking out for her...or anybody that needed his help.

He stopped walking and stared off in the distance. "My father taught me to take care of the things that matter first. Family matters. Livelihood matters." He focused on her. "People matter."

She nodded. "Yes. Of course they do." Was he trying to impress on her again the need to be careful with the pistol? Or was he saying something else altogether?

She considered him as he scanned the clearing for a suitable target for practice. Tiny lines fanned out from the corners of his blue eyes as he squinted. His tan Stetson shadowed his face. He had retied his dark green bandana around his neck in a loose knot just below his Adam's apple. His handsome appearance made it all the more difficult to keep from falling under his spell. She felt so safe in his presence—so protected. She thought back to how close they'd been while riding his horse to Molly's last evening...just the thought made her pulse quicken. It would be entirely too easy to let herself succumb to his charm. And that wouldn't be safe at all.

He pointed toward the creek. "See that dead tree?"

She shook off her wayward musings and followed his line of sight. The tree was half falling over. A strong wind or heavy snow would see it to the ground this winter or next.

He held the gun out straight before him and aimed at the center of the trunk, continuing to explain what he was doing as he cocked the lever back and fired.

"Your turn." He held out the gun to her.

The polished wood handle was warm from his hand. She gripped it and mimicked his actions, even to the point of saying his instructions out loud so that he could correct her if necessary. She cocked the hammer, aimed and slowly squeezed the trigger.

With a loud report the gun raised up of its own power and jolted her arm and shoulder. She stumbled back a step to catch her balance, and felt his sudden steadying grip on each shoulder from behind. His hands lingered there at moment, almost as if he were reluctant to let go. When he lowered his hands, she still felt the spots of warmth where his hands had rested. The feeling radiated to the ends of her fingertips.

"You could have warned me," she said accusingly, aware that he still stood quite close behind her. Slowly her heart returned to its normal rhythm.

He wasn't the least repentant. "Makes a stronger impression that way."

"Anything else I should know?"

An amused half smile appeared on his face—just a slight drawing back of the corners of his mouth. "Well...you missed. Try again."

She huffed out a breath. She stepped up to her original spot and took her stance. She aimed... and felt his warm breath tickle her neck, creating a delicious tingling sensation. She could barely concentrate. No, she thought, weighing her reaction...she could not concentrate at all. She lowered her gun. "Just what do you think you are doing?"

"Comes with the price of a lesson. Go ahead and aim for the center of the tree." She did as he asked, then he pressed his fingers on the crook of her elbow, signaling her to lower her arm slightly. "There. Try that now."

She took a deep breath and fired. This time the bullet glanced off the edge of the trunk, splintering the dry ragged bark.

"Go again," Craig said.

She fired two more times and with each shot

she came a little closer to the center of the trunk. Her ears rang with the loud noise and the gun felt heavier each time she would lift and aim, but she began to feel more confident. The last shot, however, traveled far afield to the left. She lowered the weapon and rubbed her aching shoulder.

"That'll do for today," he said, taking the gun from her.

Once they were back at the schoolhouse, Craig set the gun down on her desk. "Your turn to reload it."

Conscious of him watching, she carefully reloaded the chambers, leaving one chamber free of a bullet—the precaution he had taught her as a measure for safety. She didn't remember her father ever doing that, but then she hadn't paid much attention to his collection of guns. At least not until she had needed to use this one.

When she was finished, Craig climbed onto her chair to put the box with the gun back in its hiding place and out of sight. He jumped back to the floor. "Ready to go?"

She nodded.

He followed her out and waited while she locked the door.

From her vantage point on the stoop, the sun cast an orange-pink glow in the western sky as it neared the horizon. Pink clouds scudded across, separating the bluer heavens from the wealth of color below. Lower, the pointed peaks of pines and the gnarled branches of the oaks lining the stream were silhouetted against the sky. On the oaks, the last few leaves clung tenaciously, ignoring the fact that winter was flush upon them.

"I love this time of day."

"Yep," Craig said, but he wasn't looking west. He was looking at her with an expression that said he very much enjoyed the view.

Heat radiated up her neck. He made her feel special. It had been a long time since anyone stirred that feeling inside her. But what was she doing? She couldn't let it happen. Couldn't enjoy it even though he was the first person to make her feel alive in over a year. Resolutely, she turned away from him. "It will be dark soon. I better be on my way to Molly's or she will worry."

She felt rather than saw him hesitate. Then slowly he left her side and untied his horse's lead rope from the tie line. He led his horse to the steps, giving her the option of riding.

She tucked her heavy coat around her. "I'll walk with you," she said and fell into step beside him as they started toward town. "Thank you for the lesson, Craig."

"You could have said something sooner." He

stopped, his blue eyes pinning her. "I would rather have you safe. Don't you realize that by now?"

She blinked, taken aback by his blunt honesty and the frustration she heard in his voice. "You're upset?"

"If I had not come upon you on top of your desk reaching for that gun, would you have ever asked me for help?"

She hadn't planned to. And her answer must have shown on her face.

His grip tightened on the lead rope.

It was the only evidence of tension, but she could feel it emanating from him...crackling in the air.

They walked in silence a ways before he spoke. "Why is it so hard for you to accept help?"

Because trust didn't come easy. She had trusted the wrong man once before and look where she was now. However, she couldn't tell Craig that. "I don't like the violence and hurt guns bring."

"Did something happen to you? Or to someone close to you?"

She wanted to be honest...wanted to explain about Boston...but the fact that he was a sheriff stopped her. To tell him would ruin their tenuous friendship—a friendship she was coming to depend on more and more. She looked away from his intense gaze. "I would just rather talk my way out of a situation than use a gun."

"Can't talk your way out of a bear attack," he said, his voice flat. Then a reluctant grin teased his lips and tripped up her heart. "But it would be something to see you try."

She warmed considerably.

"So tell me, how did you grow up without ever shooting a gun? Even my mother learned as a young girl."

"Well, you grew up on a ranch. It makes sense your mother would know how to shoot. Father…" Just saying his name made her throat constrict. "Father had a cabinet that he kept locked. It held dueling pistols that had been handed down from his father. They were old and the handles quite ornate. He also had a hunting rifle—an antique that came all the way from England. I never saw Father use any of the weapons. He was a lawyer first and foremost. He reasoned with people and he was very good at it."

"Seems strange. Growing up around something like that and not using it."

"Here guns are more a necessity of life. You have bears and rattlers. To my father they were simply antiquities…ornamentation for our home and a reminder of his heritage."

Even now, a year later, it hurt deeply to recall how things had been. She'd lost so much.

Craig eyed her closely. "You miss him."

She nodded.

"Then why did you leave?"

She knew what he was asking, but one question would lead to another and she couldn't tell him the truth. "I'm here to teach the children."

His gaze narrowed. "That's not what I mean. What happened that you traveled all the way from Boston to California...and, I suspect...alone? That's unusual for a woman. Even more so for a woman who obviously had money. What did your family have to say about it?"

He was figuring out too much. If she wasn't careful he would eventually add things up and realize she wasn't who she said she was, but she should tell him something to appease his curiosity. Perhaps then he would leave her past alone.

"Mother died when I was very young. A carriage accident. I don't remember her. My father raised me on his own...with a few servants."

"And tutors."

"He died recently. It was his heart," she answered the question that appeared immediately on his handsome face.

Craig frowned. "How long after his death did you leave?"

"A month later."

"Didn't give you much time to put his things in order."

She could hear the question in his voice. "I couldn't bear the quiet. I was so close to Father. He supported me in everything I wanted to do."

Craig's brow raised.

It didn't take a scholar to recognize the look he gave her. "I was, perhaps, a bit spoiled. We discussed his law cases. He challenged me to think for myself and thought I'd make a good lawyer. I was in my second year of law school at the university when he died."

They turned from the main road of town and headed down the lane to the boardinghouse.

"They let women in?"

"There were two other women in my class."

"Why didn't you stay and finish?"

"When my father died, I had to start afresh— somewhere totally different. I'd been writing for years to Elizabeth. She wrote to me and poured her heart out in her letters as her world was falling apart. She is the sister I always wanted. When my father died, all I could think of was seeing her." She looked down at the ground. "That's when I packed a bag, closed up the house and left Boston."

"No relatives? No one tried to stop you?"

"No." Thank goodness they were nearing the boardinghouse and the twilight shadows hid her face from his scrutiny. She'd told him the truth… just not all of it.

He stopped before Molly's fence and whipped the lead strap around the top railing. Then he walked her up to the door. Molly's parlor lantern spilled light outside and onto the small porch.

"Do you ever think about going back?"

"And leave Clear Springs?" she teased at first, and then grew serious. "I may move somewhere new. But no, I won't ever go back." She knew full well what waited for her in Boston—a jail cell.

"Maybe someday you will finish law school."

That would make her too easy to track down. Women lawyers were few and far between. No… that dream had ended abruptly and was best left in the past. "Someday never comes." She pasted on a smile to take the sting out of her own words. "Good evening, Craig. Thank you for…everything."

When she turned to go inside, Craig stepped forward. "Wait."

"What?"

"You answered a few questions I had." He searched her face as though still trying to figure out more. His face was inches from her own. She breathed in the scent of leather and horse that always hovered around him. The brown stubble on his jaw caught her attention. So rough…and yet the ends gleamed gold.

"It's getting late. Molly will have supper waiting." She didn't want him to know more…see more…because if he did, he might see that she was coming to care for him even though she oughtn't. He was too smart.

With his hand to her waist, he pulled her close.

She stiffened. "Craig? What are you doing?"

He gazed at her, his blue eyes intense. "Be still."

She knew that look. It thrilled her…and yet she couldn't let him kiss her. "Craig… No. Remember," she said desperately fighting the tug inside her that drew her closer to him. "I promised Mr. Tanner? You…should…unhand me." Her words were a bare whisper and she couldn't help but stare at his lips. They looked soft…and inviting.

"I plan to." He lowered his mouth to hers, touching her lips lightly, tentatively with his. His warm breath tickled her face.

Just the lightest butterfly touch and she calmed, suspended somewhere between Boston and Clear Springs, wrong and right, despair and hope.

Inch by inch his fingers walked around to encircle her waist and then, holding her gently secure, he slanted his mouth over hers and deepened the kiss.

She melted.

Her lips tingled under his, the sensation spreading and rippling through her entire body and into her toes. Her heartbeat quickened. This shouldn't be happening. She knew this shouldn't be happening. She even clenched her hands into fists on his chest to push him away, but then found herself stopping just short of doing that and instead, grasping his leather vest, unwilling to let go. *Oh, my...*

He took his time ending the kiss.

His gaze pinned her in place even though she knew she should take her leave. For an earth-shattering moment as they looked at each other, time seemed to stop.

Then he released her. "Good night, Gemma."

He strode down Molly's path, mounted his horse and rode away.

It was then she remembered to breathe.

"Hey, now! Ain't it time for me to get out of here, Sheriff? The light is fading already."

Craig twisted around on his office chair to face Joe who sat bleary-eyed and half tilting on a cot on the other side of the bars. The young cowboy had a little time behind bars coming to him, by Craig's way of thinking. He'd disturbed the peace in Clear Springs—especially Craig's peace. Stuck babysitting a reckless drunk wasn't anywhere near where Craig wanted to be. He wanted to see Gemma. The only thing that had saved Joe from his wrath was the fact that school was in session and Gemma was busy teaching.

"Sober yet?" he asked.

"Course I'm sober. Haven't had a drop of whiskey since last night and it's practically suppertime! My head's a-pounding so much my back teeth are loose." He glared at the light coming in through the window. "And that stamp mill ain't helpin' on that account!" he yelled at whoever might be passing by the jail to hear.

Craig had no sympathy for the kid. "You ran old Mr. Green down with your horse, Joe. You put him flat on his back—and hurting. I think you being in here a little longer might give him some satisfaction. He's none too happy with you right now. You might want to consider a nice gift to smooth things over with him."

"A gift!"

"Yeah. I hear he likes good cigars."

Joe sputtered something about being broke.

"Well," Craig said seriously. "You've got enough money to buy liquor. Can't say I have much sympathy for you. You're losing everything to that blasted bottle. Today it's your freedom. What will it be tomorrow?"

Joe threw himself down on the cot and turned his back to Craig. "What do you know…"

Craig shook his head in disgust. "I'm going over to the café. I'll bring back coffee and something to eat if you're up to it."

"Suit yourself. Don't trip on your way out."

At the café, Craig relaxed over a cup of coffee before grabbing another one for Joe and a bowl of chicken and dumplings and then heading back. He liked Joe just fine when the man was sober. When he was drunk—not so much.

His footsteps pounded on the boardwalk as he strode back to the law office. He glanced at the sign nailed over the door. Sheriff/Jail. It got him to thinking about Gemma and the things she'd said about her father and wanting to go into law. Had that ambition died when he did? What had happened to all the money from her father? If he had enough for tutors for her, surely at his passing there was some left over for Gemma.

Few women would leave a nice home back East to live and work in a mining town. He could understand running to Elizabeth. It was impulsive, but Gemma had been distraught at the time. Yet the rest… Staying… That surprised him. She had more grit than any two women he knew.

Nothing like Charlotte. Charlotte compared to Gemma was about as close as a house cat compared to that cougar they had come across. Stuck inside that shed, Charlotte would have still been there sitting in a frustrated puddle of tears because he hadn't come to her rescue. Not so Gemma. She had gotten herself out and was preparing for the cold walk home.

He'd like to think his kiss had flustered her to a point she wasn't thinking straight, but that was pure ego on his part and not likely. Gemma didn't fluster easy. She got uppity easy and could be riled easy...but she didn't fluster. He regretted a lot of things he'd done in his life, but that kiss wasn't ever going to be one of them. He'd seen stars. And he thought maybe she did too. She hadn't pushed him away. Like snow on a frying pan, she had melted—quick and sizzling.

He remembered her promise to Tanner and sighed to himself. Gemma had too much character to renege on her word. That kiss had been impetuous on his part. Unplanned. He should relegate it to an enjoyable memory and leave it at that.

Except when it had happened, when they kissed...everything had suddenly shifted and fallen into place. Why he was here in Clear Springs...why she was... He couldn't exactly explain it, but everything had suddenly become... right.

Chapter Eight

The children stood at the front of the room. Gemma had placed them in order of height so that none would be lost behind another, taller child. She wished she had a piano to accompany them but she hadn't played since leaving home, and truth be told had never been very good anyway. She found the beginning note on her harmonica and blew.

"Mmmmmmm…" The children hummed the note.

With ruler in hand, she raised her hand up and then copied the motions she'd seen the conductor make when Roland had taken her to the opera in Boston. The strains of "Joy to the World" filled the room in warbling sweetness as the children lifted their voices in song. Only three more days which meant three more practices and it would be time for the real thing—the Christmas program on Saturday.

"Well done, everyone!" she said, clapping to encourage them. They had done remarkably well considering they'd only started practicing a week ago. "Now remember you'll need to wear your Sunday best and be there at the town hall by six thirty on Saturday. Remind your parents. We will give our program at seven o'clock. For today, you are dismissed."

They grabbed their coats and slates and meal tins and headed out the door, scattering like birds after gunshot. She followed, leaning against the doorpost and watching them run and skip in groups of two and three as they headed home. She really loved this job and loved the children. They gave her such hope for the future.

"Excuse me, Miss Starling," Billy mumbled behind her.

She straightened and moved aside so that he could get through the doorway. She hadn't spoken to him about the raccoon or the fight. She wanted to, but not with his sister always so near. Tara, sitting on the mule, was all ears. "I thought everyone was out."

"Tara forgot her coat."

She glanced down at the dark green wool coat in his hand.

"You take good care of your sister," she said, remembering her conversation with Craig about honey. "Your mother must be very proud of you."

He hunkered down, his shoulders drawn up to his red-tipped ears, and handed the coat up to Tara. While she shrugged into it, he untied the mule and walked it over to the steps, using them to mount up behind his sister. The two always rode bareback.

She had told him about the cougar frightening her mare after her visit to his mother. She wondered how in the world he and his sister would stay on if they came upon the big cat. "What if your mule is spooked? How do you stay on?"

He shrugged, tossing his head to swing his dark blond bangs out of his eyes. "Just hang on tight with my legs and grab the mane."

"And you hold on to your sister, I hope."

He snickered. "Yeah. Her too." He grabbed a hank of bristly mane. "Uh, Miss Starling? I put that book back."

"Did you finish it?"

"Yeah."

"And did you like it?" she asked softly.

"It was good."

She smiled.

He flipped the stiff black mane through his fingers. "Uh, Miss Starling? I'm real sorry about the raccoon. I tried to stop it."

"I'm sorry too. Thank you for telling me."

"Are you sore?"

"You mean am I angry?" She shook her head. She had been hurt, not angry. "Not now."

"You gonna punish us?"

"Yes. I'm not sure what it will entail, but yes. Don't you think you deserve being punished?"

"Maybe." He squinted as he considered his options. "You could forbid me and Duncan to sing in the program."

She laughed. Once. "Nice try, Mr. Odom. At your age that isn't a punishment. You probably *want* to get out of it, thinking you are too old and will make a spectacle of yourself. It's not true, you know. The class needs both your and Duncan's deep voices to balance the girl's high ones."

He rolled his eyes but she thought he might be secretly pleased when she mentioned his voice.

"I'll see you two tomorrow," she said to both him and Tara.

Billy expertly maneuvered the mule down the path toward the road. He was nearly to the trees when Mr. Larabee stepped into view. The old man held up a rabbit by the legs for Billy's inspection. It could be dead. It certainly wasn't moving. He stuffed it carefully in a burlap bag and handed the bag to Billy.

Gemma started across the clearing. "Mr. Larabee! May I have a word with you?"

She quickened her pace, her boot heels sinking into the soft ground and chunking up the mud. It gave her an ungainly gait. The crisp wind bit through her clothing and chilled her neck and face. She crossed her arms over her chest to help keep them warm and wished for her coat.

The old man withdrew something small from his pocket and handed it to Tara.

Before she drew closer, Billy kicked the flanks of the mule and started down the road away from the school and town. Mr. Larabee stared across the clearing at her. Had he heard her?

But no. He was turning away.

"Wait!" she called.

He didn't wait. He faded back into the woods.

Winded and frustrated, she stopped and blew out an exasperated breath. Thoroughly disgruntled, she turned and marched back to the schoolhouse to do her end-of-the-day chores.

It had been such a crazy day, only made more so by the fact that every time she turned around she thought of that kiss—Craig's kiss.

The only other kiss she had received happened when Roland kissed her once down at the boathouse. It was a bruising, possessive kiss and he hadn't wanted to stop with just one. It was as if someone else lurked beneath the surface he had shown to her. And that someone made her nervous. From that point on, she'd done her best never to be alone with him.

It was a surprise in that in almost everything else Roland had so much finesse. He was an excellent dancer, an excellent boater and he even played polo at the club. There were many young women in her social circle who had their hats set for him before he started working for her father. Suddenly, those women faded away and he only had time for her. At first she'd been flattered and then she'd been uncomfortable. He smothered her and began demanding that she do things his way. She should have exposed him to her father. He had deluded them both.

Craig's kiss was nothing like Roland's. She even hated to think of them in the same minute of time. Although insistent, Craig had been gentle. She could have pulled away if she had wanted to, but she was enchanted by it, and didn't want to move or break the spell. Even as he deepened the kiss he'd been tender, drawing her along with him in a shimmery pool of delight. She had suddenly felt energized, the air around her charged with electricity that flowed between them both. Likely her hair would stand on end if she had not worn it tidied up carefully in a bun.

Even now, just thinking about the kiss kicked her pulse up to a faster rate. Had it been that way for him?

But they had to talk. She had to explain. He had overstepped. They both had overstepped.

She remembered his persistence to accompany her to the Odom place and blew out a breath.

When it came to doing his job as sheriff he always overstepped. And…if she were truthful with herself, she had to admit that she was glad he did. He had protected her from that cougar by way of his presence and his superior skills as a horseman. That's why it was so hard to turn from him now. But if their friendship continued, eventually he would learn of what had occurred in Boston. She couldn't let that happen. The kiss had been wonderful…but it was a mistake. She couldn't let herself care for him. Not in that way—the way of happily-ever-after. She had ruined that chance with one single gunshot. Happily-ever-after would never happen for her. A family of her own could never happen. She would never put those closest to her at risk.

All she wanted was a peaceful life where she could do something productive and make a positive difference in the lives of those around her. If that were possible without the specter of Roland's death and family coming after her, she would learn to be content.

She wiped down the slate board and then repositioned the benches that had been pushed awry by her energetic pupils. Then grabbing the bucket of dirty water, she walked outside and tossed the water behind the building. On her way back, she stopped at the shed and picked out two pieces of wood for the morning's fire. After depositing those near the stove, she glanced about the room and let out a satisfied sigh. All ready for tomorrow.

After locking things up, she straightened the pine wreath that hung on the door and then hurried toward town. Tonight the quilting ladies were meeting at the town hall to finish the quilt. She was determined not to miss out this time.

Craig sat at his desk, tapping his finger on the law book he'd been studying while he waited for Joe to finish his coffee. "When I let you out I expect you to get on that horse of yours and head straight back to The Lazy L Ranch. If I catch you in one of the saloons, I'll drag you right back here so fast your head will spin. Understand? And you better think hard about apologizing to Adolph Green. He's a good man and he's been here long before you ever set eyes on Clear Springs. He deserves a word."

Joe swiped his fingers through his long oily hair. "All right, Sheriff. You made your point." He swigged down the coffee and handed the mug back to Craig. "I'm ready."

Craig grabbed the key for the cell door and let the man out.

Without another word, Joe slid his hat on and sauntered outside and across the road to the livery.

As soon as Craig was sure Joe headed out of town and not into one of the saloons, he locked up the law office and headed over to the livery himself. He nodded to Gil Jolson and saddled up Jasper. He had done all the thinking on that kiss he was going to do without seeing Gemma. He had missed her at noon thanks to Joe and that had sat sideways in his craw the entire day.

As he rode out of town two younger boys that he recognized from the area came toward him down the road. Each one stopped every few minutes to scoop up enough snow to pack into a small snowball and throw at the other. He chuckled. He'd had fun tormenting his brother the same way. There was more snow back home. Their ranch at the base of the Sierra Nevada range had been higher in elevation than Clear Springs. A day like today, with small patches of the white stuff here and there wasn't hardly enough to get excited about it.

With some surprise, he realized that the ill will he'd had for his brother had lessened over the past six months. Had time done that…or distance? Or something more—Gemma. Whatever it was, thinking about Douglas and Charlotte didn't make him burn like it once had.

He clucked to Jasper and picked up his pace to a comfortable half walk/half trot. Thinking about snow…he still hadn't come up with any clues on those footprints he'd seen by the school. But he liked a puzzle. He'd figure it out. Just had to keep mulling it over. He was sure of it.

Things looked deserted when he rode up to the school and dismounted. Someone had nailed a pine wreath on the door and decorated it with a red ribbon. Made the place look ready for Christmas. The door was ajar so Gemma must be inside. He tied Jasper to the step railing and walked up the wooden planks. She had accused him of startling her before so he thought to call out when he opened the door.

"Gemma?"

No answer.

"Miss Starling?"

He stepped farther inside. All was quiet. No sign of her.

Maybe she was practicing her aim.

He walked outside and around to the back of the school where they had been before. She wasn't in the small field and he didn't hear the report of a gun, so she wasn't practicing her aim.

He walked back up to the door and shut it firmly.

It wasn't like her to leave the place unlocked.

The situation bothered him until, on the ride back into town, he saw her walking beside Mrs. Birdwell on Main Street. He thought to ride up to her, but then realized she was greeting three other ladies. Each of them held carpet bags that appeared to be stuffed full. They chattered non-stop just before disappearing into the town hall.

He would speak to her tomorrow.

Chapter Nine

The next morning Craig rose early and saddled his horse. He'd thought things through during the night and it still sat crooked with him that the school hadn't been secured. He would just mention it to Gemma in passing. If she said anything about that kiss…well they'd tackle that subject too.

By the time he reined Jasper away from town, kerosene lamps were blazing in Becker's Bakery and in the café down the street. It wouldn't be long before kids were heading to class.

Ten minutes later he tied his horse to the tieline and headed inside the school.

"Gemma?" he called out so as not to startle her.

In the back of the room, he stopped short.

She stood behind her desk, her face as white as the snow outside—trembling. Something was wrong—terribly wrong.

All thought of what he had planned to say escaped in light of the frightened look on her face. He strode toward her. "What is it?"

She pointed to a large torn piece of brown wrapping paper rolled up on her desk.

He spread it out on her desktop.

In bold black capital letters were the words: YOU AIN'T WANTED HERE, TEECH. YOU OR YOR PUNY SKULE. QUIT NOW OR BE SORRY.

He met her gaze. "Who would do this?"

She stared back at him, her mouth half-open, her brown eyes full with anxious fear. "I…I don't know. Craig… What is going on?"

He knew she was tough, but this… His first instinct was to gather her to him. He started toward her when two of the Shalbot boys tumbled into the room laughing and shoving each other good-naturedly.

"Boys!" He used his voice to cut through their playing like a sharp blade.

Gemma squeezed his arm.

"Toby? Justin?" she said. "Wait outside. I'll call you inside in a minute."

"Aw, Miss Starling, it's cold out there!" Toby whined. "We got snow!"

"You won't freeze, but you need to go outside. Shut the door tightly behind you, please."

They both grimaced, yet minded her, dropping their slates on their desks and heading back outdoors.

She sank onto her seat and stared at the note. "I can understand that someone might not like me…a northerner. But whoever this is…what have they got against the school?"

"Good question."

"I believe your premonition has been verified. Whoever left me in the shed, did so on purpose." She rubbed her forehead with her fingers. "I really didn't want proof. Not like this."

He glanced about the room. "Anything else look out of place?"

"No. Only…" She pointed to the floor. Large clots of mud dappled the aisle.

Surely he would have noticed those last night. They hadn't been there, he was sure. "I came by last night. The door wasn't locked."

She frowned. "But I locked it." She rose and strode back to the door, checking the locking mechanism. It gave easily… *Broken.*

"That morning of the fight…" she said, a puzzled expression on her face.

"What?" he prompted.

"Billy said the door had been only *half locked* when he was able to get inside early that morning. I brushed it off. And then the fight and the raccoon happened. It slipped my mind."

Craig didn't like the sound of that. "So it hasn't been locking correctly for over a week?"

Her gaze met his. "Possibly."

A high-pitched giggle sounded as outside more children arrived. A snowball fight had begun with the small amount of snow they could scrape from the ground. Looked like seven or eight of the younger kids had joined in. He turned back to Gemma. "Maybe you should call school off for the day."

She shook her head. "I can't. There's only two days left to prepare for the Christmas program on Saturday."

He frowned. "I could tell them you are sick."

"But I'm not." As if to emphasize her decision, she untied the ribbons under her chin and removed her bonnet.

He followed her to the cloakroom. "You don't have to do this, Gemma. I'll find someone else to help the kids."

She hooked her bonnet over a peg and then pressed the hairpins back into her bun. "If I quit now, then whoever wrote this has already won. It will be twice as hard for me to return after the break if I give in to him."

"So you are thinking it's a man." He thought so too. He just wanted to hear her reasons.

She nodded and pointed at the mud. "Big feet. And the handwriting is masculine."

"Anything else?"

"Uneducated—or trying to pass himself off as uneducated." She trembled.

It made him want to draw her close against him. "It could be a student."

She frowned. "I won't believe that."

"I'm sorry, Gemma, but it could be. The only way to figure this out is by assessing the facts."

She opened her mouth to protest, but then closed it without a word.

Outside a little girl shrieked.

Gemma jerked, startled, and started for the door. When the next sound was the same girl dissolving into a fit of giggles, Gemma slowed, her body suddenly going limp.

He walked up behind her and with one hand on each shoulder, turned her face toward him. "Are you sure about this?"

She nodded. "I'll be fine. I suppose I should ring the bell and start school. It's time."

She looked so frightened and yet was trying hard to rally her courage. He wanted to help carry the burden. As a sheriff he wanted to protect her. As a man…he wanted to hold her and stroke away the fear that widened her eyes and robbed her of breath.

Everything inside him told him to back up… to keep his distance. Yet…she needed to know he was on her side and that others would be on her side. Gently, he slid his fingers along the curve of her jaw and under her chin to raise her gaze to his. "I want to know about anything strange that happens. I don't care how small or silly you think it may be. I want to know. Promise me."

She swallowed. And nodded.

He felt the muscles in her slender neck work. It was all he could do to keep from embracing her. "I know you like to handle things yourself. You are independent. I understand that. But whoever doesn't want you here may not be rational."

The door slammed open and a blast of chilled air swept into the room.

"Why ain't you callin' us in?" Duncan said. He stopped abruptly when he saw Craig. "What's going on?"

Gemma pulled away, distancing herself from him as she acknowledged Duncan. "Mr. Philmont. Yes. It is time. Go ahead and take your seat."

"I'll go," Craig said, lowering his voice. "Tanner should know about this. I'll take that note. He might recognize the handwriting." Craig folded it and slipped it into his coat pocket. "I'll be back at the end of the day to make sure you get home safely."

A tremulous breath escaped as though he'd thrown her a rope. "I'd like that."

He took her hand, squeezed it reassuringly. "Whoever this is, he's not around now."

She chuckled without mirth. "Unless he's a student."

"This note is the sign of a coward. He'll give you time to react. Be strong. I'll be back."

With that, he strode down the aisle that separated the girls' benches from the boys', stepped out the door and gave the large cowbell two strong, hard jerks.

From the start of class Gemma had a difficult time keeping her thoughts on teaching the children. The stark, harsh words of the note had been emblazed on her mind. Who wanted her gone? And why? She considered the people she'd met since coming to Clear Springs and searched her memory for someone she might have inadvertently antagonized—those in the small church, the few storekeepers she knew or the parents of the children she taught. She was unable to figure out who might have taken offense to her so strongly. More and more she feared it had nothing to do with the people here—but with her past.

As the day wore on, she leaned into the familiar role as teacher. She found comfort in hearing the children go through their rote memorization, their numbers and their spelling. They handled their parts well as they rehearsed their program for Saturday. Only two more days to go to the dance.

After the children left, she began cleaning off the slate board. She was looking forward to seeing Craig again, actually anxious, and not just to hear what he might have learned during the day. She felt safer with him near. With all that had happened, they both had not talked about that kiss…if in fact it should be discussed at all. Perhaps leaving it in the past was best.

"Teach."

She froze, her entire body tense. That word. Just like in the note. She lowered her hand and turned.

"I…I mean Miss Starling."

Duncan Philmont stood on the other side of her desk. Craig had said the note might have come from a student. She didn't want to believe so, but then she had been wrong about Duncan before. And he had been involved in the raccoon episode. Warily, she answered him. "Yes, Duncan?"

"What is going on?"

She set down the water bucket and rag. "Duncan…about what you saw this morning… Sheriff Parker was just doing his job."

He gave her a flat look. "Right."

"I'm not at liberty to say more. I'm sorry."

Duncan blew out a breath. "He is worried about something. I can tell that much. And it has something to do with you."

"I wish I could be more open with you. I just can't." She could tell he was disappointed that she wouldn't confide in him, but to do so went beyond a teacher/student relationship.

The door at the back of the room creaked open and Craig strode toward them, his boots pounding the floor planks and causing a decisive rumble. Duncan scowled, but moved back a measure. "I gotta go to work."

Gemma nodded to him, but found herself relieved when he grabbed his things and left the room. For the first time since she had started teaching here, a student made her uneasy and she hadn't wanted to be alone with him in the room. Whether it was him, or whether it was in light of what Craig had said, she wasn't sure. She just knew she didn't want to let it happen again.

"What was that all about?" Craig asked.

She shook her head. "He senses that something is going on and was asking about it."

He watched her closely. "Did you tell him?"

"No."

"Good."

She swallowed. "Craig…I'm glad you are here." With the admission, her defenses crumbled slightly. He'd kept his word. He'd come back at the end of the day for her. She hadn't realized how much she'd been striving to remain strong throughout class until now.

His eyes softened, yet it wasn't Craig who spoke next, but the sheriff within him. "Has he bothered you before?"

"Only by being mouthy in class. I see where you are heading with this, Craig, and I don't like it."

"I know you don't, Gemma, but it's my job. Right now the only people I can rule out regarding that note and those footprints are you and me. Everyone else is suspect."

"The note is not from Duncan. I would know."

"Like you knew about that raccoon?"

"The handwriting doesn't match any of my students," she said obstinately. She wouldn't back down. Her students wouldn't do something like this.

"Handwriting can be altered. And Duncan Philmont called you Teach. I heard him."

She frowned. "Just how long have you been outside?"

"Long enough to watch the children start for home."

Her mouth dropped open. She had forgotten her duties.

"I didn't tell you to upset you."

"But... I should have..." Suddenly tears welled up in her eyes. Embarrassed, she opened her desk drawer and searched for her handkerchief, her actions fumbling and awkward with her blurred vision.

"Gemma...don't..." He moved closer and squeezed her shoulder, his action awkward.

Her cheeks heated. She had to get herself together. She couldn't allow him to see her like this—undone, vulnerable. She was mortified. The heavy weight of his hand burned through her cotton blouse and heated her skin. Where had that silly handkerchief gotten to? "I'm sorry."

"Don't apologize. You've done well."

She sniffed, still holding herself rigid. Finally, she found the handkerchief and dabbed her eyes.

When she glanced up she found him studying her. Storm clouds gathered in his eyes and the lines between his brows furrowed like matching, jagged thunderbolts.

"I don't like seeing you scared. Whoever wrote that note won't get away with it."

For a moment the silence between them was

potent and thick as though more words hovered, poised to be said. Then he dropped his hand to his side. "I'll wait outside."

She understood that he wasn't angry at her. He probably felt as impotent as she did and for a man who liked to be in control of things, his answer was to rage at the situation. But she... she had wanted him to hold her...wanted him to say it would be all right. She wanted him to take away this feeling she couldn't shake of being helpless.

And she had wanted him to kiss her again...

She covered her face and breathed into her hands, trying to take hold of herself. When had she crossed the line from liking his presence to needing it? Lowering her hands, she headed for the cloakroom, suddenly needing the privacy, the comfort of closeness and of being protected, even though no one was in the building. There she leaned against the wall for support and dragged in a shaky breath. She had wanted so badly to turn to him and sink into his arms. Would it have been so terrible to lean on him?

The seconds ticked by and finally the feeling passed. She breathed easier. It was a momentary lapse into weakness. She was better now. She squared her shoulders and grabbed her coat from the peg and headed outside.

* * *

Craig watched Gemma emerge from the schoolhouse and lock the door. For a moment she'd let him glimpse the woman inside—a woman who intrigued and who lately had consumed his thoughts. But now, noting the rigid way she held herself, he realized that she'd wrapped herself in that invisible armor once again.

He knew the message. *Keep a respectable distance.* Fine by him. He'd do his job and make sure she kept safe. When this situation was over, hopefully with the culprit behind bars for his threats, they could figure out what to do with this attraction between them and put it to rest. For now, he would stick to business.

She descended the steps, slowing as she approached. "A buggy?"

He helped her up into the light carriage. He had access to the horses and anything he needed in the livery as long as it wasn't someone's personal property and as long as it was for his work as sheriff. "Thought the situation called for it."

"What…situation exactly?" She asked slowly—almost warily.

He hadn't considered that bringing a buggy might be misconstrued after their kiss. He narrowed his gaze on her. This was about her safety… and letting whoever had sent the note know that the sheriff was involved. He raised his chin. "Scoot over."

A small frown crossed her face, but she did as he asked.

He probably could have worded that better. Maybe used a *please*. He climbed up and sat next to her. When he breathed in, the lingering scent of jasmine from the morning soap she had used wafted over him. He stared straight ahead, resigned that he would be unable to avoid the image of kissing her again on the ride into town. Because he wanted to—kiss her. It just wasn't smart for either of them right now. She was too vulnerable and he…well he needed to concentrate on his work.

He looked sideways at her and took in the pale cast to her skin, the delicate slope of her nose, and then the softness of her bowed pink lips. When he returned his gaze to her own he thought she might understand. Her brown eyes softened and her mouth parted, making it even harder for him to keep to his own council. He blew out a breath.

"There's an emergency school board meeting," he said.

"When?"

He gathered the reins and dislodged the brake. "Now. At Molly's."

"Did Mr. Tanner have anything to say about the note?"

He snapped the reins. "Tanner called the meeting."

"I've been searching my thoughts, trying to remember anything unusual beyond what I've told you. The only thing I can come up with is Mr. Larabee."

When he didn't comment, she continued. "Do you know... I think the Odom children know him. He stopped them on their way home yesterday and gave them a rabbit." She grimaced. "It looked like it was dead, by the way it dangled from his grip. Do you suppose Larabee supplies some of the furs they sell?"

"Sounds like that's one more thing to bring up tonight." He tossed the reins once to hurry the livery horse along. In doing so, his shoulder rubbed against Gemma's. A moment later, she scooted farther away from him, sending up another whiff of jasmine. He set his jaw. Probably a good idea she distanced herself the way he was feeling.

They rode in silence for half a mile and then he asked, "Where were you yesterday after school?"

"I went to the town hall with Molly to help finish a quilt. After that, the women decorated the room for the party on Saturday. Why?"

"I'm glad you weren't alone. That's all."

The carriage wheels crunched over the pebbles on the road at the edge of town. "Craig. I... wanted to talk to you about the other night. When you kissed me. I...don't know what you meant by it, but I can't think about that right now. It was something I should not have let happen."

He glanced sideways at her. She was flushed, trying to word her thoughts just so. He knew she was on edge with all that was happening. He also knew that she had enjoyed that kiss as much as he had. "Nice speech. But I'm not so sure it was a lapse on my part."

"It most certainly was. We barely know each other."

He stifled a smile, thinking of the other night when she'd fallen asleep against his chest while riding Jasper. "I wouldn't say that."

"Craig. Really? You cannot even tell me what happened between you and Charlotte. I realize that it isn't any of my business, but we both have...pasts. I think we both want to be cautious." She raised her delicate brows. "Right?"

"I'm just taking in all that you are saying, Gemma. I like hearing you talk...your voice."

She flushed more. "Well, as I told you, I am not interested in any...entanglements at the moment. I've made a commitment to Mr. Tanner about teaching for an entire year."

It didn't matter what she said. He could tell by the way she responded when he kissed her that she wasn't as indifferent to him as she would like to be.

"Well? Nothing to say?"

He'd like to stop the buggy and simply kiss her senseless, is what he would like to do, but he might end up getting slapped. Which at this point, he would deserve. She had enough going on with the school and this note. She sure didn't need him muddying things up with an "entanglement," as she so aptly called it.

He shook his head in answer to her question. "Nope. Nothing to add. You're right." He flicked the reins again to speed up the horse. "For now."

Chapter Ten

At Mrs. Birdwell's boardinghouse, the Tanners and Winterses were already in the midst of a heated discussion in the parlor when Craig arrived with Gemma.

Mrs. Birdwell's kind gaze fixed on her boarder and she hustled toward Gemma, taking her hand and patting it reassuringly. "Oh, my dear. I just heard. How frightening for you. It seems to be one thing after another. Clear Springs is usually such a quiet town. I don't know what's come over people."

Gemma reached for Mrs. Birdwell and for a moment the two women clung to each other. The sight relieved some of Craig's misgivings. Gemma would do well to have Molly on her side. When she pulled back, she took a seat, murmuring a hello to the assembled party.

Tanner stood and shook hands with Craig. Once

everyone had taken a seat, he passed around the note. Gemma cringed when she reread it and then she handed it quickly to him as if the very paper burned her skin. He wanted to acknowledge her reaction...squeeze her hand or something but he knew she would hate that. She wanted to handle this on her own as much as possible. Which was probably best for him. He needed to be clearheaded— not all fogged up trying to decipher how he felt about her.

He walked over to the fireplace to address the semicircle of adults. "Any of you have an idea who could have written this note?"

To a person, they all shook their heads.

"As I see it, besides figuring out who this person is and keeping Miss Starling safe, we need to make sure the children are safe."

Mrs. Winters raised her index finger. "Absolutely. School should be called off immediately. There is only one more day as it is. The children should be kept at home until this is resolved."

Gemma's mouth dropped open. "But Mrs. Winters... What about the Christmas program! They have worked so hard!"

Craig remembered her earlier comment— about the note writer already winning if Gemma didn't show up at school. "I'm not so sure that your plan is the best way to go, Mrs. Winters. You are saying we should let the person who wrote this note call the shots and have his way."

"Yes! No! I mean… I don't want my children in any danger."

"I'm not sure that they are. This—" he held up the paper "—seems to be directed at Miss Starling. Nothing like this has ever happened with any of the other teachers, right?"

"No," Patrick Tanner answered for the group. "But the old school was right here in the middle of town at Judge Perry's carriage house. We could keep an eye on things. With the new school located just outside the town's edge we are less aware of who comes and goes."

Molly reentered the room carrying a stool from the kitchen. "Here you go, Sheriff." Then she positioned herself on a kitchen chair at the back of the room.

He pulled the stool to the hearth and sat. "Speaking of coming and going, I need more information on this Larabee. He is still lurking around the school and he seems to know the Odom kids."

Mr. Tanner's and Mr. Winters's gazes met for a moment, then Mr. Winters said, "He has land out that way although most of it is gone now—sold off in bits and pieces in order for him to survive. One of those bits is the property the school now sits on."

"But he lives here in town?"

"Yes. Behind the butcher shop."

For the six months Craig had been sheriff of Clear Springs, nothing about the elderly man had triggered a concern. Still, the silent looks that passed among the members had Craig wondering what this Mr. Larabee had done to warrant them. He didn't like them holding back and that's just what they were doing. He needed all the facts to know what actions to take. He glanced at Gemma. She looked to be of the same mind as him by the worried frown on her face. "Sounds like there's more I should know."

Another round of silent looks occurred among the school board members.

"What is it about this Larabee that has you all staring sideways at each other? Miss Starling has a right to know as much as anybody. She's the one who will have to answer for it if something bad happens to one of her students. We both should know the details."

Patrick blew out a breath. "All right. About twenty-five years ago, Albert Larabee lost his son in an accident that to this day some believe he should have been hung for. It comes down to stupidity on his part. He set a can filled with chemicals he used for purifying gold on the kitchen table and then headed out to do some panning in the creek. Before his wife realized it, their three-year-old boy took hold of the mercury and drank it. Poison is poison. When Albert returned later to the house he found his wife…well, not quite herself and holding their dead son."

Gemma grimaced, obviously shaken. "Where is his wife now?"

"She's gone too. Not long after losing his son, a fire took her and his cabin."

"There's more to it than that," Ruth Winters said ominously.

"No point throwing dirt on an old grave," Tanner said. "It's long over. And Larabee has lived among us for twenty-five years without causing problems."

"Tell me the rest," Craig ordered. He'd make his own decisions on Larabee and he was tired of this cherry-picking of which facts they thought he should know.

Tanner shared another look with Mr. Winters. "We like to look out for our own, Sheriff."

"You mentioned that when you hired me. I have no quarrel with a town taking care of its members. Matter of fact I think that's what makes a town a community. But if Larabee has broken the law or is dangerous, that's another thing entirely."

"Some say that his wife started that fire on purpose," Tanner said. "She was filled with grief and rage over her son and terrible resentment toward Albert."

"He always blamed himself," Mrs. Winters added. "For a while he took to drinking and was horrible to anyone who approached him. Absolutely horrible. I made it a point to cross to the other side of the road if I saw him coming."

"He no longer drinks," Molly said adamantly. "Even goes to church and sits in the last pew despite not being able to hear well."

Gemma's gaze settled back on Craig. "What is our next step? I'd hate for the children to give up their Christmas Program because of this."

Silently, he reread the words on the paper in his hands: YOU AIN'T WANTED HERE, TEECH. YOU OR YOR PUNY SKULE. QUIT NOW OR BE SORRY.

"I'll check out Larabee." He hesitated, wondering how she would react to his next suggestion. "Until we find this person, I don't want you to be alone. You only have one day left of school. Tomorrow you'll have an escort."

"An escort?" she echoed.

He could see her struggling to accept his announcement. Guess everybody liked to have control of their own life and in their own way. He just wasn't used to having someone only three-fourths his size question his every decision.

"Everyone is busy, Craig. No one has time to watch over me like a four-year-old."

"I do."

Her gaze flickered down. "I just want the children safe," she murmured.

"We'll stick together, dear," Mrs. Birdwell said. "Don't you worry. The sheriff will get to the bottom of this and find this culprit, and in the meantime you and I will tend to our Christmas baking."

Gemma smiled slightly. "Thank you, Molly. That will certainly make things more tolerable."

"By the time the new year starts, this will all be in the past."

At Molly's words, the Tanners and Winterses stood. Craig walked outside and shook hands with the men as they left with their wives. He looked back to see Gemma standing in the doorway.

He retraced his few steps. "About the Christmas Dance... I don't know if you already have an escort..." His own heart beat slightly faster as he waited for her to correct him. It struck him again how beautiful she was. A beautiful woman in a town where men outnumbered the women ten to one. She probably had someone taking her to the dance already. He half hoped that was the case because if it wasn't, he couldn't see how he'd get through an entire evening of being near her and dancing with her and not end up kissing her at least once under the mistletoe. "But you can't go to the dance alone."

"Oh. Well…" She pursed her lips. "A few days ago Mr. Philmont asked me."

He scowled. "I didn't think the two of you hit it off at the school board meeting last week."

"We didn't. I was just letting you know…" She pursed her lips. "If he won't do, then what about Molly? She probably already has plans to go. The two of us could stick together."

"I was thinking of someone stronger. Someone that would be able to protect you. Have you already agreed to let Philmont take you?"

Her gaze focused on his vest. "I didn't agree," she said hesitantly. "After all that's happened, the only one I'd trust myself to go with is you, Craig. But you haven't offered."

The flash of vulnerability on her face tugged at his heart. His mouth went dry as he gazed into those liquid deep brown eyes of hers. He swallowed, and then reached up to touch her face and cradle her delicate chin.

She froze, her eyes growing large as she fixed her gaze on him.

He smoothed his thumb over her lower lip, mesmerized by its softness. "I'm offerin' now."

She trembled.

Suddenly he wanted to do more than touch… he wanted to kiss her. With that look on her face, she might be thinking the same thing. Her eyes went soft and he knew—she *was* thinking the same thing.

"Craig…" she murmured, her voice slightly breathless.

Kissing her now would change everything between them. That first kiss he could explain away as impulsive. He couldn't do that with a second kiss. A second one would be a declaration of a relationship between them which was something neither one of them wanted at the moment. It wouldn't help either of them if he gave in to the impulse to close the space between them. He had to stay focused. Any distraction might ruin that, might make him soft. His job was to keep her safe.

Reluctantly, he lowered his hand and stepped back. "I'll go with you." She blinked. "As your bodyguard."

"My bodyguard?"

"That way, I can keep a close eye on you." It would be the smartest way.

By the frown emerging on her face, his words hadn't enthralled her.

"You're serious."

He nodded. Already missing the closeness

they'd just shared. "I heard what you said on the ride here. No entanglements. This will be strictly for your safety."

"But will we dance?"

"Dance?"

"For my first Christmas in Clear Springs, I'd like to dance. You do dance, don't you?"

He blew out a breath. He could dance, all right. Charlotte had seen to that. But asking him to shoot straight, or lasso and hog-tie a calf—or a criminal, for that matter—would be ten times easier for him to do than dancing with Gemma. Holding her that close might be his undoing. His resolve to stay clear of any entanglements wouldn't survive. She was special to him—and too tempting. He knew it down deep—if he would let himself hear his own selfish wants... and needs. But that wouldn't be the best thing for her.

He rubbed the back of his neck. "That's not what this is about. This is about keeping you safe."

Disappointment flashed across her face. "Safe."

He nodded.

"And you cannot dance and keep me safe at the same time?"

"I'd hate to find out that I couldn't."

Her shoulders sank. "All right. I only hope this will all be over soon so that I can enjoy Christmas without looking over my shoulder."

Relieved that she understood him, he settled his hat on his head. "I'll be here first thing in the morning. Don't leave for school on your own."

"I'll be waiting with bells on."

Her words held a whisper of bittersweet sarcasm. She sure hated to be in this position but still she smiled gamely—making the best out of a trying situation.

"Trust me. We'll get this man."

"I do. You are excellent at your job. Good night, Craig." She turned and walked back into the boardinghouse.

It was the way she had said it that bothered him. How was he supposed to keep this all about business when the thought of spending the next couple of days with her had his heart racing and his thoughts flying to forbidden places?

How?

Long into the night, even though sleep tugged at her, Gemma lay on her bed, staring at the beam that supported the roof overhead, and thought about what had happened between her and Craig. The day had been one of discovery for her. The note first...and then Craig. He did have feelings for her. She'd figured that out with the first kiss.

This evening he had wanted to kiss her again before that rigid sense of morality and office had pulled him back. He put his duty and her safety first...before any personal feelings muddied the situation. She respected him for that. He was different than Roland in that way.

Roland had seemed so sincere in his pursuit of her at first. To ingratiate himself he had humored her desire to become Massachusetts's first woman lawyer, knowing that that would be the way to her father. It was only later, after Father's death, that she'd come to realize he was simply using them both as a stepping stone...and that she had been his idealistic, willing accomplice.

Unlike her former intended, Craig hadn't lied to people to become sheriff. He'd said something once about training under another sheriff, but all in all he was a self-made man. Although she had never seen Craig use his gun, he wore it, holstered, every single day. He was prepared and ready in case there was a need. She was sure, if that need arose, he would shoot straight and accurate. In the woods, hadn't he been a step ahead of her with his rifle when they'd come across the cougar? And hadn't he been accurate with his aim when he taught her how to shoot with the gun at school?

Roland had been a master at manipulating things—her father and her in particular—but he was never helpful. Yet every time she was with Craig, she learned something new about him or about his world out here in the West. He was what others around here would call a straight shooter. Honest. Capable. Responsible. Her father would have liked him.

She turned on her side and fluffed the pillow before settling down on it.

So why was she wanting to shake up the very things she respected about him by pressing him about dancing? The thought was a wholly disturbing glimpse into herself. Was it the challenge? Did she want to see if he would relax his standards? Break them? That didn't make any sense. Those standards made him who he was.

Or was it because compared to her and the things of her past, he seemed too good to be true?

But to have him hold her close like he had when she rode on his horse sitting in front of him… To swirl around the room with him to the sound of a violin and laughter and with the aroma of fresh-cut pine boughs and Molly's apple-and-cinnamon pie… To tease him and know that she was the one putting a smile on his handsome face… To maybe, just maybe, know the touch of his lips on hers once more…

She sighed. It was a beautiful dream…and that's all it could be. Her eyes drifted closed on that disconcerting thought.

Chapter Eleven

Friday morning, when Gemma opened Molly's front door to head to school, Craig was waiting silently at the gate. Late into the night she had thought about all that had happened since she'd left Boston. She wanted to be honest with Craig about it and tell him about her past. It came down to trusting whether he would send her back there in handcuffs or whether he would believe her side of the story. Knowing him and his strict moral code, she didn't stand a chance. If he knew that she had shot a man, Craig would turn her in. It wouldn't matter that it had been self-defense. A man was dead—because of her.

She headed down Molly's front path, tying her hat ribbon under her chin while the basket of cookies that Molly had made for the children dangled heavily from the crook of her elbow.

A hawk chose that moment to glide through the

trees and perch in a pine ahead. Craig squinted up at the bird and then returned his gaze to her, studying her as she approached. A complex mix of emotions furrowed his brow. He wore his six-shooter and holster, tied with a leather cord around his thigh. She remembered thinking it unnecessary when she first came to Clear Springs. The town was quiet and peaceful. Men in Boston didn't have to wear a gun. The whole idea of it seemed barbaric. But now in light of the threatening note, she was glad he was ready. Now, his gun made her feel safe.

She shifted the basket of cookies to her other arm.

"I'll carry that," he said.

"Thank you, but it's not that heavy."

He took the basket from her anyway and hooked the handle over his horse's saddle horn, lashing it down securely with a leather cord.

"I don't know if in all the craziness, I've thanked you for all that you are doing," she said, falling into step beside him. "I know I make it hard sometimes and yet you have gone out of your way to help."

"You heard Mr. Tanner last night. People here look out for each other. You are not alone. You've got people here that care about you and the school. Mrs. Birdwell, the Tanners, the Winterses. Me."

She heard what he said, but she could only believe it to a small degree. None of them knew her. Not really. If they did, they might not offer their help so quickly. She turned down the main road with him, surveying the few buggies and horses stopped in front of the businesses. "It's just… I don't want to put any of you in harm's way and I feel like I am!"

"What do you mean, Gemma? A single note has you worried about us?"

There was no way to say more without revealing what had happened in Boston, yet if harm should come to any of the people she knew here because of her, she didn't know if she could live with herself.

"It's just a general feeling I have of impending…trouble. I want you to be careful, Craig."

He stopped her with a hand to her arm. "Tell me what really happened to you? And be honest. I don't want to hear some story about you coming here because you had your heart set on teaching. You've already told me that you wanted to be an attorney. A woman doesn't just up and leave a life of luxury unless she's forced to."

"Maybe you don't know women as well as you think you do! Or…or…"

He let go of her. "Or what? What are you hiding?"

"Me? You can't even tell me about your precious Charlotte! I have as much right to privacy as you do." She pressed her lips together, her jaw tight. She had given him just enough mystery to ensure his unending curiosity. He would not let up. And she couldn't be completely honest with him. Not ever. If she could just get through this day, and then the dance tomorrow night. Then... she wasn't sure. Maybe the best thing for her, and the safest for the children, would be to leave town. She could find another small town, another community that needed a teacher. Perhaps somewhere far north near San Francisco.

They were nearly out of town. If she picked up the pace slightly...

"About Charlotte..."

It was the last thing she expected him to bring up. She had only goaded him to stop him from digging further into her past. "I spoke out of turn. Out of frustration. Your situation with Charlotte isn't any of my business. You don't need to say anything."

"I think I do," he said seriously. "Charlotte lived on a ranch about a mile west of my family's ranch. We went to the same small school, had the same friends. Our families helped each other out at roundup time." He looked sideways at her. "I never cared about ranching the way my older brother did. He was a natural and he ate, slept and breathed ranching. I always knew I'd be leaving one day. Charlotte and I planned to marry as soon as I got a job."

"What happened?"

"Jeremiah Cash and his gang came through town and robbed the bank. I volunteered along with four other men to form a posse. We went after Cash. Never caught him, but he shot the sheriff. The sheriff pulled through, but until he was back on his feet, I took over his duties. He liked the job I did and he offered me the job of deputy. I jumped at the chance. I'd get to stay right there in Bartlett and Charlotte and I could marry."

"But you didn't. Why?"

He grimaced. "Charlotte found she couldn't handle the fretting and worrying that comes with being hitched to a lawman. When I didn't make it home, she would sit up with my family. She finally admitted that she didn't want a life of it. She also admitted that her affections had grown for my brother during those long hours that I wasn't there. He had more than eased her worries."

She sucked in a sharp breath. "I'm so sorry, Craig."

"There wasn't much around Bartlett except ranching and that wasn't for me. And I liked my job. As a sheriff I make a difference in people's lives."

He sounded surprisingly like she had when she pressed to go to law school. "But surely—"

"She married my brother," Craig said, interrupting her. He met her gaze. "It wasn't long after their wedding that I heard about Clear Springs needing a sheriff."

They had arrived at the school. Craig stopped at the line and tied up his horse.

"I'm...sorry things didn't work out."

He blew out a breath. "Yeah...well, guess it's for the best all around. My line of work is hard on a marriage. At least we figured that out before the wedding."

He moved to the saddle and unhooked the basket, handing off the cookies to her. In taking the handle, her fingers skimmed over his, eliciting a jolt of warmth that rushed up her arm.

He took his time releasing his grip. And by his expression, he'd felt something too. "I'm doing what I'm good at. Keeping the law."

"You certainly make me feel safe," she said softly. "As a matter of fact you have been rather insistent about it."

His lips twitched.

She grew bolder. "Bossy even."

"I can shoulder bossy."

That was an understatement in her mind. His shoulders were so broad and strong that he could "shoulder" just about anything. If only that meant he could shoulder the truth about her.

His grin widened. "Although I'd prefer enthusiastic. Or assertive."

She unlocked the door. "You are going for adjectives? With a teacher? How about aggressive?"

His handsome face was dangerously close. A mere stretch and she could press her lips to his smooth jaw…and to those enticing lips. For a moment she contemplated doing just that, but then noticed he too had become silent, watching her.

She pulled back, then stepped into the room and stopped short. Three giant words filled the large slate board: LAST DAY TEECH.

She tensed, angry and scared all at the same time. How dare this person threaten her! "Why have a door when just anybody can come in!" She dropped the basket on the last bench with a jolt and marched to the front of the room.

Craig rushed into the cloakroom. "No one back here," he called out.

He hadn't seen her desk.

She stared down at the dead rabbit stretched

out over her papers. Blood had congealed in a small pool by the animal's neck.

The urge to retch came fast. She bent over, grabbing her middle with both hands and trying to control it. She spun away from the gruesome sight, trying to block the image from her mind.

Craig stepped back into the main room, took one look at her face and started forward.

She wanted to hit something she was so angry. She clenched her hands, the rage bubbling up inside her and spewing out. "Why don't you show yourself?" she yelled. "Show yourself! You coward! Is this all you can do? Write notes to me? And misspelled ones at that! You horrible, pathetic creature!"

Craig had raced down the aisle when she started her tirade and now slowed upon seeing the rabbit. "Son of—"

"How dare he do this to me, to this school!" She dragged in a steadying breath and still her stomach roiled. She rubbed her forehead, trying to work through what she must do. "I cannot have this here when the children arrive. There's old newspaper in the corner of the cloakroom. If you will take care of the rabbit, I'll get water and clean off the board."

"I don't want you leaving my sight. Just wait, Gemma. Wait. I'll get the water." He strode back to the cloakroom and a second later came back, his arms filled with the newspapers. Wrapping the rabbit inside them, he also blotted as much of the blood off the desk as he could.

She picked up the bucket and together they walked down to the creek, keeping a wary eye out for anything unusual.

While Craig buried the rabbit, she stepped closer to the water and filled her bucket. She took a moment to wash her face in the icy stream.

Craig threw aside the stick he'd used to dig a small trench in the dirt. He laid the rabbit inside and covered it with dirt and then rocks. "That won't keep any animals from finding it, but I don't want to take the time to do a better job." He joined her at the water and washed his hands. "We should get back to the school before any students arrive."

He took the bucket from her and together they trudged up the hill to the clearing. He glanced her way often, his gaze searching.

"If you are waiting for me to fall apart again, I won't. I'm too angry."

"Good. I'd rather have you angry than scared."

"I'm calling off school. I can't have the children in the middle of this. Their safety comes first. I'll have them practice their lines for tomorrow's program and the two songs, treat them with

Molly's cookies and then dismiss them. I'll walk with them back to town."

"And you'll stay together as a big group." Worry etched his brow. "Promise me. This isn't a time to be stubborn and independent."

So he thought that about her? She stood a little taller, a little straighter. She could "shoulder" that. "I promise."

"I need to find out who is doing this. Once you get started on your day, I'll slip out the back. This man is a coward. I don't think he will bother you with all the children around."

Listening to him take charge, she realized with sudden clarity that she could love this man. It would be easy. If only she could be honest with him and tell him the truth. It hadn't escaped her that someone from Roland's family might be the one writing the notes. Craig deserved to know.

There was the sound of young voices on the road. The children had started arriving. She turned to Craig. His eyes had never looked so blue to her, his face never so handsome. "You be careful," she said, suddenly more fearful for him than ever.

"You be strong," he said urgently in his deep voice.

She thought about all she'd been through over

the past year and about the gun hidden in the rafters. She would use it if it came to it. "I am strong."

A slow smile inched up his face. "I already got that figured out."

Chapter Twelve

As soon as the children arrived, Gemma rang the bell to call them inside. Craig nodded to Gemma as she helped a few of the younger ones with their coats and gloves, and then he slipped out the door. He mounted Jasper and made a wide circle around the school, searching for tracks in the grass or the few snow patches that still remained on the ground. Finding nothing to follow, he reined his horse northwest and toward the land that Tanner had said belonged to Larabee. Seemed the man had a fondness for rabbits...

Ten minutes later he came across a small worn shack hidden in the woods and built up against a small hill. It sat five hundred yards from the curve of the creek. A vapid trail of smoke made its way into the sky from a narrow stovepipe in the tin roof of the cabin.

That made him curious. He'd been told that Larabee lived in town.

A stump, probably used as a seat, was knocked over on its side, near the front door—a door that swung back and forth on its hinges—unlatched. Something wasn't right.

"Larabee!"

No answer.

"Larabee!"

Then he noticed the blood. It was smeared on the side of the doorframe as if someone had grabbed there for support with a bloody hand. From there, another trace of blood—smeared again—colored the top of a boulder. He drew his Colt and quietly approached the shack. Cautiously, he opened the door.

The one-room cabin was empty, but signs of a struggle met his eyes—a filthy cotton-covered pallet had been ripped and shredded, leaving the straw stuffing scattered all over the floor. A small shallow bowl for panning had been overturned on the ground. A shovel stained with dark dried blood lay in the corner.

Heading back outside, Craig followed the blood trail and tracks through the woods. Halfway to the creek, crushed weeds and brush were smeared with drops of blood. More blood stained a patch of snow.

He scanned the trail to the water. There, half in and half out of the creek, was a man lying still as stone with his cheek against the gravel.

Larabee.

Craig checked his surroundings. Anyone could be lurking in the shadows. Then he made his way down to the water's edge. He checked for a pulse at the man's throat. At first—nothing, and then he felt the slow, faint throbbing beneath his fingers. He dragged him from the water.

"Larabee!" He shook him gently.

No response.

He rolled him over. A gash over the man's head appeared to be the reason for all the blood Craig had seen. It was now clotted with gritty bits of gravel and dirt imbedded in it.

"Albert. I'm taking you to Doc Palmer. And you better not die on me. You've got a lot of explaining to do." He lifted Larabee onto Jasper—the man was small and wiry and didn't weigh much more than a large child—then climbed on himself and turned his horse toward town.

He'd been more than half-certain it was Larabee behind the first note. It made sense. Maybe the old man wanted his land back. But now… Craig wasn't sure.

This wasn't an accident. The signs of struggle were too telling. Somebody had fought with the

man and left him for dead. It looked like Larabee
had crawled to the creek to try and care for his
injuries. Or maybe someone dragged him, planning to submerge the body. Had Craig's sudden
appearance thwarted them?

The only evidence that tied Larabee to the
notes was that rabbit and the fact his property
was nearby. It was all just a mite too convenient. If
Larabee lived, he had better supply some answers.

Gemma breathed a sigh of relief when she
looked out Molly's parlor window at three o'clock
that afternoon and saw Craig ride down the road.
She opened the door and stood on the porch until
he tied his horse and strode up the path from the
gate. Her heart caught just a little at his strong, sure
stride and the determination she read on his face.

"Did you find out anything?" she asked without preamble.

"I'm starving. Care to talk over a meal at the
restaurant?"

His change of topic confused her at first, but
she hurried back inside, explained where she
would be to Molly and then slipped her dark blue
coat off the peg by the door.

They stopped at the livery just long enough
for Craig to hand over Jasper's reins to Mr. Jol-

son, and then they walked the two blocks down the main street to the Miningtown Restaurant.

She felt Craig's hand on her lower back as he ushered her into the main room. He seemed to know where he wanted to go and stopped at a table against the wall. As he held a chair out for her to sit down, she realized that this was the first time they had done anything "normal" together. A trip to where a woman aimed her rifle at them, racing through the woods from a cougar, and shooting lessons did not constitute a regular acquaintanceship. By comparison, eating a meal with him was tame.

A pretty young blonde sashayed up to the table.

"Miss Starling, this is Daisy Finley," Craig said. "You'll find she is the best cook in Clear Springs. We'll take your special with a piece of your peach pie."

"Sure thing, Sheriff." The young woman winked at him and smiled.

So this was where Craig took his meals… "Is she sweet on you?" Gemma asked when Daisy left to get their plates.

"She only sees my badge," he said, brushing off the observation. "Things go okay for you at school? Anything happen?"

And just like that he was back in work mode. "Nothing unusual. We practiced the Christmas program for tomorrow and then I dismissed the children. They were very excited to have an extra half day off."

"I bet."

"But I got to thinking… What if the note is right? What if this is the last day I will teach here?"

"It isn't," Craig said, his blue gaze serious. "I won't let it be."

"If the Tanners and Winterses think I'm the cause of this, it could be. You heard them. They are worried for the children. They might ask me to go." Just saying the words out loud made it more of a possibility—more real. Looking at the man across the table from her, she knew leaving him would make it hard. She would hate to leave Clear Springs, but perhaps it would be providence. Leaving still would be the best thing for her. Saying it was her way of preparing herself.

Daisy returned with two steaming plates of roasted chicken and potatoes. When she had slipped back toward the kitchen, Craig leaned forward, pinning Gemma with his gaze, his dark brows drawn together. "Don't talk like that. You aren't defeated. You are strong."

"What I am is practical," she said, her hushed tone matching his. "Did you mention today's warning to Mr. Tanner?"

"Yes."

"And the rabbit?"

Craig nodded once.

"Then it is only a matter of time before they decide a different teacher might be the better course."

He pulled back. "Is that what you want? To leave? Because it's sure not what the children want. It's not what I want."

At his admission, she met his gaze. His words thrilled her and terrified her all at once. She didn't trust herself to answer immediately. To have the interest of this man would make any woman's pulse race. She had never felt this way about any man before and strongly doubted that she ever would again. He was everything a man should be...

What he'd said was momentous, considering his past with Charlotte. She should say something to acknowledge it, yet all she could do was shake her head in mute answer to his questions. She wasn't worthy of his regard. Her past stood in the way. It would break her heart to leave Clear Springs, but even more to leave him. She took a bite of her food—food that tasted like ashes with all the turmoil happening inside her.

Craig attended to his meal too. When he broke open his roll, steam swirled up between them. He stared at it for a moment before speaking. "About today…" Then he told her about Larabee.

"Could he have fallen? Hit his head?" she asked when he was done.

"Doc Palmer thinks someone attacked him. So do I. His injuries were too severe to be caused by a fall."

"Then the notes probably weren't from him. There are still no answers," she said. More and more she had begun to suspect that the threats had everything to do with what she had done in Boston. Somebody was toying with her. But then why would they attack Mr. Larabee? It didn't make sense. Perhaps what was going on was actually separate. It was selfish on her part to hope that, but she didn't want to be responsible for anyone getting hurt.

He nodded grimly. "There are answers, but they are locked inside Larabee. Only he can supply them. When he wakes, we'll know more."

"*If* he wakes," she said, dully. She was getting more discouraged by the minute.

He reached across the table and covered her hand with his. "We're getting closer, Gemma."

She stared at his hand. So big in the way that it hid hers. So strong. "Who has the upper hand, Craig?"

He grimaced, then squeezed her hand once before releasing her.

"I'm sorry," she said. "That wasn't very encouraging, was it?"

"It was true. He's making all the rules to this game."

She sighed. "But he didn't read the rulebook. I'm the one that likes the control."

"I can tell." His smile was spare as he stood and paid for their meal. "Lot of rules, Miss Starling. Come on. I'll walk you back."

Once outside, they started to Molly's. "Teachers live by the rules. Lawyers too for that matter, so I think I'm doubly allowed."

"I'd allow you just about anything."

He said it softly, so that she almost didn't hear it. His words caught at her, gently pulling her, but they were words and feelings neither one of them could afford. He didn't know her. "Craig…"

"I'll wait." The words were a challenge.

"What for?" she asked, almost afraid to hear his answer.

"You."

Chapter Thirteen

"He's coming up the walk, dear," Molly said, peering through the front parlor window. "And, oh, my, does he look dashing. I don't think I've ever seen the sheriff dressed up before in his Sunday best. Not even on Sunday." She bustled over to the door, ready to let Craig in as soon as he knocked.

Gemma stood by the hearth, her back to the glowing coals, warming herself. She was a bundle of excited nerves. Something about the things he'd said yesterday…that he cared…that he'd wait…had infused her with new hope in spite of all that was going on. With that realization she had determined that this evening she would put the craziness of the week behind her and enjoy herself at the dance. After all, Christmas was almost upon them.

Glancing down one last time at her dress, she

smoothed the material for the umpteenth time. It was from Boston—the fanciest dress she'd brought with her. The rich cranberry shade of red taffeta rustled when she walked. In the front, the skirt drew up to a bow over each of her knees which revealed a ruffled cream-colored second skirt beneath. At the end of her elbow-length sleeves the same cream-colored lace was gathered loosely to drape down gracefully. She checked the stiff bow at the back of her waist, worried now that perhaps the entire thing was too fancy for a mining town like Clear Springs.

"You look lovely," Molly said, noticing her fidgeting. "Now, don't fret. Nothing is going to ruin tonight. The children will do a wonderful job and we will both be there to help you." At the sound of Craig's light rap, she opened the door.

Craig stepped inside and removed his black Stetson. "Hello, Mrs. Birdwell. You're looking very fine this evening."

Molly said something in reply as she shut the door. Gemma wasn't sure what because she couldn't take her eyes off Craig. He looked like a silver dollar, all spit-and-polished. He'd had his hair cut and he had shaved. His black boots gleamed with a recent polishing, and he wore new black pants along with a crisp white shirt and black silk vest. With his broad, strong shoulders, dark blond hair and blue eyes, his handsome features diminished any of the men she had ever met—in Clear Springs or in Boston.

He stepped farther into the room, his leather coat slung over one forearm and holding his hat at his waist, and stopped when he caught sight of her. His eyes lit up with warm appreciation, leaving her tingling wherever his gaze touched her.

The socially appropriate action for a schoolteacher would be to draw her black-beaded shawl demurely closer, but she was too giddy for the night ahead. She loved dressing up, loved dancing, and it had been an eternity since she'd had the opportunity. She lowered her wrap off her shoulders, letting it loop down below her bustle bow and spun around once. The skirt flared out at her feet, revealing her eyelet petticoat.

"You are…" he murmured, then blinked and closed his mouth.

A thrill shot through her. "I've rendered the sheriff of Clear Springs speechless?"

"Your concerns that you might not get a chance to dance are groundless, Miss Starling. Every young cowboy in town is going to be vying for a dance with you tonight. I have a feeling it's going to be a long night of vigilance on my part."

"I don't mean to make your job more difficult," she said with studied innocence.

His mouth twisted into a grin. "Oh, I think you do, but I'm not disappointed. I'm up to the task."

Satisfied with his response, she gathered the shawl back up onto her shoulders. Perhaps she would get a dance from him after all. After the children performed, she just might make that her main goal for the evening.

"Sheriff," Molly said, coming back into the room from the kitchen area. When had she left the room? She was dressed in her best, a dark blue woolen skirt and matching blue blouse. The gold brooch at her throat sat slightly askew. She already had on her hat and her heavy shawl and was toting a cloth-covered platter. "There's more to carry on the table. I'd appreciate a hand."

"Yes, ma'am."

Gemma followed him into the kitchen. A large tray of cookies and a crock filled with eggnog remained.

"Looks like Mrs. Birdwell intends to feed the entire town," he murmured as he picked up the crock. He indicated the cookies with a nod of his head. "Can you manage those? I'll hold the door."

"There will be more, just wait and see. Sue is bringing more pies from the bakery and Eileen from the dry goods store is bringing molasses bread. You won't go away hungry."

"At least not for food," he murmured, as she

passed by carrying the tray. His low, suggestive voice sent shivers through her again.

They walked at a brisk pace the two blocks to Main Street. The night was clear with stars just making their appearance in the eastern sky. When they turned toward the town hall, a few people she didn't recognize were already gathered outside, the smoke from two of the older men's pipes floating up into the crisp, cold air.

As they approached the door, a younger man broke off from the group. He looked to be Gemma's age—a handsome young cowboy, fresh-shaven with longish blond hair slicked down. A green neckerchief fluttered as he jumped to open the door to the party. "This your famous apple pie, Widow Birdwell?"

"It is, Chet Farnsworth and don't you be helping yourself until a word of thanks to the Almighty is given."

"Oh, no, ma'am," the young man said, grinning. "Wouldn't think of it." He winked at Gemma as she passed by. "Miss Starling."

She smiled at him. She'd never been introduced to him before but he seemed quite pleasant. "Thank you, Mr. Farnsworth."

He tipped his dark hat. "My pleasure. Hope you'll save me a dance."

"Certainly," she said, delighted. A dance with

Chet would be fun, but it would be nothing compared with being in Craig's arms. Craig was, despite wearing his best suit, still acting as her bodyguard. She certainly hoped as the evening wore on that he would relax his restrictions on his duties as sheriff.

Craig cleared his throat as they all stopped just inside the door. "I thought Daisy was taking up all your time these days, Chet."

"That's a fact, but I got time for a dance or two with the teacher while Daisy takes her turn seeing to the refreshments. Don't want Miss Starling to rest too much neither. She's looking real purty tonight."

"I can keep her busy," Craig muttered, turning away to head for the table where he could set the crock down. Bemused at the exchange, Gemma watched Craig stride away. When she turned back she found Chet studying her.

He removed his hat. "I'll catch that dance later," he said, grinning. Then he winked at her and sauntered off.

Gemma looked about the room. A few more decorations had been added to the ones she and the quilting ladies had put up—namely a swag of small pine branches tied together and draped over the door. Someone had also brought in a pine tree and propped it at the front of the room.

By the looks of it, children had decorated the lower branches and adults the upper part. Wide, cranberry-colored ribbon swirled down each side from a huge bow on the top. It scented the room with pine. Mixed with the fragrance of the sweet bread and warm pies from Becker's Bakery and the large crock of eggnog on the table, now it truly felt like Christmas was upon them. She inhaled, enjoying the mix of different scents.

Craig was acutely aware of Gemma as she stepped up beside him and set the tray of cookies she held down on the adjacent table. She bumped against his arm and a frisson of electricity shot to his fingers. She glanced up at him, her smile dazzling, oblivious to her effect on him. "Pardon me."

The woman *had* to know of her effect on him. Being this near to her and yet chaperoned by half the town would be an exercise in restraint. "I'll take your wrap." He assisted her with its removal.

Before he turned toward the cloakroom, he caught her watching him. The trust and warmth in her gaze reached deep inside him, and caused his chest to expand. He had better remind himself that he was on duty tonight—often. He had to keep his wits about him in spite of the fact she looked like a vision. He broke contact with her eyes and let his gaze travel down to her lips, the sight of them so soft and inviting that his pulse sped up at the memory of their kiss. The wine-colored material she wore tonight set off the creaminess of her skin. Her neckline was slightly lower than usual, showing off her delicate collarbones and the pulse at the base of her neck. Tonight he'd have no trouble keeping his eyes on her. Others would too. She was a magnet—radiating charm and warmth and excitement.

He had a feeling tonight would be a challenge to keep from whisking her off to a secluded corner and stealing a kiss...or three. He hung up her shawl and his coat in the cloakroom.

When he returned to the main room Gemma was searching the assembly and counting which of her students were already there. Craig stood back, admiring her as she efficiently gathered them into a group and began coaching and encouraging them for the program ahead. As she talked, she placed small sprigs of holly in each of the girls' hair and helped each boy pin one on his shirt or suspenders. The children looked up at her with expectant, excited faces, scrubbed and polished. They reminded him of baby birds in the nest waiting openmouthed for morsels of food from their mother. It was obvious the younger ones liked their teacher. No issues there.

He searched the room for Duncan and Billy. Those two, he'd be sure to keep an eye on tonight. They hadn't arrived yet...if they were actually going to show up at all.

In the corner, Mr. Winters and his daughter stood warming up their fiddles. His oldest son, Jordan, was picking softly at his banjo. They were usually called upon for shindigs like this as their entire family was musically inclined and they played all the best melodies. The ladies from church had hung three large quilts on the walls. Molly had explained that one was to be auctioned off for funds for the school and the other two would go to needy families in the area as Christmas gifts. She had wanted his input on who those two families might be and he had suggested the Odoms for one of the quilts.

Just then Billy and Duncan sauntered in together and joined the other students at the front of the room. They made their way to the back of the three lines, and stood one on each end, winded and with reddened faces. They tried to look bored, but completely failed and were looking guiltier than anything. Where had they just come from? They'd been up to mischief, he suspected.

"Sheriff?" The preacher gained his attention at the front of the room. "If you'll call in those standing outside, we'll get the evening started."

He nodded to him and stepped out to alert the few lingerers outside. They came in bringing a rush of cold air sweeping through the hall. A few of the more delicate women raised a clamor to *hurry up and shut the door!* All in good nature.

"I'll say a word and then the Christmas program by the schoolchildren will commence," the preacher called out in a voice that boomed through the entire room. The talking and laughter quieted down to a more hushed level and then silence.

Looking around, Craig realized he knew many of the people in the room and he liked most of them—a good sign for his first Christmas here. He wondered what Gemma thought of the town now that she'd been here a couple of months. She stood with her hands folded, keeping a quieting eye on the children as the preacher finished up. When he was done, she stepped forward.

"Thank you all for allowing the children to add to tonight's festivities." Behind her one of the girls giggled and a boy coughed. Gemma turned to face her students and raised her hands to start the first song. Jordan Winters picked his banjo softly, playing "What Child Is This?" as the children began to sing. After one verse of the song, each student said a memorized short piece about what they liked in school and then added what they planned for Christmas break. The boys spoke of riding, hunting and games over their break. Billy, surprisingly, admitted to wanting to read a new book. The girls looked forward to sewing and cooking and visiting friends and family.

When they were finished, Gemma stepped forward, her gaze focused on the back of the room. "Thank you again for letting your children participate. They have enjoyed putting this together for you. We have one more song and would like all of you to join in."

She nodded for the music and everyone started singing "Joy to the World." Craig followed her gaze and found that Mrs. Odom had shown up and stood alone at the very back of the room near the door. She wore an old knitted sweater over a faded cotton dress and had pulled her hair up into a small bun at the nape of her neck. She crossed her arms over her chest as if she wasn't all that comfortable, but she was here and her eyes were shining with emotion as she listened.

"Glad to see you made it, Mrs. Odom," he said, stopping before her. "Your little girl sure can sing."

"I didn't know my Tara had a voice like that,"

she said, her own voice filled with wonder. "She don't sing t' home. Sings like an angel, don't she?"

"That she does. Billy too."

"Billy too," she murmured awestruck, turning her attention back to the performance.

The lamplight shone on her cheek and revealed a deep purple bruise that was slowly fading to a brownish yellow near her eye. She had covered it with a sweep of her hair but the thin strands had separated enough for him to notice.

The song ended and she turned back to him, catching him studying her face. She hurriedly patted her hair back in place.

"What happened?" he asked.

"Oh, had me a tussle with one of my chickens and fell against the coop is all. Happens all the time, the ground is so uneven right there."

"I remember a run-in with an ornery rooster myself growing up," he said. "I hope your hen made it into the stewpot after that."

A light came to Mrs. Odom's face. "That she did, Sheriff. And tasted mighty good too."

Tara came running up all excited and flushed with happiness. "Mama! Mama! Did you hear me?"

"Yes, yes, child. You was good. Real good. Now, it's time to get Billy and git home." She gently shoved Tara's shoulder. "Go tell your brother, now."

Craig wondered if Gemma would want to talk to Mrs. Odom before she left. He scanned the room for her and found that one of the parents had stopped her halfway through the room and was now deep in a one-sided conversation. Gemma looked distracted for a moment but then set her attention on the woman talking to her.

Nearby at the refreshment table, Mrs. Birdwell must have heard the exchange and she started toward them. "Edna! How good to see you! Won't you have a little pie before heading out into the cold?"

Mrs. Odom looked almost afraid as she answered. "Now, Mrs. Birdwell, you know I can't. I got to stop by the doc's real quick-like and then I got to get home."

"How about I wrap up a few pieces for you and the children."

"That would be all right, I guess. Thank you kindly."

"You're going by Doc Palmer's?" Craig asked. What did Mrs. Odom have to do with Larabee? Or was there another reason? Medicine, maybe?

Mrs. Odom nodded but didn't explain further.

Molly hustled over to the table and loaded

pieces of pie into a tin. By the time she came back to Craig, Billy and Tara had joined them.

"I know Miss Starling would like to see you," Molly said. "It means something to her that you chose to come and let Tara and Billy participate."

Edna Odom glanced at Craig, looking all the more fearful. "I heared her thanks already. I got to go now."

Molly pressed the pie tin into her hands. "You just have Billy bring the tin back to school when it starts up again. Say hello to Albert for me."

"I'll do that. Good night." And she and the children slipped out the door.

Craig turned back to Molly. "Albert?"

"Edna is Albert Larabee's niece," Molly said. "Her mother was his sister."

"She look scared to you?"

Molly shook her head. "She has always looked scared. That's just her way. Growin' up her father was a mean man. Then she foolishly married a man just like him. I only hope Tara fares better."

"They get along? Larabee and the kids?"

"Oh, he always did have a soft spot for Edna and her children. But he don't get along with Elias. Not one bit—like oil and vinegar—so he stays clear of their place."

A few things started making sense, like Gemma's story of seeing Larabee hand a dead rabbit to Billy. He could have been supplying them meat for a meal—and the skin for bartering. "He's probably glad that Elias has left for the silver mines," he said, testing how much more information he could get from Molly that might help him figure out who was bothering Gemma.

"I'd say so. I'd say they are all breathing a sight easier knowing he's gone." Molly's attention was drawn by something over his shoulder. "Now, would you look at that. Mr. Tanner has finally got around to hanging the mistletoe and look who is making a beeline for it."

Craig looked up, not really interested, only to find that Gemma was in her first dance of the evening, and who should be twirling her right toward the offending plant but Ryan Philmont.

Chet strolled up and stood beside Craig, eyeing the scene speculatively. "You hungry?"

Chet shoved a plate of Molly's apple pie at him. He grabbed on to the plate just as the pie slid over the edge and splattered at his feet.

"You men. Good work gone to waste!" Molly fumed. She hurried over to grab a dishtowel and slapped it in Chet's hand. "Now, you just wipe that up, young man."

Chet grinned. "Sure, ma'am. Just testing the sheriff's quick-draw reflexes." He squatted and cleaned up the mess.

"Hope you never find out, either," Craig muttered.

"So…" Chet said as he stood. "Are you gonna dance with that purty bird or should I take her for a spin on the floor?"

"I'm on duty."

Chet wrinkled his brow.

The dance came to an end and with only a beat or two of rest before the Winterses started up another tune. He looked around the room and found Tanner standing with his wife on the perimeter of the dance floor. They didn't seem to notice that Gemma was now on dance number two with Philmont. Hadn't he been worried about losing her to marriage because she was so comely?

"They make a tolerably good dance couple," Chet said. "He's keeping her moving. Think I'll cut in and take that dance she promised. Can't have Miss Starling narrowing down her options so early in the year. I consider it my community duty to help her out. I just hope I can keep up with her…me with my war wound and all."

Craig chuckled. "Your war wound from the gold heist was in the shoulder. I doubt that affects your dancing."

Chet grinned.

"Enough, you two!" Molly's eyes twinkled with mirth. "I'll go myself."

And to Craig's surprise, she did just that. Molly marched right up to Gemma as the dance was ending and told her that she needed help passing out water and eggnog for a spell. Gemma looked happy to comply. Her cheeks were flushed and her eyes were bright…but as she begged off another dance with Philmont, she searched the room…and stopped when she found him.

The tightness in his chest might have eased some at that. He watched her make her way toward him and the refreshment table. She had to be the prettiest woman here, bar none. He held out a glass of water for her. "Figured water would quench your thirst better than eggnog after dancing like that."

"Are you saying I was agile in my dancing?" Her eyes sparkled.

He held back a grin. "You were smooth as butter. Philmont is the one who looked like a one-legged chicken."

She brought her fingers to her lips, covering up a smile. "You, Sheriff, have a mean streak. I never would have guessed."

"Only when it comes to you dancing with Philmont."

"Then maybe you should ask me. I haven't danced the Virginia reel since Boston."

He liked seeing her eyes light up. He hadn't

seen her like this—happy and teasing. The moments they had shared up to now had been serious and at times frightening, especially for her. She deserved an evening of fun. Seemed like things were calm enough for now. Maybe he could spare her a dance or two. "Sounds like there are a lot of things you haven't done since Boston."

"Oh, but there are new ones."

"In Clear Springs?" That seemed unlikely. How could a mining town compare to a big city like Boston?

She ticked off a few on her fingers. "Riding astride instead of sidesaddle, learning a bit of marksmanship, being chased by a cougar and…" Her eyes softened as her voice trailed off.

He wondered what she was thinking as she stared at him like that with the brown of her eyes an unfathomable depth. "And?"

She blinked and dropped her gaze. "Oh. And teaching. The children did well tonight, don't you think? I was so proud of them."

"They like you."

"I like them too." Then her eyes clouded over slightly. "Craig, we just have to find out what is going on. I don't want any of them hurt. I want this over."

She had said *we*. Finally, they were a team. They were rowing together. She trusted him enough to give up a measure of control and let him help. He liked this Gemma Starling so much more than the rigid woman she had been at first. Yet he didn't want her to dwell on the worry that hung over her and the school. At least not tonight. Tonight was for putting those concerns behind her for a few hours and having fun. He took her empty glass from her hand and set it on the table. "Dance, Miss Starling?"

She immediately grew more serious. "I thought…"

"Don't. I want to dance with you." He wanted more than that, he realized, as he gazed into her face. A lot more. For starters, he meant to kiss her before the night was over good and proper, leaving no doubt in her mind that he was interested. He ignored the part of his brain that told him to be cautious because there were things he still didn't know about her. It was just a kiss. Not an engagement.

He followed her to the dance area of the room and then excused himself to speak to Mr. Winters. When he returned to Gemma he answered the question in her eyes. "If I'm only getting one dance then I want a slow one."

She arched a brow.

"I'm not implying anything by that other than I want to keep up with you, Miss Starling." He said it lightly, teasingly, but he knew it was a slow one that he wanted. He wanted to hold her in his arms. He wanted to keep her safe, tucked in like she had been on his horse that night. As he held out his hand to begin, the small band started playing an old-time waltz.

Perfect.

Chapter Fourteen

She placed her right hand in Craig's and excitement skittered through Gemma, causing her breath to grow shallow and uneven within her corset. He'd hadn't promised any more than one dance. It didn't sound like he was going to let himself be lax in his duties. She loved that about him…and it frustrated her when she knew all she really wanted was to be in his arms the rest of the evening. Likely, thinking that way was folly, but that's how she felt and she couldn't deny it any longer.

She drew up the hem of her taffeta dress and petticoat with her left hand. Her pulse raced as he slowly smoothed his right hand around her waist to her back. Could he tell?

Only the hint of a smile played about his mouth as the music began. He gazed at her as if there was no one else he'd rather be with, tightened his grip on her hand and then whirled her into the music. The intensity blinded her. She dropped her gaze and focused on the knot in his bolo tie at his white shirt collar, the steps she was taking, the music. The other dancers became blurs of color swirling around them. The waltz was such an intuitive dance that it was easy to get lost in the sweet sound of the violin and depend on his strong lead.

A gentle breeze disturbed the tendrils of hair on her neck and she glanced back to see the Tanners moving quickly away from her. Clarice smiled and waved two fingers at her. The other dancers and those watching on the edges of the dance floor blended into a kaleidoscope of bright Christmas colors of red and green and gold. She glanced up at Craig. The colors blurred and faded under the blueness of his gaze.

This time she didn't look away. Dancing afforded her the perfect excuse to look right at him and have it not be considered untoward by those watching. It was only a matter of keeping her feelings from showing. The dare of doing so was all it took for her to accept the challenge. She admired his strong jaw and the straight profile of his nose, his thick dark brows that seemed not to match his blond hair and yet somehow did, and the reflection of the lights in his eyes.

"Miss Starling?" Craig's deep voice, along with a chuckle permeated her thoughts. "The Winters are taking a break."

He slowed to a stop at the front of the room as the music came to a close.

"Thank you for the dance." She sank to a curtsy.

He stepped back and bowed. "I think I am the one who is supposed to say thank you."

She realized that some of her students were watching from only a few feet away. Two of the girls twittered behind cupped hands, telling secrets. "I could use another glass of water—or perhaps punch this time. It's getting so hot in here." A drop of perspiration trickled down in front of her left ear. She fanned herself with her hand.

He walked with her to the refreshment table and handed her a glass of punch. The large crock of punch had been sitting outside so the liquid was cool and refreshing as she swallowed. Closing her eyes for a moment, she held the glass against her temple, hoping to absorb some of its coolness. When she opened them, Craig was returning from the cloakroom.

"Let's go outside," Craig said, his voice husky and near her ear. He wrapped her shawl around her shoulders and took her glass, setting it aside on the table with his own. She noticed that he had put his hat back on.

Outside the air was immediately crisp and invigorating.

"We'll probably catch our death doing this," she warned him. "However, it does feel lovely."

Craig offered his arm. She tucked her hand into the crook of his elbow and walked with him toward the end of the boardwalk. Three men loitered across the street in front of the saloon. They glanced her way once and then returned to talking among themselves.

At the next cross street, Craig stepped around the corner of the dry goods store and into the deeper shadows, backing her up to the building's brick wall.

"Just what do you think you are doing, Sheriff?" she teased. "This isn't the sort of place a prim and proper schoolteacher should find herself."

"I mean to kiss you."

He wasn't teasing. Not at all. Her heart sped up. "But you forgot the mistletoe." It was an inane thing to say.

"That I did," he said, leaning closer.

His warm breath tickled her neck. She shivered.

"Perhaps we could go back and get it?" Her words came out a bit breathlessly.

"I'll manage without it." He smiled slightly

and then leaned closer to whisper in her ear. "You don't need to be nervous, Gemma."

"I...I'm not." He seemed so in control. And she was slipping under the spell he was weaving.

"You should know—the first time I kissed you was a mistake."

She parted her mouth, surprised at his words.

He brought her hand to his chest, held it there and studied her with an intensity in his gaze she'd never seen before. "In my line of work having a woman on the side doesn't make sense."

She felt the strong beat of his heart through his silk vest. The slow, constant rhythm, so steady, where hers was probably skittering all over the place. "I agree. And I for one won't let myself *be* on the side, as you so eloquently put it. Yet I understand about a man's work. My fath—" She broke off her words. She was chattering.

"We both have good reasons to stay clear of entanglements." He searched her face. "You have your word with Tanner."

She swayed slightly closer. "I do." And there was another reason too, but at the moment it seemed vague and far away and she didn't want to think about it. His mouth, his lips, loomed just inches from hers and pulled her like a butterfly to milkweed.

"Gemma," he said, a soft warning in his voice

as if he too was affected by their closeness. "I'd like to say I'm giving you a chance to step back…" He slipped both hands down, one to each side of her waist and held her firmly. "But…I'm not."

He bent down and pressed his mouth firmly to hers. His lips were surprisingly soft and his kiss surprisingly tender as he slanted his mouth over hers. It wouldn't be so hard to escape. A smart woman…one with a past like hers…would try. She would push away and rush back to the dance where it was safe. But *this* woman only tilted her head and lost herself in the tingling sensation that started where he touched her and spread throughout her body. He slipped both hands behind her back and drew her against him.

This kiss was so different from the first one. She understood him now. The first could be explained away as an aberration—a moment of passion. This was so much more. Without saying a word, he was claiming her. A sigh fluttered up and through her lips as that thought centered within her. An odd sensation swept through her and her joints felt loose and weak as he concentrated on first her top lip and then her lower lip with the sweetness of his own.

"Craig…this isn't wise. Anyone could see…" she managed to whisper.

He stopped and pulled back slightly.

Cool air swirled between them but did little to diminish the heat in her cheeks—or the heat in his eyes. A million questions lingered in that gaze. And she knew, eventually, she would have to answer them.

Footsteps sounded on the boardwalk.

She had the sudden urge to flee, but knew it was of course too late, and only hoped the person striding toward them would pass them by. With some relief she realized Craig's hat brim had blocked any view of their kiss, although it wouldn't take a genius to know what they'd been doing, considering how close they stood.

"Sheriff! *Psst!*"

Craig turned slightly, continuing to shield her with his body. "What do you want, Chet?"

"They're callin' for Miss Starling back at the dance if you, ahem…" he cleared his throat "…happen to know where she would be."

Craig chuckled, his eyes twinkling by the light of the saloon window as he looked down on her. "When I find her, I'll be sure to tell her."

"I'll let Mrs. Winters know."

The sound of footsteps headed back to the dance and they were alone again.

Amused at their calm exchange and feeling more herself, Gemma managed to stifle a giggle. "I imagine your teachers had a time with you."

"I only care what one particular teacher thinks."

She straightened her bun, pushing pins back in that he had knocked askew.

"She thinks you are as incorrigible now as you must have been then. But she might be inclined to amend that assessment if you would step aside and let her pass."

"I don't think I want to let her go," he said, seriously.

Her breath caught. "Craig…you said…we can't…" She stumbled over why they shouldn't pursue this further. They…they simply couldn't. They'd been caught up in the moment. It was a Christmas kiss. A very special Christmas kiss… without the mistletoe.

She leaned back against the brick wall as the reality of the situation sank in. She could no longer deny what was happening. Oh, my, but she was playing with fire.

He moved aside. "You had better find out what it is they want."

Her cheeks felt hot when she started back. Likely she was as flushed as when she had left the town hall only this time it had nothing to do with exerting herself during a dance.

On entering the building, Clarice Tanner waved for her. She stood with the other school board members. "Miss Starling? Would you please come up here before we start the children's games?"

A few groans emerged from the younger children standing by the Christmas tree. Several of them held what appeared to be new scarves or mittens and a quick glance at the bottom of the tree revealed that the wrapped presents were gone.

"Douglas P. Winters, I heard that," Ruth Winters scolded. "You can wait quietly for two minutes or you won't play."

What was this all about? Gemma glanced at Molly to see if she knew. The woman raised a brow. *Wonderful.* Aware that Molly would speak her mind eventually, Gemma imagined she might be listening to a conversation on proper etiquette during a dance before the night was over.

Everyone turned to watch as she made her way to the front of the room. A few students caught her eye and smiled. A few townspeople looked on expectantly. Halfway to the front of the room, she heard the door behind her open. A blast of cold air swirled in again and then the door closed. She hoped it was Craig who had entered.

When she reached the front of the room, Clarice Tanner held out a small tin box.

"The school board wanted you to have this as a token for all your hard work," the woman said.

"We realize the first year for a new teacher is difficult, and your last couple of weeks have been particularly so. We want you to know that we believe in you and the school." She added softly, "I hope you like it."

Gemma was stunned. Hadn't she just been contemplating what she would do if they let her go? She certainly hadn't expected this! She gripped Clarice's hand, her eyes blurring with the sudden sting of tears. "You have no idea what this means to me."

She took a deep breath and lifted her voice to the rest of the people in the room. "Thank you. I truly enjoy teaching the children of Clear Springs. It has been a pleasure."

The children gathered close to watch her open the box, as did the board members. She glanced up to see Craig standing by a post near the back, his arms crossed in front of him, a half smile on his face. She was glad he was here to share this with her.

A bit self-consciously, she pulled the ribbon and opened the lid. Inside, nesting in a swath of cotton batting was a thick domed piece of clear blown glass. Suspended in the center of the glass was an apple seed.

Gently she withdrew the dome from the box and held it up on her palm for the room to see.

"It's a paperweight," she said, delighted with the gift. "Thank you! This is a lovely improvement on the lead washer that I use now."

Several people in the room chuckled.

"May I ask what the seed means?" she asked.

"Well, we had to think about that some," Mr. Tanner said. "A gold nugget seemed more the thing, considering this is a mining town, but that probably wouldn't have lasted long on your desk before someone swiped it."

Someone snickered in the back of the room. "And yer too all-fired tightfisted, Tanner!"

Mr. Winters stepped forward and glared at the man who had spoken. "It's an apple seed for those that can't see, Jessop." Then he cleared his throat. "And it's the symbol of a start here. For you. For the school. For the town."

She held it up once more. "It's lovely. I'll treasure it." She put the dome back inside the box.

"Here's another one!" Jordan Winters said as he backed out from beneath the Christmas tree. "It's got *Miss Starling* written on the paper."

"All right, son. Bring it on up here."

Jordan brought the box to Gemma and then stood there to watch. Although this box was simply that—a box with her name—it was a long, thin, rectangular. She turned it over to see if there was anything written on the bottom to ascertain the giver. Nothing.

She glanced up at Craig and then to the curious onlookers. "There's no name except mine."

"Well, open it and see!" Jessop called out from the back. "Some people want to dance before the sun comes up, dagnabit!"

"Quiet, Jessop!" Mr. Philmont said as another wave of soft chuckles filled the room.

She smiled, feeling more and more comfortable with their quips and goodwill.

She opened the box.

Inside sat another note.

Craig heard Gemma's scream and saw her horrified face at the same time that Chet came barging into the hall yelling something about seeing smoke outside. It took less than a split second for Craig to start toward Gemma. *If* the two were related, she was what was important. The smoke could be nothing more than that—smoke.

While everyone else in the room rushed for the door, Gemma stood frozen in place, shaking like a leaf. The contents of the box had spilled out in disarray on the floor. Craig pushed against the strong current to get to her. It was a bad dream that wouldn't stop. He needed to be at her side and here people pulled him toward the door assuming he would want to know if there was a fire.

"Sheriff! This way!" Old Jessop yelled and grabbed his arm.

Seeing Gemma slowly raise her frightened gaze to his, Craig jerked free. "There's more going on here than a fire," he growled. He plowed ahead and then rushed up to her.

She reached for him and hid her face against his chest at the same time that he wrapped her in his arms and pulled her close. Whatever was on the note, something inside her had died upon seeing it. He hated to see her so broken. "Oh, darlin'. It's all right. You're safe," he murmured, holding her tight. "It's just words on paper."

"Why doesn't he stop? Why?" she said, the last sounding close to a sob.

He helped her into a nearby chair. "We'll figure him out. Then we'll have a better chance of catching him."

He found the note on the floor and picked it up. Fresh blood splattered the paper. He'd like to crush whoever was scaring Gemma like this. She didn't deserve such treatment...nobody did.

Quickly he unfolded the note: TOO LATE. YOU HAD YOR CHANCE.

Inside, a cold lump of anger congealed in Craig's gut. Whoever this man was, he was a coward. But what did it mean? What did he intend to do to Gemma?

The door banged open and Chet called out. "Sheriff! The smoke is comin' from out by the school!" He motioned for him to come and then turned back to the people in the street. "Everybody grab a bucket and get out to the school!"

"The school?" Gemma pushed away from his hold and looked about the now empty room.

"You should go, Craig. People will need your cool head. And you might find out something about who is behind all this. You might see somebody you haven't seen before."

So she'd figured out that the two incidences were probably connected. "You're right. I have to get out there. If it is the school, we've got to save as much as we can. There is still a chance the fire has nothing to do with the person writing these notes."

"Oh, really?" she said flatly.

He took it as a sign that she was recovering from her shock. "Slim," he admitted with a grimace.

Just then Molly bustled through the door and started toward them. "You better go, Sheriff. Something is happening and I think the town needs you. I can stay with Gemma."

"I'm not leaving her. Whoever sent that note

could be lurking around here. She has to come with me." He rushed to the cloakroom and grabbed her shawl and another that he hoped was Molly's. He tossed Gemma's over her shoulders and then took her hand as the three of them rushed outside.

"We'll take a rig. There's bound to be one at the livery," he said, pausing on the boardwalk to check for a wagon or buggy sitting unused on the road.

As luck would have it, there were two rigs. One down by the doc's house that must have been Edna Odom's and one in front of the saloon. That one probably belonged to someone too soused to help anyway. He started to step down from the boardwalk when he realized Gemma was staring northward. Although no flames could be seen through the dense trees, gray smoke billowed up over their spiked silhouettes into the night sky, lit entirely by what had to be the burning of the school.

A few choice words not fit for the ladies grumbled through his brain. "Come on," he said, tugging Gemma's hand. Together they headed for the buggy outside the saloon.

The crisp air had reviving effects on Gemma, or maybe it was the wild carriage ride or the fact that it was *her* school that was burning that finally pushed out all thoughts of the ugly note. He drove the horse as fast as it was safe, doing his best to avoid ruts in the road, low branches and the people who were running to the clearing on foot.

When they arrived, flames sputtered and danced along the eaves of the building and the fire shooting from the inside and through the broken windows lit up the night sky with chaotic sparks.

"Oh, no!" Gemma and Molly uttered in the same breath.

He was stunned. How had the fire gotten so large without anyone seeing it or smelling the smoke? Plenty of partygoers had come from the north. On their way into town they would have ridden right by the school. Someone should have noticed the smoke early on. Seemed like the fire had sprung out of nowhere.

Kerosene.

A host of people, neighbors, cowboys and miners alike, worked to put out the flames. A line had formed that reached the stream, across the field and up to the schoolhouse. As the men and women filled buckets with the water they'd hand the bucket off to the next in line, sending it on a journey all the way back to the fire. There the last person in line tossed the meager amount of water on the edge of the fire. It would only keep it contained, Craig realized. The fire would have to burn itself out. It was already too big to stop and save much.

Craig jumped from the carriage and then helped Gemma and Molly descend to the ground. "Stay together," he ordered, as they hurried off to help with the bucket brigade. "I'm going to see if I can salvage anything from inside." He headed to the other side of the school, where it looked like a pile of items was forming.

A large man lunged toward him, a black silhouette against the flames that jumped behind him. Craig braced himself, thinking that here might be the man responsible for the fire, but then Chet's smoke-streaked face emerged.

"We got a few things out," he told Craig. "The bookcase. One bench. A few odds and ends. Not much. The rest is too far gone. And it's too hot to go back in now."

"All right. I don't want anyone hurt," Craig said. "We will keep the fire from spreading, but otherwise just have people stay back. I walked the ground two days ago. It was wet from the snow to the point of being soggy. The fire may smolder and smoke like crazy, but I think it will burn itself out before it travels far…as long as the wind doesn't pick up."

"Does this have something to do with Miss Starling?" Chet lifted his chin toward Gemma who was marching toward them with an out-of-breath Mrs. Birdwell in her wake.

Craig nodded. "Keep an eye out for anyone or anything unusual."

"Will do, Sheriff." Chet tipped his hat to Gemma and Mrs. Birdwell and then headed back to the other side of the building.

They stood, along with most of the people who had been at the dance, watching the flames devour the building. Mothers, fathers, children, miners and ranchers—they all stood back, their forms illuminated from the glow of the fire, their faces sweaty and blackened from the soot and smoke and heat. The heat from the fire kept them at a safe distance. The men and women who formed the bucket brigade one by one lowered their buckets after a last dousing of the edge of the flames and quietly moved back, heads hanging, their shoulders stooped, spent of their energy.

"Well this is a fine way to end the night," Mrs. Birdwell said, her hands going to her hips.

Gemma clenched her hands. "I just can't believe someone would do this on purpose! It would be so much easier to understand if the fire had started from lightning or because I did not douse the fire in the woodstove, but this…this is irrational! What kind of person is angry at a school? It just doesn't make any sense." Her chin trembled with emotion as she stared at the flames enveloping the building. "Why didn't he just come after me? Why the school? It was brand-new! And after all the work everyone put into building it."

Craig slid his arm around her shoulders. A person crazy enough to do this…even a coward… might come after her in the din and confusion. Might have even planned it that way.

Gemma leaned into him. Her shoulders rose and fell on a large sigh. "At least the children weren't here. At least none of them were hurt."

She took his supportive touch for all of a minute before he felt her body stiffen with renewed tension. "If this person expects me to stop teaching because the building is gone, he is wrong. I can still teach. I *will* teach if there is a place the children can gather out of the weather, even if it means sitting on bales of hay in the livery until a new school can be built." She shrugged out from under his arm.

Craig stared at Gemma, impressed by her grit. Any other woman would be ready to quit, yet here she was already making plans for the children despite what had happened. He admired her spirit even as he feared she could still be a target if she continued teaching. If Gemma was the person the arsonist was angry at, a school in the livery could go up in flames even faster than way out here and a fire there would threaten the entire town.

He had to find out who had done this.

He looked back at the fire. "For now, you two should head back to town. Take the carriage. Whoever was in the saloon is probably looking for it. There's nothing more you can do here and neither one of you is dressed for the cold."

"But—" Gemma started to protest.

"I'm staying until morning...until the fire burns down all the way. I need to make sure the fire is out and I need to see if there are any clues to how it started left behind. I can't see those until the sun comes up."

He walked back with them to the wagon and helped Mrs. Birdwell up to the spring seat. "Do you have a rifle or gun at your place?"

She nodded. "My husband's. Ain't had no call to use it since he passed but I sure can use it if I have to."

"Good. Might want to have it handy. I'll find Chet and send him along in a few minutes. I want him to stay the night there. Don't make him too comfortable. I want him awake and alert until morning." He smiled grimly. "And don't shoot him when he shows up."

"You be careful, Sheriff." Molly scooted over to allow room for Gemma.

He took a moment before helping Gemma up into the seat. He hated separating this way. He wanted to stay with her, but he had a duty to the people of Clear Springs and he couldn't be in two places at once.

"It's all right, Craig. I understand."

She may as well have read his mind.

"Don't worry about me. I'll be fine. And I'll be careful."

Her words were so opposite of what Charlotte would have said. They were strong, independent, stubborn... She constantly amazed him. He kissed her hard, just once, not caring that Mrs. Birdwell sat watching. Then he helped her up into the buggy.

When he handed her the reins, she clasped his hand with both of hers. She gripped him hard—not as if she were frightened, but as if she were trying to instill her strength into him. "Find him, Craig. Be careful for yourself, but find him and stop him once and for all."

Chapter Fifteen

Sleep came near dawn for Gemma. Her mind was in turmoil and every time she took a breath she detected the odor of smoke on her clothes. Even though she had removed her taffeta gown, her corset, stockings and chemise still carried the scent—a reminder of all that had happened. Not long after she had closed her eyes, a Steller's jay started cawing outside her window. She hissed at it to be quiet. Here she was warm and toasty under her covers and finally sleeping and it disturbed her. Already it was morning.

She counted backward from five. At the count of zero, she flung her blankets off and sat up, rubbing her face. At a noise from down the hall, she slipped into her slippers and threw a robe over her shoulders, cinching it at her waist. She tiptoed from her room to see who was stirring.

In the kitchen, Chet sat at the table drinking

coffee while Molly scrambled eggs for him. His hair was tousled and the way his eyelids drooped it looked like he hadn't slept a wink.

"How long before church?"

"An hour, dear," Molly said. "I didn't think we would be going today, considering all that happened. I'm sure you could use more sleep."

"Thank you for the kind thought, but I have to be there. There will be questions people have."

"There might also be folks who are angry along with the questions," Molly said. "Are you sure you are up to it?"

"I'm not sure. But that doesn't matter now. Things cannot be hidden behind a board meeting any longer. The people have a right to know. It's their hard work and money that built the school. It's their children. And I'm the teacher."

"If you're going then I'm going," Chet said. "Sheriff said to keep an eye on you and I intend to."

She wasn't about to argue that it wasn't necessary... Never again. Craig knew what he was doing and what was necessary to protect her and the town. She trusted him completely. "Thank you, Mr. Farnsworth."

"It's Chet. And you might have to nudge me to keep me awake through the sermon," he added.

She smiled, feeling as sleepy as he looked. "Agreed. As long as you will do the same for me."

She headed back to her room. A moment later, Molly bustled in with the teakettle. "I'll just leave you some warm water and some soap. I'm glad you're going. Might want to give some thought for how you'll be answering to the questions."

An hour later, the church bells rang out and Gemma joined with the families heading into the whitewashed church on the corner of Third Street and Pine. Many of the men were notably absent, having fought the fire and then stayed into the wee hours of the morning to make sure it didn't spread any farther—especially toward town. The pastor announced his intent at the start and agreed to let her speak at the end of his service.

At that, several faces turned toward her. She wouldn't say that they were all filled with Christian goodwill. Some looked curious, but more than a few looked angry. The pastor announced that two of the men were being treated by Doc Palmer for burns and he offered a prayer for them. There was no mention of Craig other than to say he was still out at the school property.

It was difficult for her to pay attention to the sermon, which was on the good news of Christmas. She wasn't feeling much joy now. So much had changed because of the fire. She felt the culprit who had started it had robbed her of her Christmas joy. At the end of the last hymn, she walked up the aisle and faced the congregation. Before her sat mothers, fathers and children, older widows like Molly and her friends and a few miners. Women whispered behind cupped hands to their neighbors and some men stared at her, their thick brows drawn together in suspicion.

She took a deep breath to prepare herself before beginning. "In view of the loss of the school and of the threatening notes I've received, I think it best to suspend class until further notice. However, in the hopes that it won't be a long break, if any of you know of a building that the children and I can use to continue our studies for the remainder of the school year, I'd appreciate it if you would let me or one of the members of the school board know."

As she spoke, the back door opened and Craig stepped inside. His good clothes, his hands, his face were blackened with soot. His shoulders drooped with fatigue. He removed his hat and stood holding it against his chest.

A man stood up in one of the middle pews. "So you admit you received a note even before this happened?" The anger in his voice was unmistakable.

"Yes."

Low rumbling among the seated people grew louder.

This might get ugly.

"I'd have kept my son out of school if I'd known this was going on. He could have been hurt! Why didn't you let us know?"

She wished someone from the school board were here to support her. "At first we thought it was a one-time occurrence by a coward," she said. "Someone—perhaps even one of the students— who had received a low grade or who I had unintentionally offended."

"Did Mr. Tanner know?" A woman halfway back in the sanctuary asked. "He's head of the school board. You should have told him. Sounds like you were acting on your own. You don't have authority to do that. Not when it comes to our children's safety."

Authority? She had authority to teach the children all day, but no authority to use her own brain? This was quickly getting out of hand. She didn't want anybody to point fingers or place blame. It wouldn't help matters. The enemy was the man who'd done the threatening—not her, not Craig and not those on the school board. "I don't blame you for being upset. I will tell you that the situation was discussed at length with the board members, but—"

"Tanner knew," Craig said, effectively cutting off other grumblings that were gaining in volume.

He strode forward, joining her at the front of the church. "And this isn't a witch hunt. The person who set fire to the school hasn't been found. If anyone knows anything, come to me with the information."

He stood by her side, answering the questions that he could. Relief filtered through her as he expertly diffused the upset crowd with calm reasoning for the next ten minutes. His badge, his demeanor and the fact that he was covered with soot and had worked all night lent all the authority he needed. The people respected him...and it showed by the way they stopped interrupting each other and stopped trying to foist the blame on her.

"That's all the time I have," Craig said, and taking Gemma by the arm, he walked with her from the church.

Just like that.

"Thank you," she said once they were outside. "You know, you could easily go into law the way you handled that." She took a closer look at him. The whites of his eyes were bloodshot. "You need some sleep."

He rubbed the back of his neck. "Heading that way soon. First I need to check in on Larabee."

"May I come?"

He nodded.

She glanced around for Chet. "What about Chet?"

"I sent him home."

The sky was overcast and dreary as they walked to the doctor's house. It would be a perfect day for sleeping—once Craig was able to finish his duties. Gemma couldn't believe he was still managing to make sense of anything considering his lack of sleep. He was dedicated, and though she understood that about him and respected it, she wished he could step away from his job and just be himself. She sighed, thinking of his kiss. She didn't know where Craig left off and Sheriff Parker started. All she knew was that she was coming to care for the both of them—very much.

She wanted to help him with some of the burden that he shouldered. He shouldn't have to give his lifeblood to everyone else without having a bit of comfort for himself. If only there was a way she could be that comfort…

Dr. Palmer's residence was around the corner and down the street from the church. It didn't take them long to reach it. The Doc had been in Clear Springs for five years. He'd been hired by the mine owners originally but after a year when his contract was up he had stayed on. He was in his fifties—with salt-and-pepper hair and a slender build. His wife helped him run the office, which was basically the dining room and one extra room.

Craig held the door open for her to walk inside. "I want to talk to Doc Palmer. Go ahead on in to see Larabee."

She left him with the doctor and walked into the small side room. The green shades had been drawn despite the fact that the day was cloudy. Mr. Larabee lay still and silent, breathing easy, and he had another little visitor at his bedside.

"Tara! What a nice surprise. Are you here all alone?"

"I'm not alone. I'm with my uncle."

Gemma smiled gently. "Did you come by yourself?"

"Mama brought me. She went to the store."

"But the store isn't opened on Sunday."

"Mr. Gilliam will open it for her."

"That's good."

Craig slipped into the room.

"Well, you are growing up if she feels you can take care of your uncle." Gemma stepped closer to the bed, studying Mr. Larabee's face for any type of reaction. "How is he doing?"

Tara stroked her uncle's hand lovingly and shook her head as any grown-up might, letting out a deep sigh. "He is tired yet. Mama brought soup but he won't wake up."

She was such a cute little waif and so solemn, acting in such an adult way. "Oh. Soup is always good when a person is not feeling well. Especially chicken soup."

"That's what Mama says. She makes it for me too."

"With all those chickens you have, that makes good sense."

"Papa hates it. He don't like Mama to fix it."

"Oh. Well, then..." She didn't quite know how to respond to that information. She was saved from trying to when Edna Odom hurried into the room.

She carried a bag from the dry goods store and looked suspiciously from Gemma to Craig. "What are you a doin' here?" she asked sharply.

The woman had been so pleasant last night at the dance. Gemma couldn't understand the change. "We just came to see how Mr. Larabee is doing."

"Sorry to startle you, ma'am," Craig said. "We hoped he'd be awake by now. I'd like to know who did this to him."

Edna shifted the bag in her arms, turning away. "I got to get home now. Tara, come with me."

Tara ran from the other side of the bed to join her mother and the two quickly departed.

Gemma frowned. "She was friendlier last night."

Craig studied Mr. Larabee. "No change, I take it?"

"No." She looked closer at Craig. "You really need to get some rest yourself."

He rubbed his face. "Yeah. Guess so. Once I take you to Tanners'. Patrick and Clarice have agreed to watch out for you while I get some shut-eye."

It was the first she'd heard that she wouldn't be staying with Molly.

He slid on his Stetson. "Ready?"

She pressed her lips together. He had taught her about guns. Molly had the rifle. She didn't want to be a bother to the Tanners. Yet…she respected his expertise.

He held the door for her and then followed her outside. They walked to the end of the boardwalk and then turned down the side street toward the Tanners' house.

"You can't be watching out for me for the rest of your life."

He shot a spare smile her way. "This arrangement is only for today."

"Molly and I were going to bake."

"Molly knows. She agrees it's the safer course too. I'd feel better with a man watching over you."

She wrestled with what he'd done…commandeering her day…her life…her heart. She glanced at him, walking beside her with his face set. He wouldn't budge. She knew that much. He lived his life like that—determinedly…passionately. He had even kissed her like that.

"You can't be watching out for me for the rest of your life."

"Once I catch this coward, that's exactly what I intend to do."

She stopped walking and stared at him. "What did you say?"

"You heard me."

He *intended* to watch out for her? Was that some kind of a proposal? "Craig Parker! You can plan all you want, but I think that I will be in charge of my own life."

He gave a tired smile. "That's what I like about you."

He stepped up to the Tanners' door and rapped against the wood.

And she stood there stunned. "You haven't even asked to court me or…or…" she sputtered, her thoughts and words a-jumble.

He raised a brow, his gaze speculative.

"This is not how it is done in Boston!"

"We skipped over that part…last evening."

Her cheeks warmed at the thought of how

he'd kissed her at the dance…and how she'd responded. This definitely wasn't how it was done, but she had been a willing partner.

"We'll talk about it later," he said as the door opened.

Mr. Tanner stood there. "Come on in, Miss Starling. Clarice has some cake and tea she made in the kitchen."

She started to enter, but noticed that Craig remained out on the porch. He didn't plan to stay? Not even for a few moments? Not even after saying such an earth-shattering thing?

"You been over to Doc Palmer's?" Tanner asked.

"Larabee is still out of it. Doc says, the longer he's like this, the harder it will be for him to recover," Craig said. "It's going on forty-eight hours. I'll check on him again after I've had a few hours of sleep."

Craig looked back at her. His gaze lingered and for a fleeting minute dropped to her mouth. He wouldn't kiss her in front of Mr. Tanner, she was sure, but the way his gaze caressed her lips, she certainly felt like she'd just been kissed.

No more kisses! She couldn't think straight when he worked his magic on her.

She pressed her lips together and remained

silent as he tipped his hat, spun on his foot and strode down the path.

He was witty, charming, stubborn, at times exasperating…and…special. He had done everything in his power to make sure she was safe and protected. How easy it would be to love this man. How very easy it was…

And just that simply, she realized she loved him. She wanted a future with him. She wanted… him. And she wanted to be his.

She breathed in sharply. What had happened? What had she let happen? Even if he did propose, she couldn't marry him. Not with what she'd done. A marriage couldn't be built on lies. He didn't know about why she'd left her home. If he ever did find out he would hate her for her deception.

And she couldn't stand that.

They had to talk. She'd let things go too far without being honest. She had to explain to him about Boston and about what she'd done. All she had to do was summon up the nerve.

Her chest tightened, filling with a pressure of her own making.

She was afraid now of doing just that. Afraid of losing the one man she truly loved.

"Oh, Craig—" she murmured.

She must tell him about Boston…or she had to leave.

* * *

Craig woke with a start and focused blearily on the shadows that crept across his room behind the sheriff's office. He swung his feet over the edge of his bed and sat there a moment, herding his thoughts into what lay ahead. He rubbed his face, trying to wake up further. With the waning sunlight shining through the window it looked like he had slept the day away—probably just what he needed—but not what he had planned. He had things to take care of and had wanted to be about them before dusk.

He pumped frigid water from the spigot at the sink and washed and shaved, then put on his last clean shirt and pants. He finished dressing— boots, then holster—and then checked the bullets in his gun before slipping it back into his holster. He'd gotten so used to wearing it as sheriff that it felt unnatural to him to leave it off.

He stopped at Tanner's first to make sure Gemma was all right. A gnawing need to see her filled him. Once he set eyes on her he could see to his duties.

"I just got back from Doc Palmer's," Tanner said, as he ushered Craig into his parlor.

"And…?" He wanted to know about Larabee, but he was glancing over Tanner's shoulder looking for Gemma. Where was she?

"No change."

He blew out a breath. The hope dwindled that the old man would be able to help clear things up. "Any visitors?"

"No."

Craig felt bad for Larabee even though he didn't know him. He'd had a rough life.

"Miss Starling?"

"She's fine. Widow Birdwell stopped by with another friend and they took her to the café for supper. Seemed safe enough. They just left, if you want to catch them."

He had other things more pressing. "No. As long as she's with a group, she should be safe."

"My thoughts too," said Tanner. "By the way, Chet offered to stay the night at the boarding-house again. He said he would understand if you came and kicked him out."

It would be Craig instead of Chet. No question there. But after that kiss he had shared with Gemma during the dance, he would be sorely tempted to pay more attention to her than to the situation at hand. Good thing he'd caught up on sleep. He had to stay sharp.

"I'll do that," he answered Tanner as he walked to the door. "I'm going to get a bite to eat, then I'll catch up to Miss Starling. Thanks for today."

"It's the least I could do. I hired her. She's easy

to have around and as I mentioned once, easy on the eyes."

"Don't I know it," Craig mumbled.

Tanner laughed. "You've got it bad, my friend."

"Don't I know that too." He tugged his hat down on his head tighter, hunched his shoulders against the deepening cold and stepped out into the night.

At the restaurant, Daisy whipped up eggs and pancakes for him.

"You could slow down a mite," she said, a hand on her hip, as she watched him wolf down her fine meal.

When he was finished, he fished in his pocket for a quarter, and then thumbed it into the air toward her.

"Thanks for the food." He slid his hat on and headed for the door.

He crossed the main road and walked down two blocks until he came to the Butterfield Café. Through the front window panes, he could see the three women talking. Widow Birdwell was laughing about something the other woman was saying. Gemma looked relaxed.

The café had been decorated for Christmas, a pine wreath on the door and a swag of pine boughs on the mantel of the large stone fireplace toward the back of the room. Each tabletop held a center decoration made up of pinecones and red-and-gold ribbons. It made him pause. Here Christmas was coming in two days and things had been happening so fast he didn't have anything for Gemma.

Talk about putting the cart before the horse, he'd all but told her he intended to marry her and they hadn't even exchanged ages or birthdays. She knew that he had a brother, but he knew nothing about her family other than both her parents were gone now and she was an only child. He didn't even know her favorite color. It was all off-kilter.

With Charlotte, he'd known everything right down to the mole she had on her back because he'd seen her swimming in her undergarments once when she was eight. He didn't know a thing about Gemma—not even if she preferred tea or coffee. Coming from Boston, he imagined it would be tea. He smiled to himself at the thought. He looked forward to learning all about her once this note business was resolved.

Gemma's lips turned up in a gentle smile as she listened to the two other ladies. Mrs. Birdwell and her friend seemed to know how to keep the conversation going on and on. Gemma's eyes sparkled, like she was privy to a secret that no one else knew.

"You gonna stand here all night or go say hello?" Chet said from behind him.

Craig jerked, his hand going to his gun in an automatic response as he spun around.

Chet stumbled back with his hands out in front of him. "Whoa, now. It's just me. No need to shoot anyone."

Nothing like feeling the fool. "I'm not going to shoot you, Chet, but make it a point not to sneak up on me like that again or I might."

Chet grinned. "Sneak! Not hardly! I just strolled up like anybody would this time of evening who was looking to eat. You're the one who was so far gone in thought a rabid dog could have run down Main Street and you wouldn't have noticed."

Chet's words registered and were an uncomfortable fit. It was true. He hadn't been careful. What did that tell him about staying the night at Mrs. Birdwell's? If he was smart, he should head right back to his one-room shed behind the jail and let Chet do the honors of guarding the place again. If he was smart…

"What?" Chet asked, when he didn't respond.

Craig shook his head. "I'll be staying at the boardinghouse. You're off the hook for tonight."

"Hmm," Chet said, then grinned. "You gonna sleep?"

"With one eye open."

"All righty. Guess that opens up my evening to see Daisy." Chet turned and sauntered across the street at a leisurely pace toward the hotel.

The door behind Craig jostled.

"Crai—I mean, Sheriff Parker!" Gemma said, looping her dark green scarf snug against her neck.

She looked pleased to see him, which lightened his mood considerably. "Good evening, ladies. Thought I'd escort you back to the boarding-house."

"That would be lovely, Sheriff," Mrs. Birdwell said, and then added, "By way of Mrs. Hornsby's place, if it is all right?"

"Best to keep everyone together," he said. As much as he didn't want Gemma outside and exposed from all sides, he wouldn't be comfortable letting the older woman walk back home by herself after dark.

Mrs. Hornsby's place was the opposite side of town, but although the night was cold, it was not windy. As they walked, he checked down the darkened side roads. No one jumped out at them or bothered them. By the time they left Mrs. Hornsby and then headed back to the boarding-house, he felt confident that no one was going to bother Gemma. At least not on the main road.

About halfway to the Widow Birdwell's, he

grasped Gemma's hand and tucked it into the bend of his elbow. She didn't pull away. It felt right to him—her at his side, strolling along on a wintry evening. He wished things could be so simple, but he knew until he found out who had left the notes and burned the school, nothing would be simple between them.

Except that kiss. That had been as perfect as a kiss could be. It broke through every boundary he'd put in place, cut through every argument and silenced him. When she had given in to him and kissed him back with such passion he'd known that he couldn't let her get away. She was worth the risk.

Gemma wasn't Charlotte, but he still knew, down deep that loving a sheriff came with a load of hurt and worry. Not many women could handle it. Maybe Gemma would rethink things after this crazy situation had passed and decide she didn't want to be hitched to so much uncertainty.

It was that worry that kept him from completely trusting her. That…and the fact she still pulled away at times and closed herself off from him.

They arrived at Widow Birdwell's and he helped the ladies remove their coats and hung them on the coatrack near the door.

"Will Chet be staying with us again?" Mrs.

Birdwell asked, removing her hat and hanging it on the coatrack as well.

"It'll be me, ma'am," Craig answered.

"Well, that'll be fine, Sheriff," Mrs. Birdwell said. "Wish I'd known and I would have made supper instead of going out. It's been a long time since I cooked for my husband and I like to cook for a man with a healthy appetite once in a while. Miss Starling here has been eating barely enough to keep a baby chick alive."

He relaxed slightly at the woman's matter-of-fact attitude. He'd wondered how she would react about him staying since she had witnessed him kissing Gemma at the fire.

"I'll just put a kettle of water on so we can all have some tea in a bit. Get the fire going, will you, Sheriff?" She disappeared into the kitchen and he heard the squeak of the water pump at the sink as she worked the handle.

He turned to Gemma. "Are you all right with this?" Suddenly it all felt awkward.

She raised her dark brows. "Isn't it a bit late to be asking me?"

Now, what did she mean by that? He raked his fingers back through his hair.

"You are very good at telling me how things are going to be. For example, when you said you intended to make me your future."

She sounded peeved, but not overly much. He vaguely remembered her saying something about courting. He'd been tired and hadn't paid close attention. "Only to keep you safe."

They stood there, staring at each other for the space of a second and then in one stride he pulled her to him, hugging her fiercely.

He took her face in his hands and kissed her forehead. That's all he planned to do, but then his lips skidded down to her cheek. Just this cheek, he told himself. It wasn't enough. He slipped across the silken softness of her closed eyelids and over to her other cheek. Smooth—so smooth. "You've haunted my dreams since we parted. I couldn't wait to see you again."

"Craig." She let out a shivery breath and whispered, "The fire. You are supposed to be seeing to the fire."

He smiled against her lips, nuzzling her, teasing her. "I thought I was. I'm definitely warm."

She offered up her mouth, her eyes mere slits under heavy lids.

He tilted his head enough to seal his lips to hers and kissed her hard.

She was the strongest, most beautiful woman he had ever known, and at this moment, she was all his. The empty place inside him filled to the brim. Her breath caught. When she exhaled, her body rested against him.

A few moments later, the clatter of china in the kitchen reminded him of his whereabouts and reluctantly he pulled away. "We'll continue this later."

Gemma looked like a woman well kissed, her lips slightly swollen. He'd done that.

By the time Mrs. Birdwell came back in the room with the tea, he was crouched before the hearth, lighting the kindling.

Chapter Sixteen

The back door closed and a moment later Craig strode into the parlor.

Gemma lowered her knitting into her lap. She had forgotten the number of stitches she had taken. Again. It was the second time he had slipped outside to check around the cabin when he'd heard a noise and with each time her unease grew.

He deposited his coat and hat on the coatrack and then returned to his seat on the settee. "Everything is quiet," he told her and Molly.

Gemma lowered her knitting needles into her lap. "Do you think anyone will bother us while you are here?"

"No."

His answer, simple and direct, still left room to worry. She didn't want to be placated. She wanted the truth. "You're not just saying that?"

"No one will bother you, Gemma. My presence will scare them off. If not?" He shrugged. "I'm not going to let anybody hurt you."

His confidence made her feel that much safer. That much more protected. She had once known that kind of self-assurance for herself—when her father still lived. Ever since she left Boston that comfort was beyond her reach. It helped so much to have Craig near. She glanced once more out the parlor window, her thoughts returning to how she should broach the subject of Roland once they were alone.

The firelight from the hearth flickered and started to wane. Mrs. Birdwell, sitting closest to the fire, rocked slowly, rhythmically, in her rocking chair. For the past half hour Molly had struggled to stay awake and continue with her mending.

"I was looking forward to Christmas," Gemma said. "But now with all that has happened it seems so hard to get back into the spirit of the holiday." She glanced at the small pine tree on the tea table. It looked a bit forlorn without any decorations. As she spoke she noticed Molly's head tilt down and her eyes shutter closed. The poor woman should go to bed but was trying to do her duty as a hostess.

"Molly," Gemma said softly.

Molly startled awake with a snort.

Gemma held back a smile.

Molly cleared her throat and then set aside her sewing. "I believe I'll head to bed. Sheriff, there's pillows in the trunk there. Gemma—good night, dear. I hope it's a quiet one." She stood and turned down the lantern.

"I hope we can all sleep," Gemma said.

Molly removed her eyeglasses and set them on the mantel. Then she peered into the wooden bowl that sat next to Craig. It had been full of popcorn at one time. She pursed her lips. "Why, not a kernel remains! You ate it all, didn't you? That's the last time I leave you with a full bowl, young man. You shirked your job. Now how will I decorate our tree?"

Craig grinned, offering no explanation. "Something will turn up, ma'am."

Only Gemma knew he had strung the popcorn and hidden the two long strands in the cupboard.

After Molly had gone to her room, Craig patted the space beside him on the settee in an open invitation.

Gemma could think of nothing she wanted more than to be near him. She laid aside her knitting and moved across the room to sit with him.

He slipped his arm across her shoulder and pulled her against his side.

She hesitated a moment before she snuggled

closer. They watched the flames dance on the wood until it slowly crumbled to embers.

"Do you want to ride out and see the school tomorrow?" Craig asked.

She wasn't certain. "It would be hard to see it reduced to ashes."

"Think about it. If you want to go, I'll take you."

He drew her against him again and smoothed his thumb over the back of her hand, over and over in a soothing caress, sending tingles up her arm.

"I meant what I said before. I want you in my life...by my side. Being hitched to a sheriff is hard on a woman. I told you about Charlotte."

She nodded against his chest.

"Unexpected things come up in my line of business. I'm not going to lie—it won't be easy. If you have misgivings, you should listen to them."

"Just what kind of a proposal is that? It is only slightly better than this morning's when you said you intended to watch out for me. It is inevitable when you care for someone that you worry for them," she argued. He was building an unsurmountable case *against* marrying him. Why would he do that? "With one hand you are offering and with the other hand, pulling it all away."

"Because I won't build our future on coercing you to stay," he said seriously. He huffed out a breath, the sound rumbling through his chest under her ear. "I don't think you are the type of woman that can be tricked anyway. You are strong inside and out. That gives me hope that you could one day see your way clear to be my wife."

She wasn't as smart as he thought. She had been tricked, and tricked in the worst way. His was the first real proposal she had ever received. She swallowed. She wanted a life with this man and in this town.

But as he was being honest with her, she had to return it.

The time had come. She couldn't let things continue between them without telling him what she had done. And to tell him...well...once he knew the truth, she would lose him, her teaching position and possibly her freedom. As sheriff, he would have to act. There would be no way he could look the other way or forgive her for what she'd done.

She had hoped that she'd run far enough to be safe from her past. Here in Clear Springs she thought she had. She would have been content here as long as she could teach. She'd never counted on a man like Craig to come along. Why did he have to be a lawman on top of it? And of all things why, why, *why* had she let things get this far? All she had wanted was a new beginning. She hadn't expected…him. And now…now it was too late to leave.

She loved him. But did she love him enough to be honest with him? Enough to give up everything for a chance at a future with him? All she knew was that in loving him, she could no longer live the lie.

"I was deceived once," she said quietly, focusing on the dying embers in the hearth. "And before you say another word about 'us' you need to know about it. It may change things."

Beside her, he tensed slightly—enough that she knew she had his full attention.

"I told you that my father died a year ago and that is when I decided to come West. I… There is more to it than that. As you pointed out once, a well-bred woman of means rarely leaves her comfortable life behind to teach in a mining camp. I didn't really have a choice." She took a deep breath. She would see this through. All the way.

The circles he'd been making on the back of her hand ceased. "Go on."

She looked up at Craig's face as the firelight danced shadows across him. He looked wary—as though he weren't sure he wanted to hear what she had to say. "My father's assistant, Roland Wilkins, had aspirations to one day be a full law partner and then go into politics. Roland was handsome and flashy and exciting. He could talk a banker out of his gold. He had a rather coarse upbringing. His one fault was his impatience. He looked for the fast way to an end, which was not always the best way. At times he'd say things that shocked me, especially when he was frustrated or angry. He was careful to curb that tendency around my father, but it slipped out when he was with me or with the staff."

Craig raised his brows. "Staff?"

"Two. Mrs. Horne served as our housekeeper and cook. Mr. Ross was our butler and driver. They'd been with us since I was very young."

"Tutors. House staff. Gemma...you didn't have a house, you had an estate."

"No, just a very nice house in a very old and established area of Boston near the university."

"Do you still own it?"

"I don't know."

The disbelief on his face made her feel very young and foolish. *You don't know?* it said. *Why not?*

She turned away from him and stared at the red embers. "When Father passed away, Roland wanted to marry immediately. To look after me, he said. I was distraught...lost in my grief...but I was also my father's daughter and I knew that to make such a momentous decision during my time of mourning was unwise. It was when I was going through my father's things that I began to suspect Roland had stolen money from us. When I questioned him, he said it had to be a miscalculation on my part. He became insistent that we marry. Right then."

Craig exhaled, long and slow. "If you married him, you couldn't accuse him."

She nodded.

"What happened?"

"He had papers drawn up. I was in father's study when he approached me and said we had to go to the church. When I refused to move, he grabbed and shook me. I still refused. It made him even angrier." She closed her eyes. She'd been so scared. "Then he slapped me—hard. I reeled across the room and fell against my father's gun cabinet. Suddenly I was surrounded by broken glass and guns. I snatched one up. I didn't know whether it was loaded or not. I just knew I had to protect myself. Roland just laughed and dared me to stop him. He said I might be going to law school but I wasn't strong enough to pull the trigger. He came at me again...and I closed my eyes...and squeezed."

"No witnesses?"

"Mrs. Horne was downstairs. She rushed in

afterward but she didn't see what actually happened. We were both frightened. Roland was a powerful man with powerful connections. I... I ran to my room, filled my trunk with what I needed for a long trip and Mr. Ross drove me to the train station. He didn't want to know which train I got on. We both wanted it that way. I told him I would contact him after I was settled."

"What happened to Roland?"

"Mr. Ross said he would take care of the body."

"So you ran."

"Yes."

His chest rose and fell with a breath. He took another.

She looked up at him. At his set, tense jaw. "I'm sorry I couldn't tell you before."

"What made you say something now?"

"Because you professed your feelings for me. I know you. You won't be satisfied with the holes in my history. Besides, I have come to have strong feelings for you. I don't want to hide the truth. There is a time for honesty and it is now."

"Are those the only reasons?"

She averted her gaze. "No. But it's enough." She wouldn't tell him it was because she loved him. That would only rub salt into the wound of her duplicity. He had trusted her, protected her and cared for her. And she had betrayed that trust.

What must he think of her? Through her entire confession he'd offered no sign of his thoughts.

He was quiet for a long time. The fire went completely out. The only light in the room was the soft glow from the kerosene lantern at the window.

Craig readjusted himself, extracting his arm and then the rest of himself from her. "I have to check things outside." He rose to his feet.

"You have nothing to say?"

She watched him put on his coat and then his hat, half wondering if the next thing he was going to do was insist on taking her to the jail.

"It can wait until morning. You should get some sleep." He turned and headed outside.

As he walked away, the balloon of pressure that had been building the entire time she told her story suddenly deflated. He must be disgusted with her. He had to be. She'd put him in a bind. He had to make a choice now—ignore his conscience and let her continue teaching in Clear Springs or turn her in. Either way, marriage or love was out of the question. She was sure of that now.

Tears burned in her eyes. She blinked them away and rose to her feet. At least her conscience would no longer accuse her. She had had all she could stand of that. She gathered a blanket and a pillow from the old Pennsylvania trunk and left them for him on the settee. Then she made her way to her room and closed the door.

Early the next morning, the sound of footsteps on the front porch woke Craig. Then someone rapped insistently on the door.

"Sheriff! Wake up!" Chet called softly.

He rose from the settee and opened the door. "What is it?"

"Larabee is rousing. Thought you'd want to know. I'm heading out to tell Mrs. Odom."

"Good. She's been worried." By the amount of daylight it must've been around seven. An ominous red shaded the eastern sky. "I'll get right over to Doc's."

He shut the door and walked over to the settee to put on his holster. He could have slept in Mrs. Birdwell's last vacant room, but he had worried a real bed would be too comfortable and he'd sleep too soundly. As it was, he was up checking the house and yard every few hours throughout the night. Until this was finished he had the feeling a good night's sleep would be elusive.

"Who was that?" Gemma said from the hall doorway.

"Chet. Larabee is coming around." He finished the buckle before looking up at her.

He forgot to breathe. Beautiful didn't begin to describe the way she looked. She leaned against the plaster, holding her cream-colored robe tightly closed at the lace collar. Her rich brown hair fell over her shoulder in a thick, loose and messy braid. It dawned on him that here was the sight he'd be greeted with every morning if she'd have him, if—

And then he remembered all that she'd said last night and he went numb. It had been the same last night when she first told him. He had quieted as he reeled from her revelation. Better that than railing at her in anger and frustration. Her words had ruined the tentative dreams he'd built for the two of them.

"You are going now?" she asked.

He nodded.

"May I come?"

He didn't want to wait, but he still had to protect her. Just because he had learned a few more facts about her didn't mean he could shirk his duties. "How fast can you get dressed?"

She dashed to her room.

In the kitchen he found some bread and cheese and made himself a quick sandwich, and then washed it down with water. He made another for Gemma. He'd never been completely sure if the threat was more about the school…or about her.

Now…with all she'd told him it had larger ramifications than he'd first imagined.

"Ready," Gemma said a few minutes later from the doorway. She was already in her coat and tying the ribbons on her bonnet beneath her chin.

He handed her the sandwich.

"Are we going to talk about last night…?" she said, taking the sandwich.

She looked so apprehensive, so…uneasy. He wanted to tell her everything would be okay, but he couldn't. He was still angry that she hadn't been honest with him from the first. He understood why, but that didn't make it any easier to swallow that the woman he cared for had been so duplicitous. And the fact remained, stark and blatant, that she had run. She had not faced the consequences of her actions. His entire life, his entire being was a daily reminder of those consequences in his effort to keep the community safe.

"Did it ever occur to you," he said carefully, "that someone in Roland's family might have come looking for you and that is the person sending you the notes? It could be their way of revenge…striking back."

It was plain to see she had thought that through by the look on her face. "But how would they have found me? And if they did, wouldn't they have me arrested and send me back to Massachusetts to stand trial?"

"This is the West. Things aren't so proper out here." They could tease her with notes until she went crazy. They could play cat and mouse for as long as they wanted, if that was who was threatening her. They could also wait until she was isolated and simply shoot her. The eye-for-an-eye code of revenge. He was angry with her and in a coarse way he wanted to strike out at her. Yet he also understood why she'd kept her silence. Fear that he'd send her back, fear that he'd incarcerate her, had held her tongue. In her shoes, what would he have done?

He thought he loved her, yet now he was rattled on that count. How could he love someone whom he didn't really know? He recalled the times he'd hesitated, wondering about some of the things she'd said, but then his heart had not listened. It would be so much simpler if he could wash his hands of her…but he couldn't. And last, and most important—he had sworn to uphold the law. A fact that didn't bode well for her. "I can't talk about last night now, but I have not forgotten. We'll take one thing at a time. For now, let's go see about Larabee."

Slowly, she wrapped the sandwich in a cloth

napkin and tucked it into her satchel. "I'll eat later." Her voice broke on the last word.

He held the door for her as they left, and they walked in silence all the way to the doctor's residence.

"He wakes for a few seconds, maybe up thirty seconds, and then he slips back under," Doc Palmer said when Craig asked about Larabee. He backed up to allow them room to enter his home office, nodding to Gemma as she passed.

When they entered the spare room, Mrs. Palmer was dabbing a damp cloth over Larabee's face. That roused him for a second and while he was awake, she quickly held a small cup of water to his lips. The water dribbled half in and half out of his mouth. He coughed—a weak, pitiful choking type cough and then closed his eyes and lay still again.

"That seems to be about all the excitement he can handle for now," Doc Palmer said. "Maybe later in the day he'll have more fortitude."

"He hasn't spoken?" Gemma asked.

"No. Nothing."

"Can he hear?" she asked, glancing at Craig. He knew what she wanted to know. Had this man left her in that shed because he hadn't realized she was there…or had it been on purpose?

"Not much," the doctor said. "A mine explosion ruined his hearing. But he's fair at reading lips."

"Any other visitors besides the Odoms?" Craig asked.

Doc Palmer shook his head. "I've got my breakfast getting cold. You can stay if you want. Have a seat. Call me if you notice a change but I'd appreciate it if you wouldn't bother him. He needs the rest if he is going to improve."

"We'll stay a few minutes." He motioned for Gemma to take a seat. He then sat down in the only other straight-backed chair. He leaned over, elbows on his thighs, his Stetson in his hands, and waited.

After ten minutes with no change in Larabee, Craig had had about all the waiting he could take. It wasn't productive, and he wanted to get out to the school property and look around a bit more. He stood. "I'll take you back to the Tanners. Given the situation, you're safer there than at the boardinghouse."

She rose, nodding her head in agreement.

Craig walked outside with Gemma and started down the boardwalk. The closer they got to the Tanners, the slower Gemma walked.

At the door she said, "I really hate to impose on the Tanners."

He started to touch her under the chin and then

thought better of it and stuffed his hand in his pocket. It had been so easy, caressing her, kissing her last night before he knew. He had wanted her heart, but now…? Everything had changed in the light of her confession.

"I'll be too busy today to keep an eye on you." He knew his voice sounded distant, maybe even cold to her. It did to him.

She shrank back from him. "I understand. It's just…" She drew in a shaky breath and then smiled—a tremulous smile. "I understand. It's okay. Clarice and I plan to bake today anyway. We didn't get it done yesterday and after all, Christmas is tomorrow."

"You bake?" The words came out flat and cynical. He should have questioned that yesterday when she spoke about baking with Molly. She had been raised with a silver spoon in Boston. He had trouble believing she could even use a stove.

"Mrs. Horne taught me a few things."

She wasn't who she said she was. He didn't know who she was anymore. "I have to go."

She reached for his forearm and held it. "Be careful, Craig."

He couldn't allow himself to feel anything for her. She had put him in a compromised position by confessing to what she had done. He should be putting her in jail right now, but he couldn't

bring himself to do it. One moment he wanted
to kiss her and the next…he wanted to turn her
in. In his gut, he realized it had been self-defense
on her part. But she hadn't stayed to see things
through. She had run and he couldn't get past
that. He tightened his jaw and looked down at
her hand on his arm.

She released him.

He left her, standing in the doorway.

Chapter Seventeen

In the livery, he saddled Jasper and then mounted. He reined the horse toward the school property and urged him into an easy lope.

While he had waited there at Doc Palmer's for Larabee to rouse, he'd realized that he needed to get back out to Larabee's shack and see if something would make sense to him that hadn't the other day when he'd come upon the old man. That day, he'd been caught up with footprints and the second note, but once he'd found the injured miner, he'd been worried about getting help for the man. The burning of the school and Larabee's attack might not be related at all—but he had a deep-down gut feeling that they were. At least he could take Larabee's name out of the short list of suspects.

This time instead of going straight through the woods to get to Larabee's claim, he decided to ride along the bank of the creek. According to Gemma, she'd seen Larabee use this route more often than the more direct one through the trees. Craig kept Jasper to a walk as he leaned over slightly, checking the ground for anything odd or telling.

When he arrived at the place where he had dragged Larabee from the water, he heard a muffled noise. Reining Jasper to a stop, he listened. Metal striking stone. Someone was using a shovel or pickax.

And they were on Larabee's land.

Craig dismounted quietly, ground-tied Jasper and drew his Colt. He made his way through the brush carefully, counting the draw between the strikes. It sounded like one person...a man by the sounds of the grunts. Still, there could be another one standing by. The shack loomed ahead.

"Oof!" The grunt sounded near.

The sounds were coming from inside the small shack.

He crept closer. No sign of a horse. He worked his way around a few trees and tall brush and came up on the side of the shack. Stealing closer, he peeked in through the partially open door. On the back wall, a tan, dirty tarp had been pulled to the side like a sash and beyond that, instead of a wall of wood like the other three walls, a tunnel had been carved into the hillside.

Inside the tunnel, stooped and making his way toward Craig as he stared at a piece of quartz in his palm, was Duncan Philmont.

Craig trained his gun on him. "Hello, Duncan."

Duncan froze. His jaw slowly dropped open. And then closed.

Craig motioned with the barrel of his gun. "Come on out. And don't try to run. I'd hate to have to explain that to your father."

Duncan moved another ten feet to where he could stand up inside the shack. "What are you going to do?"

"Outside. Head toward the river. I've got a few questions for you." Craig whistled sharp and brief.

"Can't you ask me right here?"

"No."

Jasper trotted out from the trees and stopped in front of Craig. The sheriff pulled handcuffs from his saddlebag.

Duncan's green eyes widened and he backed up a step. "You already saw me, Sheriff. I ain't going anywhere."

"I'm arresting you on suspicion of attacking Albert Larabee with the intent to kill." He cuffed Duncan's hands behind his back.

"What? I didn't do it!" Anger and something else—fear—shone on the boy's face. The piece of quartz Duncan held dropped from his hand.

Craig retrieved the rock and turned it over in his hand. A rich strain of gold shot through one corner of it. "You are in deep trouble, Mr. Philmont. Trespassing, claim jumping, attacking a defenseless old man, maybe even arson. You might want to have your father get you a lawyer."

"I didn't do it, Sheriff. I swear I didn't."

"Which part?"

The Adam's apple in the boy's throat slid up and then back down as he swallowed hard.

Craig wished he could believe the boy. He just had too many doubts. "We'll sort it out at the jail."

He helped him up into the saddle, and then took the lead line and started toward the road.

They passed the remains of the school and he circled the perimeter of the charred boards looking for anything that might help him figure out or even prove who had started the fire. In places smoke still rose up from the piles of ashes and wood. In other places, the fire had jumped over entire sections. The plank with two rows of offset hooks that had been used for hanging up coats in the cloakroom had burned only halfway, leaving a usable piece. The pungent smell of burnt wood hung in the air.

The few items rescued were grouped together in the grass in front of the building—a bench, the bookcase, the globe from Gemma's desk. It wasn't much considering all the things that had been inside.

"When you and Billy Odom came into the town hall on Saturday night, you both looked like you had been up to no good. Then later I hear that the school is on fire. Is that a coincidence? Did you and Billy take on another dare?"

He watched Duncan's expression for any signs of emotion—remorse would be nice.

Duncan's jaw hardened. "No."

Craig hadn't expected the boy to own up to it.

The school's door lay flat on the grass a short distance from the rest of the charred building, almost as if it had exploded away from the rest in a blast of dynamite. He walked up to it and shoved it over.

Still recognizable and intact hung the wreath that Gemma had fashioned and nailed there.

Measuring the ingredients and fashioning the crust for the pies had kept Gemma's mind off her circumstances. Although she had made pies before, she had benefitted from some of Clarice's baking tips. It occurred to her that she had never thought about the time that went into preparing all the good food she'd eaten while growing up and she determined to write a long letter to Mrs. Horne in the next day or two. But now, as the afternoon slipped away, and the pies were cooling on the table, she found herself at loose ends.

She needed to talk to Craig. He'd been angry that morning and he had a right to be. She wasn't looking forward to facing that again, she needed to find out what he was going to do. She couldn't bear this state of not knowing something decisive. Surely by now he'd come to a conclusion of what to do with the information. She had to know what he planned for her. Throughout the day the idea of running, of leaving town, had grown more attractive. The longer it took him to talk to her, the stronger the impetus became.

Her well-thought-out plans of four days ago when she received her first note made her cringe. She had been ready to stand firm and fight back against whoever was writing those horrid notes. Where was that woman now? Father would not recognize her. Yet she knew in her heart it wasn't the notes, it wasn't the fire and the loss of her school that had crushed her spirit so completely. It was Craig's distancing of himself that hurt the most. Whether he knew it or not, he had already judged her.

She hadn't meant to fall in love. And now there was nothing she could do to fix what she herself had broken.

It was just after noon when she finished helping

Clarice dry the dishes they had used for baking and began to put them away. Someone knocked at the front door and Mr. Tanner spoke in low tones to the visitor. She was curious, wondering who it might be, but continued at her task. A moment later, Patrick Tanner came to the kitchen.

"That was Chet Farnsworth. Sheriff Parker has a suspect at the jail."

She put down the dish towel. "Who?"

"Duncan Philmont."

"Duncan! I can't believe…" she started to say, but then remembered his fight against Billy. He did have volatile emotions. Still, she had a difficult time believing he'd go so far as to burn down the school.

"Caught him red-handed at something this morning. I'm heading there now to find out more."

"I'm coming too."

Gemma hurried up the main street of town, keeping pace with Patrick Tanner who wore a grim look on his face. "One of the students!" he kept muttering. "I just can't believe it!"

"Nor I," Gemma said, and braced herself for seeing Duncan as well as Craig when she entered the jail.

It was her first visit to Craig's office. The large room was split by the bars of the jail cell. Approximately one-third of the room was the jail cell and the other two-thirds was the law office. On the wall behind Craig's desk a map of the area had been nailed up. On the wall opposite, wanted posters were pinned. She wondered if, since learning of her past, he had looked through the flyers to see if her picture was there.

Craig stood up immediately and stepped from behind his desk. "Miss Starling."

She would so much more like it if he called her Gemma, but they were both figuring out where they stood with each other it seemed. "Hello, Sheriff. Mr. Tanner informed me that you were holding Mr. Philmont. What is this all about?"

Craig's dark look veered from her to Mr. Tanner standing behind her. He nodded to the man. "Patrick. Come on in."

"I didn't do nothin'!" Duncan yelled, jumping up from his cot and pressing his face against the bars. "You gotta believe me, Teach!" He gripped the two vertical bars on either side of his chest with white-knuckled ferocity.

Gemma moved closer to the jail cell. She'd never seen Duncan frightened before—angry, hostile, often cynical, but never frightened. It disturbed her. "Where is your father in all this? He should be here."

"He left! But you'll stay, won't you? You'll

help get me out. I don't think I can stand being cooped up like this."

"That's enough out of you!" Craig's stern voice cut through the room. "Your close surroundings didn't matter when I caught up to you so you'll forgive me if I don't have any sympathy. Now, settle down."

Gemma had never heard that deep authoritative voice from Craig before. Her face must have revealed her shock because when Craig turned back to her and Mr. Tanner, he wouldn't look at her but for a brief second.

"Ryan Philmont was here. He has gone to obtain the services of a lawyer."

Her gaze flew once more to Duncan who grimaced and plopped himself back on his cot, glaring daggers at Craig.

"Don't you think that's a bit extreme?" Mr. Tanner said. "Why is Duncan being held?"

Craig's gaze narrowed, in essence letting Mr. Tanner and her both know that they were now in his domain. This wasn't the school or a board meeting where he would hold back in respect for the other's position. This was his office and his town.

"Have a seat, Mr. Tanner. You too," he motioned for Gemma to use his desk chair. When they'd settled, he directed his words to her. "Remember the times you saw Larabee after school?"

"Yes."

"You said he handed Billy a rabbit. And he gave Tara something. It was small and you couldn't see what it was from the school steps."

Gemma thought back and the image came to her of Larabee pulling something from his pocket and handing it to Tara. "I remember."

Craig opened his top desk drawer and withdrew a piece of quartz. "This is from Larabee's property. I found it there—in Duncan's hand."

Mr. Tanner removed his hat and leaned forward on his chair. "You found Mr. Philmont here out at Larabee's old claim?"

"That's what I said—with a pickax."

"Larabee abandoned that claim years ago. It wasn't producing."

"That may be…or it could be he quit prospecting for a while because of what happened to his wife and son. Whatever the reason, there is still gold to be had there."

"How would Duncan know about any of this?"

"He works for his father at the land office. All the claims in this county are filed there. But I'll be honest. I can't prove if that has anything to do with it. What he says is that Tara dropped a small rock. When he picked it up for her, he noticed the gold strain through it and put two and two together. He had seen Larabee handing pretty rocks to Tara in the past."

Gemma glanced over at Duncan. She still didn't want to believe that he had done such a thing as attack Mr. Larabee. He had turned over and was now lying face up on his cot with his fingers laced behind his head, studying the ceiling boards. She was sure he was listening to everything even though his expression didn't change.

"It's all circumstantial evidence," she said, returning her attention to Craig. "You don't have any proof that he hurt Mr. Larabee. You still need proof to keep Duncan in jail."

"I caught him trespassing on Larabee's claim. That'll keep him here until we can sort through everything."

"He's just a boy."

Craig's gaze hardened. "He's old enough to know right from wrong."

The way he said it, he could as easily have been speaking about her. He was a stranger to her—this overly righteous, overly zealous sheriff. And yet—he was Clear Springs's choice—and hers—for protection. "May I speak with him?"

Craig didn't answer immediately. His brows drew together as he considered her. "Stay back from the bars."

She rose from her seat and stepped closer to the cell. "Duncan…tell me the truth. Did you send me those horrible notes? Did you burn down the school?"

Duncan swung his feet to the floor and ran a large hand through his oily hair. "Honest, Miss Starling, I don't know anything about any notes. I could tell something was going on because the sheriff was hanging around more. That's all." He hung his head.

"What about the fire?"

"You can't pin that on me. You just can't. I know I don't like school much, but I wouldn't start no fire."

"You do see how this looks, don't you Duncan?"

He grimaced and looked away to the floor. "Yeah. Not good."

"No. Not good at all."

"I didn't hurt anyone. All I did was look for a little gold. And what I found, Sheriff Parker took away from me." He looked so young and scared now that she almost forgot how he'd treated her a time or two with his attitude in the classroom.

"Is there anything you can tell us that would help?" she asked gently.

"I don't know anything else. Honest."

"You are wasting your breath, Miss Starling," Craig said.

He spoke to her as though they hadn't exchanged intimate words yesterday, as though they hadn't kissed, as though she were a stranger. It hurt.

Mr. Tanner stood. "I better get back home. Clarice expects me to take her to pick out a tree for Christmas before it gets dark." He looked expectantly at Gemma. "Are you ready to go?"

She glanced at Craig. She'd hoped they might get to talk…but considering things now, it wouldn't happen. At least not tonight. He would be staying here with Duncan and they certainly couldn't talk in front of the boy. She didn't believe the fire was Duncan's doing, but she didn't know how to fix things for him. "The sheriff seems to believe he has his culprit. I don't think I need to be chaperoned any longer."

Craig's sharp look hardened on her. He held the balance of power and they both knew it. For all he seemed to care, she might as well be sitting with Duncan in the jail cell. "I should be safe to wander about on my own. At least in town."

"I don't know…" Mr. Tanner said slowly, glancing to Craig for his reaction.

It only made her that much surer of her course. She had to leave town. "Nonetheless, it is time for me to look after myself. I've imposed on you and the good sheriff long enough. With Christmas tomorrow I have a lot to do to get ready. If you need me for anything, I'll be at Molly's."

The more she talked, the tighter Craig's face became.

Tension hung in the air, thick and roiling. Craig's attitude hadn't softened toward her. Not one bit. That generosity of spirit he'd once shown was no longer directed at her.

Mr. Tanner glanced from her to Craig before putting his hat back on his head. "We'll go then."

Without another look at Duncan or Craig, she stepped outside and walked away.

Craig rubbed his roughened chin, only barely registering that he could use a shave as he thought about the situation with Duncan. He had a lot of respect for Gemma's instincts regarding her students. He just felt he was missing something. He glanced over at Duncan who was slouched on the cot, his back against the wall.

"Seems Miss Starling cares a great deal about you, Mr. Philmont. She believes in you and your potential. Mentioned that to me last week. And she believes you didn't do anything other than trespass on Larabee's land."

He shrugged. "Doesn't do a lot of good what she believes now."

"It might."

Duncan rubbed his nose with his sleeve. "How?"

"I'm trying to sort that out. Something isn't sitting right in all this."

The boy laid back down on his cot and turned toward the wall. "Let me know when you figure it out. I'd like to go home for Christmas."

Craig stared at the boy, all the while not really seeing him, but traveling in his mind back to the first day he'd really talked to Gemma—the day he'd found Tara playing hooky. He tried to piece together every incidence he could of what he knew about her. Slowly a thought took hold and he had a hunch it might lead somewhere.

"How far back does that tunnel go that Larabee dug into the hillside?" he asked Duncan. "Did you get to the end of it?"

"It was too dark and I didn't have a lantern."

"He's had forty years to dig it. You think it went all the way to the school property?"

Slowly Duncan raised up slightly and turned to look at him with a curious expression. "It could, I guess. It might."

Craig slipped his Stetson on. "I'll be back. I need to talk to your father." He closed the door on his way out. Up until today he had considered the land Larabee owned was not of any real value.

It was rocky and filled with scrub brush. But if there really was gold on it...

Ryan Philmont had closed up the land office, likely because his son was in jail and that took precedence. Considering all of Duncan's cater-wauling he should be happy to hear of his father closing shop. After a brief search of the town, Craig found him at the judge's house, already pleading his case for his boy while the judge ate a late lunch.

"What is it, Parker?" Philmont growled after stepping outside. He closed the judge's door behind him. "Haven't you done enough?"

"Who stands to benefit if Larabee is out of the picture? Who does the land and the claim pass to?" If it was Edna Odom...or her children...

"I wouldn't know. Larabee filed that claim before my time here."

Craig felt an urgency driving him that hadn't been there before. Suddenly things were starting to crystallize. "Then I want to check your records. I'll walk with you to your office."

Philmont didn't budge. Instead he tilted his head toward Judge Perry's house. "I'm trying to get my son out of jail before nightfall here. That's more important at the moment."

"Then I'd think you would be more obliging," Craig said. He fixed the man with a cold, flat stare. "You may be sitting on the information I need to do just that."

Philmont balked for a moment and then let out a long breath. "All right, Parker. You win. Let's go."

At the land office, Ryan unlocked the door and stepped inside. He went straight to the bookcase and after sorting through a few old ledgers, pulled out one from thirty years in the past. He plopped it on his desk, causing a cloud of dust to fly up. Slowly he scanned down the list of names and corresponding parcels of land notated using his bony index finger to keep his place. "Here it is."

He swung the ledger around so that Craig could read it. Beneficiary: Edna Connor Odom.

A few more things were making sense. "Thanks. I need to check something out."

"What about my son?"

"He still trespassed on a claim. He's where he belongs." He headed out the door.

"I helped you, Parker. You owe me!" Philmont called after him, hurrying to lock up the office again.

"I'll take that into consideration."

"There weren't any signs posted. How was he supposed to know it was private property?"

"A man doesn't post No Trespassing signs inside his own house. You know that, Philmont."

He strode to the jail and snatched his rifle from its rack on the wall and then loaded it with cartridges from his desk. Then he checked his Colt for a full load of bullets and stuffed it in his holster.

Duncan stood, his face against the bars again, and watched Craig. "What's going on?"

"Nothing I want you anywhere near." He stepped to the bars and met Duncan's gaze to emphasize his words. "I think you are as close to being guilty as you can get. You were caught on Larabee's property, and everybody knows you can be a hotheaded bully. But a few things don't add up. If my hunch plays out, you'll have Miss Starling to thank for being so pigheaded about your innocence. I respect her opinion…among other things."

Ryan Philmont appeared in the doorway.

"I'll be back," Craig said to him. "I'm leaving Chet Farnsworth in charge here until I return. You are welcome to stay with your son."

Ryan's jaw dropped open, but he didn't say anything more as Craig strode out the door.

Craig stopped at the livery, saddled his horse and rode out of town. For a moment he considered stopping at the boardinghouse to let Gemma know his suspicions, but with the way they had parted he thought it better to let things be for a bit. Neither one of them was seeing eye to eye at the moment and he had a job to get done. Besides, that would give Boston time to respond to the telegram he'd sent earlier asking for more information on Roland Wilkins.

About five minutes outside of Clear Springs, he stopped by the Palisade Mine on the way to the Odoms' property. When Craig rode up, Chet was bent over a mine car, replacing a broken wheel.

He straightened when he saw Craig and wiped his greasy hands on an old rag. "Hey."

Craig got right to the point. "I'm riding out to the Odoms' place. I want you to keep watch over things at my office. Duncan Philmont is in the cell. He stays there until I get back."

"You know…keep this up and you may have to start paying me."

He'd thought the same thing. Maybe he should bring it up at the next town hall meeting. He turned over his keys to Chet. "I'll be back in a few hours."

As he rode away from the Palisade Mine he mulled over how he would approach things out at the Odoms'. Mrs. Odom had been sporting a bruise on her cheek at the Christmas dance. He had accepted her story of falling at the chicken coop without suspicion, but now, in light of things, that bruise could mean her husband Elias was back in the area. If that were the case…Elias might have a few things to answer for.

Slow and cautious came to mind. He'd need to handle things slow and cautious.

Chapter Eighteen

Gemma marched to Molly's boardinghouse with her thoughts racing. She had put Craig in a difficult place with her confession and each minute she remained, he wrestled with his conscience. She could feel his unease every time that he looked at her. At this rate he would grow to hate her. And she couldn't abide that. So she would go. If she got away soon, perhaps she could salvage the pieces of her heart he had already stolen.

Until a year ago, she had never been the sort to run from her problems. Running now would make her that sort and she didn't like what that said about her. But she had a plan. She might be running away from Clear Springs, but she would be heading back to Boston. She had left a mess and it was time for her to fix it. She couldn't allow her past to ruin every bit of her future and that was what it was doing.

First she would rent a horse and buggy. Then she would stop at the schoolhouse. She wanted to see for herself the destruction. It would be a lasting image for her to take with her. Not a pretty one...but a memory of what would happen again if she didn't straighten things out. She would never know whether the fire had anything to do with her personally. She still couldn't believe that Roland's family had found her. It was too fantastical. Nonetheless, something was amiss here and she had been targeted.

Her biggest regret—besides deceiving Craig—was that she would have to leave the children, and in doing so break her promise to Mr. Tanner. She felt an obligation to them. And she cared about them. She just didn't know how to make it work anymore!

"With these clouds it looks like we may have a dusting of snow for Christmas!" Molly said when Gemma arrived. "No matter how old I get, I still long for a little bit of snow for the holiday." She hooked a small red bow on a branch of her tiny tree.

Molly's actions reminded Gemma about the popcorn strings that Craig had made. She set down her satchel and strode to the kitchen. Rummaging far back in the pantry, she found the tin she had hidden and brought it out into the parlor. "Here you go, Molly. You'll need this for the tree."

Molly opened the canister. "Well, that man! He sure had me going! He didn't eat them after all!"

Gemma smiled and tried to hold back tears that threatened. "No. You were dozing. It was a bit of a game to him to see if he could string an entire string to the end without you catching him."

Molly chuckled. "He certainly did that!" She leaned toward Gemma, staring. "Are you all right, dear?"

"Of course! Just missing my father. He'd have a huge tree in the room each year."

"Well in that case, this is quite humble for you." Molly draped the popcorn string onto the tree, fussing with it to make it hang just so.

"It's lovely," Gemma said, smiling.

"I'm going to get a few things at the bakery for tomorrow. Perhaps later this evening you and I can go to the Christmas Eve service."

"I'd like that."

"I've invited Selma Hornsby for Christmas. I didn't want her to spend the day alone."

Gemma was glad to hear that. She didn't want Molly to be alone either. She herself would be gone.

"And I think while I'm out and about that I

will stop by to ask the sheriff to join us. Is that all right with you, dear?"

Gemma swallowed. "Certainly." The image of the three of them at the table without being there herself put a catch in her throat.

"I'll be off then," Molly said and spread her cloak over her shoulders.

When the door shut, Gemma hurried to pack. She wouldn't take much…not nearly what she had arrived with. Just what the carpetbag could hold. The trunk would have to remain behind. She left a note, saying she would write when she was able. Then, when she was finished packing, she threw on her coat and bonnet and slipped out the back door.

From the spring seat of her buggy Gemma stared at the remnants of the schoolhouse. Blackened, charred wood, some boards still partially standing, some leaning at odd angles and some half gone into ashes littered the area. She sighed in disbelief as she looked on the shed. In an ironic twist of fate, the shed had not gone up in flames like the rest of the school. The outside was charred decoratively and the broken door still wobbled on its broken hinge in the light breeze.

She wrapped the long driving reins around the brake lever and climbed from the buggy. Walking slowly, she made her way through the pile of rubbish and over to the few items that had been saved. She smoothed her hand over the globe. Then she spied the box that held her gun. When she picked it up, half the box crumbled into ashes. She drew out the gun and turned it over in her hand. She checked the chambers. Still loaded. A wave of relief washed over her that no children had found the gun before her.

The thought stopped her. In leaving, she would certainly miss Craig and Molly, but she would also miss her students. Tara's pretty singing and little Moira Bishop and her stutter. What would happen to them?

She had learned something in her first teaching assignment. Given the choice of teaching or the law, she knew she could make a difference at either place. Both were noble professions. With teaching she had more of a chance to establish good traits in students so that they would not need to answer to the law later. Maybe, someday, she could do both.

If she didn't end up in jail the rest of her life.

She tossed the gun onto the floor of the buggy and then turned to climb in. It was a long way to the train station and she had better get started. She would go as far as possible today before it got dark. If luck would favor her, she would find a seat on the next train headed east.

Suddenly the hairs on the back of her neck stood up.

"Seems you don't know when to leave."

She didn't recognize the voice, but the very nature of its low, gravelly tone sounded menacing. She turned to face the stranger.

He stood at the most thirty feet away. He was big. Taller than Craig and leaner, his arms corded and sinewy beyond his rolled-up shirtsleeves. His dungarees were faded and torn, and like the plaid flannel shirt he wore, too large for his frame. His prominent brow and cheekbones gave him a gaunt, hard appearance and he watched her now as though nothing she did would escape him.

"Didn't you get my calling card, Miss Boston?"

For a moment she was confused. How did this man know her? "How…?"

A slow, evil smile grew on the man's gritty face.

The notes! He was talking about the notes! "Are you the one who burned down my school?"

"*Your* school! Now, ain't that a fine way to think of it? *Teech*."

That prickly feeling exploded down her spine. The urge to storm up to him and, hands on hips, upbraid him with a verbal hailstorm of Boston anger nearly got the better of her. Her anger thundered on the inside, but giving in to that urge would be folly. This man had no regard for her status as a teacher, no regard for her status as a woman or even a human being. She felt it in her bones. He would merely cuff her like the overgrown bear he was and then laugh as she shattered on the ground.

Father's gun.

She took a step closer to the buggy. Dare she use the gun to protect herself? Craig had said hesitating was the worst thing she could do. If she picked it up, she had to be willing to shoot. At this distance she could easily miss.

"Are you the one who left me locked in the shed?"

He let out a whoop. "Whoo-eee! I knew you heard me. I knew it! You got real quiet all of a sudden."

"You seem to know me well, but I know nothing about you." She took another step closer to the buggy. "Have we met?"

He snorted. "People don't forget me."

She swallowed. He was bigger than big. He was huge.

His cold gray eyes watched her as if she were a bug he wished to squash.

"Why did you destroy the school?"

"It's on my land."

"It's Larabee's land. He donated it for the school."

"Had no right to do that. It's mine. I got the papers to prove it. So you and the little brats can just find another place to do your schoolin'."

"Are you including your son and daughter in that? Tara? Billy?" It was a wild guess, but something about the way the man stood and talked reminded her of Billy Odom.

His eyes narrowed. "You leave them out of this."

A cold chill went through her. So this was Elias Odom. No wonder the last time she'd seen Edna, the woman had acted different. Scared. He had come back. "Why would you hurt Mr. Larabee? He's family."

"Plain and simple. My own family comes first and he was in the way."

"But Mr. Larabee helped your family when you left them."

"He doled it out—puny man. Thought he was so smart. Now I can have all I need."

The gun was right there, within grasping distance. All she had to do was reach out and grab it. She stalled, even as her heart pounded in her chest. "People around here would help you if you needed it. The town is full of good people."

"I don't take charity."

"No, you just take lives and livelihoods. That's worse." The words were out, bitter and biting before she thought to stop them. It was foolish to talk to him like this. She could tell by his expression that he grew angrier with each syllable.

"I don't rightly think much for your opinion, Teech. It's too bad you know who I am. Would have gone better for you if you would have left right off. I can't let you go now. You and me is goin' to have to take a ride." He started for her.

Her heart thumped wildly as she stumbled backward. "I'm not going anywhere with you." She grasped the gun and held it up in front her, pointing right at him. She steadied it with both hands and stepped back another step. Her breathing came fast and shallow. She clutched the gun tighter. "Stay away from me, Mr. Odom. Don't make me have to shoot."

He stopped advancing.

She glanced down at the gun. It wobbled back and forth with all the shaking she was doing.

Mr. Odom smiled. "You ain't gonna use that on me. You're shaking all to pieces cause you don't have the guts."

The irony of the situation nearly made her laugh. Which scared her. She had to be calm—

not hysterical. "Are you willing to risk it?" She took another step backward and found herself pressed up against the buggy.

His leer grew larger. "Yer gittin up in that ride like I told you." He stormed toward her.

She screamed, cocked the hammer and fired. Nothing happened. Elias kept barreling toward her. Heavens he was almost on top of her! *Think!*

Of course! The empty chamber! She cocked the hammer again and fired. The sound reverberated across the clearing, sounding almost like two shots. Elias jerked, but kept coming. He swatted her hard on the side of her head. Her head snapped around and she reeled, the gun flying from her hand before she collapsed in a heap on the charred grass.

Elias landed on top of her with a guttural grunt and a wheeze. She struggled to break free but he was heavy—too heavy. He wasn't moving, but any minute he might. Her only thought was to escape—to get away! She wiggled and pushed against him, but her weak attempts only seemed to rouse him.

He grasped her arm, squeezing hard until she thought her bone might break in two. "You done it now, girl! You...done...it...now..." Each word came out slower than the last and his grip loosened in measure. And then he stopped moving, his body going limp on top of her as he exhaled in one agonizingly long wheeze.

"Get off me!" She rolled him off her and pulled her skirt free. Her entire body throbbed as the world spun around her.

Hooves pounded the earth. A horse and rider galloped on the road toward her.

She panicked. The gun! Where was the gun? She searched in the grass beside her. Her heart racing, her breath coming in jerking sobs.

"Gemma!" Craig called out. And then he was beside her, dropping to his knees. "It's me!"

And suddenly she recognized him.

She grabbed onto his coat. How had he come to be here? She couldn't get enough air. She couldn't breathe!

He cradled her to him, enveloping her in his arms.

Craig was here. She was safe now. But she was shaking uncontrollably. Why didn't her heart slow down? She peeked around his shoulder and stared at Mr. Odom. He lay with his face down in the grass—and he didn't move. "Did I kill him? Is he…dead?" she asked, horrified at the thought.

Craig rose from his crouched position and walked over to Odom's body. He bent down again and felt for a pulse in the man's neck. "No. He's got a pulse."

The news only served to make Gemma more anxious. She covered her face with her hands; she had to breathe, had to relax.

Craig rolled Odom over and examined the wound in his shoulder, then gave the man a disgusted look and walked over to his horse. He pulled handcuffs from the saddlebag and clipped them on Odom's wrists.

His eyes narrowed on her as if just noticing her difficulty. "What's wrong?"

She grasped the tall grass, trying to hold on to something real, something solid as her thoughts spun out of control. "It's happening again! Don't you see?"

"What are you talking about?" Craig asked and then his expression changed. "Gemma, this isn't Boston. I saw what happened. This was self-defense. No court is going to charge you with doing anything wrong. You're safe. Everything is okay. You're safe."

She let out a long, slow breath, and tried to calm herself down.

Craig helped her up, looking her over critically. "He hit you hard. Are you hurt?"

She rubbed her ear. It still stung from Mr. Odom's strike. She worked her jaw, open and closed. Gingerly, she touched her cheek. The left side of her face felt puffy and swollen and bruised.

A lower tooth was loose and she tasted blood. She was sore, but she would be sorer tomorrow.

He wrapped her in his arms. "I should have put everything together sooner." Frustration laced his voice as he raked his hair back with his fingers. "I'm sorry I wasn't here."

"How is it you are here at all? I thought you were with Duncan."

"Chet's with him. I had a hunch it might be Odom. Edna Odom's bruises bothered me. They were fresh. I rode out to her place and was on my way back when I heard voices…and then the gun."

She looked down on Mr. Odom. He was moving slightly. Moaning. "He tried to kill Mr. Larabee, so he could get control of the mine."

"Which runs under the school property."

"It was never about me."

Craig shook his head. "No."

For the first time, she felt a measure of relief, a measure that things were finally going to be clear. It wasn't her fault. Not this.

"What are you doing out here by yourself? Aren't you carrying your freedom too f—?" Craig shifted his gaze to the carriage—specifically to her travel bag in the carriage.

She saw the moment his expression changed. The moment it closed her out. "Craig…I can…"

"We better get back to town."

"Craig…"

"Get in the buggy, Miss Starling. We need to get Odom to Doc Palmer," he said, his voice suddenly tired and weary.

He walked over to Mr. Odom and grabbed the man's arm, pulling him to his feet. "Get up. You're not hurt that bad. I'm taking you in." He pushed him toward Jasper.

Mr. Odom stumbled, weaving sideways. "She shot me! I'm bleeding out! How do you expect me to get up on that horse?"

"Should he ride in the buggy?" Gemma asked.

"After nearly killing you?" Craig scowled. "Not up front. I don't want him anywhere near you. He can ride in the boot." He walked him toward the back of the buggy. "You wouldn't be hollering so loud if you were bleeding out. Now get on up there." Mr. Odom plopped into the boot with Craig's forceful help.

"I'll take you to Doc Palmer's. You have a lot of answering to do for your crimes. You are one sorry example to those kids of yours, Odom. I sure hope they take after their ma." While he spoke, he tied a line from his horse to the back of the buggy.

Gemma scooted over as he pulled himself up and sat down beside her. For a moment more they surveyed the scene before them—the charred remains of the school—then Craig flicked the reins lightly, turned the buggy around and headed back to Clear Springs.

Chapter Nineteen

⁓⁓⁓⁓

Gemma climbed from the buggy with her travel case and waited while Craig turned the conveyance over to Gil Jolson at the livery. They had already dropped off Mr. Odom at Doc Palmer's with Chet standing by as guard. Mr. Larabee and Mr. Odom under the same roof. The thought was worrisome. But between the doctor and Chet, she imagined they'd keep things in order.

Craig led his horse back to a stall in the far corner. When he returned to her, his next words were cold, distant. "I need to check on Duncan."

So that was it? He hadn't even looked at her as he spoke. "I…I don't understand, Craig. There are things to say. Do you want me to come with you?"

"You were leaving. You were running," he accused. "What is there to talk about?"

"I thought that's what you wanted. You wouldn't look at me or talk to me. I…couldn't stand it. I had made a mess of things. All I could think of was to go back home and try to fix what I could. If that meant I'd go to prison, then that is what I would do. I just knew I couldn't face you or anyone else here in Clear Springs again and hold my head up." She had to look away. Her entire being ached with wanting him to understand. With wanting…him.

His jaw tightened. "It's not that easy. I took an oath."

"Oh, Craig." Her voice broke on his name. "Have I ruined everything?"

He stepped forward, at first reaching for her, only to pull back with clenched fists at his sides. "We should go. I need to check on Duncan and relieve Tanner." He picked up her travel bag.

Something crumbled inside her. She had known deep down that he wouldn't be able to look the other way about her past. It had been a vain, foolish dream. She turned and walked numbly to the door.

Outside, evening clouds scudded the sky. Craig stopped. "You can go back to the boardinghouse, but don't leave again."

She shook her head. "I appreciate that you trust me not to leave. You said that Mr. Tanner was at your office. I suppose I should tell him about Boston and get it over with. There is no point hiding it any longer."

He studied her a moment, his blue gaze penetrating. "Suit yourself." He spun around and headed to his office without waiting, still holding on to her bag.

She followed at a slower pace. It mattered little whether she arrived with him or a few paces behind. He was at odds, it seemed, with how to treat her, what to do with her. And because of it, he was being a brute. Here she was trying to do the right thing and he was being so...hurtful! How could he go from asking her to marry him one day to...to this?

You hurt him, her conscience said, accusing her all over again. *You lied and then ran away.*

But I didn't have to tell him about Boston in the first place!

Didn't you? You would have kept that from him?

No. If she were honest with herself, she had done the only thing she could live with. Holding in a secret like that would have eaten away at their love and twisted it into something ugly. Holding on to it would have tainted their relationship beyond hope. It was too late to change anything now even if she did want to go back somehow and make things right. It was done and over with.

She shut out the incriminating thoughts and concentrated on what she would tell Patrick Tanner. She was done with carrying this secret. It was too heavy and big. Craig had had a right to know and as head of the school board, so did Tanner.

"Tanner," Craig said, striding into his office. She entered a moment behind him, to see him set her bag down by his desk.

Mr. Tanner startled awake, uncrossed his ankles and lowered his boots from the desktop to the floor.

Craig grabbed the keys from the top drawer and strode over to the jail cell.

A lump lodged in her throat. He didn't mean to put her in there with Duncan, did he? It was an off-center, incoherent thought and it only proved to her that her grip on things was loose and tenuous.

"You're free to go, Mr. Philmont. Don't let me catch you trespassing on Larabee's property ever again."

Duncan jumped from the cot and grabbed his jacket. "What's going on?"

"I figure one night is enough for trespassing. *This* time."

"It won't happen again."

"I have your word on that?"

"Yes, sir."

"Then you might want to hear that the gold Larabee has been giving to Tara was found years ago. There's no more in the mine. I'll be keeping my eyes on you, Philmont. You might want to know that if it weren't for Miss Starling being so sure of your innocence, and her capture of the arsonist just now, you would still be in here. Happy Christmas."

"Miss Starling caught him? Are you serious?" Duncan turned to stare at her in awe. "Wow! Just wow! Happy Christmas!" He stumbled out of the office. A second later, a loud whoop sounded on his way down the main street.

Craig according the capture to her was the last thing she expected. She looked back to him. He still held on to the cell door.

Tanner stood and looked from one to the other. "It was Odom then. Like you thought."

"Yes," Craig said.

"I'm glad it had nothing to do with you, Miss Starling. You didn't deserve all those scares. Hope it won't sour you on our town."

"Thank you, Mr. Tanner," she said. His kind words after the way Craig had been treating her nearly made her break down.

"And Larabee's awake enough to say all that you just said to the Philmont boy?" Mr. Tanner asked skeptically.

Craig shook his head. "He's better, but not that much better. And he didn't talk. I got that from

Edna. He's been helping out the family for a while now so that they can make ends meet. Elias only just discovered that she was hiding the gold and using it as she needed for her and the children to survive."

Mr. Tanner turned to Gemma. "And you stopped him?" he said, admiration in his expression. "How?"

"I…I knew too much, he said." She couldn't bring herself to say that she'd shot the man. "He was forcing me into the carriage to…take me away."

"But he's half again as big as you." He watched her, skeptical now.

She glanced at Craig. There was no getting around it. The entire town would know soon enough. "I shot him. And…you should know… it's not the first time I've shot a man."

Mr. Tanner slowly sat back down. "I think you better explain that one to me."

She swallowed.

Craig walked over and shut the office door. At least no one would be eavesdropping from the street. "Have a seat, Miss Starling."

She pressed her lips together. She wished he would call her Gemma. She missed hearing it from him. She took a deep breath and launched into what had happened in Boston, telling Mr.

Tanner everything she had told Craig the day before. When she finished he was silent, steepling his fingers and apparently mulling over her story.

She looked askance at Craig. *Now what?*

"Lots of the people who come West come here to find a better future for themselves and their loved ones. Others…like you…have a past they are escaping. It sounds like a clear case of self-defense to me, Miss Starling. If what you're saying is true—and I think it is—we need to find out what happened after you left Boston. That's the piece of the puzzle that is missing."

"I came to that thought myself just recently. I thought it was time I write a letter to Mr. Ross who is managing my late father's estate. I could ask."

"That's a good idea. It seems a bit strange for this to come out now. What happened? A case of Christmas guilt seems unlikely. What prompted you to tell Sheriff Parker all of this now?"

Craig just stood there, his face a blank mask.

She squared her shoulders. This was on her. Not him. "Because I love him."

"You don't say." Mr. Tanner shot Craig an accusing look. "And how does the good sheriff feel about you?"

"I…I'm not sure," Gemma said honestly, watching Craig shut the cell door with a decided clank. "We've not talked much since I told him about Roland."

"So just the three of us here in this room know about what happened in Boston?"

"Yes. Is it necessary to tell anyone else?" She really hoped not.

"I don't see why we need to go any further here in town with the information. Maybe I'll be lucky and you'll finish out the year," Mr. Tanner mumbled, then looked at Craig. "You said you'd keep your distance."

Craig ignored him. "A letter is a good idea. A telegram better and faster. This morning I sent a telegram—one to the police station in Boston and the other to Mr. Ross."

The bottom dropped out of her world. Elias Odom had been scary enough. What if Roland's relations came after her now? "Oh, Craig! Tell me you didn't."

He pressed his lips together and for the first time since returning to town appeared affected by her predicament. "Chet handed the replies to me at Doc Palmer's."

He took papers from his back pocket. Opening the first one, he read out loud. "Mr. Wilkins has recovered from the wound you inflicted. He chose not to press any charges and has moved to

Washington, D.C., where he is setting up his new attorney office."

The room tilted. "Roland didn't die?"

"No."

"But… What does that mean? Am I…could I be…exonerated?" Could she honestly be free?

Craig nodded.

"What about the funds he stole from my father?"

Craig waved the second telegram. "From Mr. Ross. 'Miss Gemma—It is safe for you to return home. Come. Mrs. Horne and I miss you.'" Craig looked up at her. "He also wired a hundred dollars to the bank here so that you would have the funds to travel. And a ticket."

The weight that had been crushing her for the past year slowly lifted. "It's over? I'm free?" She could scarcely believe it. She needed something to hold on to. This was astounding. "I guess the only thing that has been chasing me is my own guilt," she said in wonder.

"You are free to do what you want," Craig said. "It's up to you. So you see, you don't have to run. You can go home." He met her gaze and for the first time she saw acceptance in his eyes.

"Home!" she repeated and imagined what that would be like.

"Guess that means I better start looking for another teacher," Mr. Tanner said with a mock scowl. He didn't seem too upset, which she thought was very gracious of him...considering. "Let me know what you decide, Miss Starling. I'd hate to lose you, but with everything you've been through, I realize you need to do what's best for you."

She was still reeling as he stood and strode from the office.

She stepped to the only other chair in the room and sank into it.

Craig watched her carefully. He walked over to his desk and settled into his chair, removing his Stetson and placing it on the desk. "Changes things, doesn't it."

She suddenly registered that he was talking to her. "Everything. Everything is changed. I'm still stunned. May I see the telegrams?"

He leaned over and handed them to her. They were her tickets to freedom. She didn't think she would ever let them go. She reread them...twice, and then flattened them to her breast.

"Guess this means that you'll be leaving. Heading back to Boston. Maybe even finishing up law school."

"I...don't know." Suddenly it hit her, why he'd been so closed off. At first she had thought it was because of her choice to leave Clear Springs... to leave him. But now...now she realized he had

had this information all along. "You are worried that I'll go, aren't you?"

"How can Clear Springs measure up? Life in a dusty mining town instead of in a beautiful house in Boston…with servants?"

"When you put it like that, it does sound a bit unlikely."

He didn't say a word.

It was clear that he wasn't going to beg her to stay. It wasn't his way. But she did want to know if he still wanted her. She rose. "This is too much for me to take in all at once. I need time to think."

He stood also and walked from behind his desk.

They stared at each other from across the short expanse of pine flooring. The only sound came from the tree outside as the wind rustled its branches and they scratched against the roof.

If he hadn't sent the telegram she never would have known! She would have traveled all the way back to Boston scared and nervous. She owed this man so much. "Craig. Thank you." She took a deep breath. The words sounded so inadequate.

She took one step. Then another. And then she couldn't hold back any longer. She rushed into his arms. "I'm sorry, Craig. I put you in such a difficult position. Please forgive me. I feel like I am finally waking up after a long nightmare."

He stroked her hair back from her face and then slipped his strong arms around her.

She squeezed her eyes shut to ward off the tears that threatened while she gulped in shaky breaths.

"Gemma," he murmured. "It's over. It's over."

It was all it took and she was weeping in his arms.

He held her tighter. And kept on holding her.

What utter relief! The pressure released from inside and seeped out through her pores, like a stream of cool water running over her and carrying away the heat of the day. This was a hundred times better. The wonderful, amazing gift of being free.

After a time, she quieted.

He slipped his handkerchief out of his pocket and offered it to her.

She dabbed at her eyes. Then she smiled softly, a bit self-conscious. "I must look a sight. All swollen, red eyes."

"You look beautiful," he said, his eyes going soft.

"Good. Because it's all your fault."

A half smile tilted his mouth. "How do you figure that?"

"You sent that telegram. I was too scared to do that."

"You told me the truth. That took guts."

She sighed happily. "I guess we both made it happen."

He nodded.

She thought of the trip to the Odoms', the cougar, the notes and all that had happened since she'd been teaching at Clear Springs. "You and me…we are better together than we are apart."

"You should have told me about Roland sooner. Should have trusted me. But it's over now." He pushed her hair back from her face again. "Do you have any other secrets to get off your conscience?"

"No."

"Good. Now that I know the real you, Gemma Starling… I love you."

At his words, joy skittered up her to grasp on to her heart.

He leaned down and kissed her. A swift, strong kiss that told her all her fears about him not wanting her came to naught. When he drew back, she gasped in air, the room spinning. "I'm giving fair warning. I'm not going to make it easy for you to head back to Boston."

She slipped her hand behind his neck and pulled him close. "Good."

Something was different when Gemma walked into the Molly's parlor on Christmas Day after the church service. The scent of pine permeated the room. Strangely, it was mixed with a tinge of acrid smoke. Not unpleasant…just barely noticeable. The small pine tree sat on the small table under the front window, its boughs covered in strings of popcorn and small bows of red-and-gold ribbon that Molly had made.

Still that didn't explain the odor of smoke.

She looked around the room and her gaze stopped at the fireplace. The wreath she had made for the school was tacked above the mantel.

She walked into the room and fingered the pine needles and then straightened the singed red bow. Craig must have salvaged the wreath from the school property. Her eyes burned, and then filled with unshed tears. It was such a sweet gesture.

"Now, none of that, dear!" Molly said. "The sheriff will be back in no time with Mrs. Hornsby. Help me with the sweet potatoes."

The tiny cabin didn't have a formal dining room so the kitchen table had been prepared with a pretty bouquet of pinecones and ribbons in the center. The ham was cooked and waiting on the sideboard, scored and basted so that the aroma of cloves and honey scented the air.

"I have so much to be grateful for this Christmas," Gemma said, her heart overflowing with hope and thanksgiving as she rearranged the centerpiece. "Molly, you've been so wonderful through everything. I don't know how I could have managed without you."

"Oh, tosh. You would have done just fine. You're young and strong and sensible. And you'll come to the right decision for yourself about whether to stay or to go home. Don't you let anyone push you into anything too fast."

"No. I'll be careful."

The front door swung open. "Molly? Look what I found on the street," Craig called.

Molly wiped her hands on her apron and walked into the front room. Craig had just entered, his gaze going directly to Gemma. He winked.

"Two lost souls…" Chet said, stepping inside and shrugging out of his heavy leather coat. "Hope you don't mind."

"Why, Chet Farnsworth! 'Course you're welcome. Who is that you are hidin'?"

From behind him, Daisy Finley peeked out. "The restaurant is closed for the day."

"Come in! Come in!" Molly waved her hand. "I'll just set extra plates. This'll be just fine! I haven't had so many faces around my table since my husband and boys were here. Daisy, the sheriff tells me that you are the best cook in Clear Springs. You deserve a day off from the kitchen and certainly Christmas Day of all days!"

Gemma soaked up her enthusiasm as everyone

took their seats and grace was said. She looked about the table at the smiling, friendly faces. In Boston, Mrs. Horne and Mr. Ross would always join her and her father for Christmas Dinner. This too felt like home. Beneath the table, she grasped Craig's hand. She didn't think anyone was fooled by the fact both she and Craig used only one hand apiece to eat throughout the entire meal.

When they were all stuffed with Molly's excellent cooking, Craig tilted his head slightly, indicating he wanted a word with her in the other room.

While Chet and Daisy helped Molly with the dishes and Molly and Daisy talked recipes, Gemma followed Craig to the hearth where the fire burned steadily.

"I have something for you." He drew a small black velvet pouch from his shirt pocket.

"Oh, Craig. In all that has been going on, I don't have anything for you."

"Just make up your mind to stay here in Clear Springs. That will be enough."

She cocked her head. "You're already starting?"

He grinned. "That's not pressure." He gave her the pouch.

She loosened the drawstring and turned over the contents of the bag into her hand. A pretty silver ring spilled out with a small rose quartz stone. Confusion overtook her as she looked up into his eyes. "I thought I had a bit of time to think about things. You aren't playing fair."

"It's not what you think."

"Enlighten me."

"This ring is my promise to you—that I'll wait, I'll hope, and I'll love only you. No more and no less. I'll fight to keep you here, but only on your terms. The way to honor how I feel about you is to give you the freedom to choose."

She recognized what he was saying and it made his pledge that much more precious. "Then," she said simply, holding the ring out to him. "I accept."

He took her hand in his large one and slipped the ring on her finger.

She raised it up to look at it in the light. "It's perfect." Then she raised up on her toes to kiss him lightly on the cheek. He turned his face at the last and caught her offering with his lips, instead.

"Your kisses..." she said. "Unfair advantage."

"Merry Christmas." He grinned and crushed her against him.

Epilogue

Six months later Craig rode Jasper out to the school property. Since Christmas, Gemma had held school in the old carriage house at Judge Perry's while volunteers had slowly cleared away the rubbish of the burned building. Now all that stood of the old school was the small shed. Beside it, a pile of new wood had been stacked in preparation to construct the new school over the summer.

The sun was high in the sky and the meadow filled with wildflowers. It was the last day of school and Gemma had decided to have mainly games and fun activities to celebrate the ending of the school year. A few parents had joined in the fun too, bringing treats and helping with the games. From his position at the edge of the clearing he could hear the laughter and giggles. He recognized Mrs. Odom pouring lemonade. She had put on weight since her husband's incarceration and was joining in more with the happenings in town. Beside her, Albert Larabee sat on a stool and watched the children.

Craig dismounted and slowly made his way toward the small gathering, still amazed that Gemma had chosen to stay. He couldn't believe that she'd given up Boston and her life there to remain here with him. She had wanted to wait to marry until the end of the year so that she could keep her word to Patrick Tanner. He was already interviewing for a new teacher to take her place.

Tomorrow Craig was taking Gemma to meet his family.

He approached quietly. They were playing blindman's bluff and Gemma was the one wearing the blindfold. The younger children danced about her, moving just beyond her fingertips. Every time she would reach for them and they would get away, peals of laughter erupted. Gemma's hair tumbled down her back in a rich river of coffee brown, the sunlight glinting off it in places to reveal a lighter gold. Her light blue gingham dress swirled about her as she spun this way and that, dashing after the children. He chuckled to himself. Even Duncan and Billy had joined in.

He stepped closer, holding a finger to his lips, warning the children not to say anything about his presence. He handed Jasper's lead line to Clarice Tanner. The woman flashed a delighted smile.

Then he joined in the game. The other children moved back. Way back.

"Where are you?" Gemma called out. "I know you are there."

He stood still. Behind him, Duncan coughed lightly.

"Aha!" Gemma cried out and turned toward him. With her arms extended in front of her she made her way across the small game area. "I recognized that, Duncan. You'll be it next."

Her fingers touched his chest. "Got you!"

"You certainly did," he said grinning. Then he swooped in and kissed her.

She quickly pulled off her blindfold. "Sheriff Parker! The children!" she said, scolding him although the sparkle in her eyes revealed her true feelings. "Set a good example. Please!"

"I never did take to being told what to do by my teachers," he admitted. "They had a word for it."

"Incorrigible?" she said, with an arched brow. "Stubborn?"

A twitter of giggles erupted behind him.

"No…none of those," he played along.

She focused on him. "Frustrating?"

"Give me a second. Independent. That's what it was."

She smirked. "How like you to think so highly of yourself."

He grinned. Neither one of them would be independent for long. Marriage had a way of changing that. But they were better together. They had sure found that out.

"You and your independent ways, Miss Starling. I love each and every one of them."

Right there in front of her students and everybody, he kissed her again. Long, sweet and...*his*.

* * * * *

If you enjoyed this story, you won't want to miss these other great reads from Kathryn Albright:

THE ANGEL AND THE OUTLAW
THE REBEL AND THE LADY
TEXAS WEDDING FOR THEIR BABY'S SAKE
THE GUNSLINGER AND THE HEIRESS
FAMILIAR STRANGER IN CLEAR SPRINGS

MILLS & BOON®

HISTORICAL

AWAKEN THE ROMANCE OF THE PAST

A sneak peek at next month's titles...

In stores from 29th December 2016:

- **The Wedding Game** – Christine Merrill
- **Secrets of the Marriage Bed** – Ann Lethbridge
- **Compromising the Duke's Daughter** – Mary Brendan
- **In Bed with the Viking Warrior** – Harper St. George
- **Married to Her Enemy** – Jenni Fletcher
- **Baby on the Oregon Trail** – Lynna Banning

Just can't wait?
Buy our books online a month before they hit the shops!
www.millsandboon.co.uk

Also available as eBooks.

MILLS & BOON®

EXCLUSIVE EXTRACT

Wealthy gentleman Benjamin Lovell has his
eyes on the prize of the season. First, though, he
must contend with her fiercely protective sister,
Lady Amelia Summoner!

Read on for a sneak preview of
THE WEDDING GAME
by Christine Merrill

'I merely think that you are ordinary. My sister will
require the extraordinary.'

The last word touched him like a finger drawn down
his spine. His mind argued that she was right. There was
nothing the least bit exceptional about him. If she learned
the truth, she would think him common as muck and
far beneath her notice. But then, he remembered just
how far a man could rise with diligence and the help of
a beautiful woman. He leaned in to her, offering his
most seductive smile. 'Then I shall simply have to be
extraordinary for you.'

For Arabella.

That was what he had meant to say. He was supposed
to be winning the princess, not flirting with the gate-
keeper. But he had looked into those eyes again and had
lost his way.

She showed no sign of noticing his mistake. Or had
her cheeks gone pink? It was not much of a blush, just

the barest hint of colour to imply that she might wish him to be as wonderful as he claimed.

In turn, he felt a growing need to impress her, to see the glow kindle into warm approval. Would her eyes soften when she smiled, or would they sparkle? And what would they do if he kissed her?

He blinked. It did not matter. His words had been a simple mistake and such thoughts were an even bigger one. They had not been discussing her at all. And now her dog was tugging on his trousers again, as if to remind him that he should not, even for an instant, forget the prize he had fixed his sights on from the first.

She shook her head, as if she, too, needed to remember the object of the conversation. 'If you must try to be extraordinary, Mr Lovell, then you have failed already. You either are, or you aren't.'

Don't miss
THE WEDDING GAME
by Christine Merrill

Available January 2017
www.millsandboon.co.uk